Falling

Is

Like

This

Falling

Is

Like

This

KATE ROCKLAND

THOMAS DUNNE BOOKS
St. Martin's Griffin ❧ New York

THOMAS DUNNE BOOKS.
An imprint of St. Martin's Press.

FALLING IS LIKE THIS. Copyright © 2010 by Kate Rockland. All rights reserved. Printed in the United States of America. For information, address St. Martin's Press, 175 Fifth Avenue, New York, N.Y. 10010.

www.thomasdunnebooks.com
www.stmartins.com

Permission granted by Righteous Babe Records for use of Ani DiFranco's song "Falling Is Like This" to appear in this book's epigraph.

Book design by Sarah Maya Gubkin

Library of Congress Cataloging-in-Publication Data

Rockland, Kate.
    Falling is like this / Kate Rockland. — 1st ed.
        p. cm.
    ISBN 978-0-312-57600-4 (alk. paper)
    1. Rock musicians—Fiction.   2. East village (New York, N.Y.)—Fiction.
3. Chick lit.   I. Title.
    PS3618.O35446F35 2010
    813'.6—dc22

                                                                    2009047595

First Edition: May 2010

10 9 8 7 6 5 4 3 2 1

This book is dedicated to my parents,
Michael Rockland and Patricia Ard,
for instilling in me a great love of books.

Acknowledgments

Falling Is Like This would never have existed if it was not for my agent, Ryan Fischer-Harbage. You rock, Ryan.

Katie Gilligan at Thomas Dunne is not only beautiful but a whip-smart editor. Thank you so much for making my dreams come true!

My buddy from high school Kevin O'Donnell over at *Rolling Stone* helped me figure out Harper's conversation about film that she has in the Veselka diner.

My friend Mike Cavallaro of Sticks and Stones fame lent Nick his last name and gave me advice on Nick's mannerisms before leaving on tour.

My friend Dana Spencer read an early draft of this book and told me it was the best book she'd ever read. Thank you for lying! And for supporting me.

Thursday

You give me that look that's like laughing
with liquid in your mouth
like you're choosing between choking
and spitting it all out
like you're trying to fight gravity
on a planet that insists
that love is like falling
and falling is like this

—Ani DiFranco, "Falling Is Like This"

I am going to tell you about the worst thing I ever did, which in relative terms, isn't all that bad. It's probably the meanest thing a middle-class girl from the suburbs of New Jersey could set about doing. And don't think that because this involves the end of one relationship and the quick, hot flash of another means my story is a bunch of girly bullshit. It's about the hardest decision I ever made in my young life: I deserted my smart, caring boyfriend and fell hard for a punk-rock star.

Here's how to leave a man: with shopping bags. Like a leaky faucet that eventually forms a rust stain in the sink, over the last two weeks of September I stuffed random stuff like clothing, jewelry, a rubber-band ball, and my extra hair dryer into Whole Foods bags and brought them to my parents' house in Madison, New Jersey. I did this almost unconsciously, and didn't admit to myself that I was leaving Andy until he was taking out the recycling one night and remarked that we were out of paper bags. Our brief, two-month cohabitation took place in a one-bedroom on Seventh Street near First Avenue. After dating two years, and watching our rent trickle through the system, we decided to suck it up and move in

together. (Living arrangements in Manhattan are often nonroman-
tic. They are more likely to be dull and practical.)

To schlep our stuff, we used one of those "man with a van"
ten dollars per man per hour deals you see advertised on telephone poles. It's well known they're a rip-off because they send
six guys to do the work of two, but I used them anyway. (I'm a
sucker for a pole advertisement. You can ask anyone.) Move-in
day was late summer. I'd felt sick to my stomach with the sticky
city heat, but looking back, it could have been the big ole ball of
doubt beginning its slow rot in my belly.

A few days before I left Andy, I absentmindedly stroked the
velvet on the back of a photo frame while he played *Halo 3* on his
Xbox, shooting an alien's head off. The *rat-a-tat-tat* of the digital
machine gun unnerved me. He played video games day and night;
it was a constant source of tension between us. Once, I tried to get
him into bed for some humping and he asked if he could finish a
level on his game first. Um . . . awesome. So, when he called out
from his seat on the futon: "When are you going to put pictures
in those frames, Harper?" the reason came to me so suddenly I
flinched: The move in together had been a colossal mistake, and I
had no intention of hanging up photos with our grinning mugs.
Why do so if you weren't staying long?

As September bled into October, the signs that our relationship had disintegrated were all around us. The space in our tiny
apartment felt half as big as it had before, the futon loomed large,
Andy's flat-screen television on the wall felt like it was sucking
out all of my energy. Even the air tasted stale. I'd open the door
to the closet we shared to grab a sweater and get tangled up in the
hangers. It felt like the apartment was turning on me. When Andy
would go out with his friends from college for a few beers, I'd walk
down to Houston and catch a movie at the Sunshine theater,

or sit on a bench in the Tompkins dog park, watching other people's dogs play. Spending time alone helped me realize just how much Andy and I had drifted apart. Made me realize it was *over*.

As I'd pick and choose what things to bring back to my folks' house in New Jersey, the memory of a beautiful Indian girl in my ninth-grade history class swirled into my thoughts. She had become pregnant and let months slip by without getting medical treatment or acknowledging her expanding belly. She walked slowly around the hallways, face lit like chalk. She wore extra-large sweatshirts, not maternity clothing. I once saw her walking into class, her coffee-colored bump peeking out of the bottom of her blouse. Her pregnancy was the elephant in the room. It was hard for our young minds to fathom a baby growing inside our classmate, its body suspended in her womb, legs folded like a colt's. The roundness of her stomach frightened me. We whispered about her behind our hands; her catatonic state seemed crazy to us. I now understood her reluctance to embrace reality.

Part of me wanted it to work with Andy, so I kept up pretenses. Similar to using the man-with-van guys, it's just easier. He knew something was eating at me, but we lived our lives and didn't talk about the giant question mark, asking what were we doing together when we obviously weren't in love anymore. I'd take NJ Transit's Dover Express train from Penn Station to Madison, where I grew up. I spent most of those rides gazing out the window, squinting against the setting sun. Trying to figure out how I was going to leave Andy. Assessing how I'd handle him hating me for it. While I sat on the train and watched New York recede into the background and the Meadowlands flit by, I'd think back on past relationships that also hadn't worked out.

I hadn't had much luck finding a boyfriend during the past

four years while attending Rutgers University. The guys were meatheads, with spiky hair and a reverence for the campus gym. They had little interest in ideas or art, and I'd slept around out of sheer boredom, hoping for some kind of spark to ignite. None had. My dating pattern before meeting Andy went like this:

1. Meet a cute guy at a bar.
2. Take him home and have mediocre sex with him.
3. Decide mediocre guy is my one and only soul mate and jump into a relationship that lasts about a year before the inevitable dramatic breakup where I'd go slightly bananas and feel the urge to stalk him, which would quickly end when I'd meet a new, cuter guy at a bar.
4. Return to #1.

I had one boyfriend who actually attempted to force me onto a reality television show. Not too many people can claim that. Like having a third nipple or being double-jointed, it's rare.

It was sophomore year at Rutgers and I'd begged the school paper, the *Daily Targum,* for a writing gig, any job at all. In my junior year I'd nab the much-fought-over job of music editor, and even branch out to start my own zine, *Thrash,* about the New Brunswick punk music scene, but as a lowly sophomore I was given the title Reporter at Large, which called up images of some kind of Frankenstein, lurching around the campus, peering around doorways and living out of trash barrels. I was assigned to the men's wrestling team. I don't think there was a women's team, so I suppose I can just say "wrestling team" and leave it at that. Either way, what was the editor in chief thinking? Me, with thirty sweaty, strong men?

These were sweet boys, and they alternated between wanting to protect me like a sister and rip my clothes off. I'd travel to away games with them, where I would sleep on a cot in the middle of the room. Should anyone try any funny stuff, everyone would know it. After a game, I'd tuck my tape recorder and notebook away in my purse, change into my favorite purple-and-white polka-dot flannel pajamas, and lay awake for hours, listening to their snores, like a testosterone symphony.

It was a great gig, just interviewing the coach and two or three of the top athletes before and after each game. I grew to love their cauliflower ears, pushed in and squished-looking from years of having their faces pounded into the mat. Brian became my boyfriend on the bus between Rutgers and Delaware. He was a mediocre wrestler and none too bright, but he was built like a refrigerator and could pick me up with one hand. Brian was also obsessed with "making it," as he put it. This didn't seem to include being All-American for wrestling, which he already was. It meant becoming a famous actor, which with his three-time broken nose, I wasn't entirely sure was the best career choice. Frustratingly, he had no desire to try out for any plays at Rutgers. He wanted to simply be "discovered." He wanted to shoot straight to Hollywood royalty. He had head shots taken in the city; I'd helped him lick hundreds of stamps and send them out to hundreds of agents who probably threw the envelopes directly into hundreds of trash cans.

He was a reality TV buff, watching *American Idol* and *Jersey Shore*. He once asked me if he should get his nipple pierced, and I'd stared out the window, pretending I hadn't heard. He'd take the train into the city and go on MTV castings, where they'd make him take off his shirt and dance around in a cold, colorless boardroom to Kanye West with other people our age who also thought they had what it took to be on a reality show.

During finals week, I was particularly stressed because I had to turn in an article on the team and finish a fifteen-page paper for my Shakespeare class that compared the plot of *As You Like It* to an early episode of *The Fresh Prince of Bel-Air*. When Brian asked me if I'd come into the city with him for dinner I begged out of it, but he was persistent, tempting me with chocolate cake for dessert. We went to some Italian restaurant in Little Italy, and I remember taking pictures of the red, white, and green banners decorating the streets that later came out blurry.

Whatever else you could say about Brian—that he was simple, etc.—he was always kind to me. So when he started unabashedly flirting heavily with our hostess, a not particularly beautiful woman with implants and a black dress tight enough to be a scuba-diving suit, I was very taken aback. Then I was pissed off. When he asked her what she was doing later, I was furious. "Hello!" I yelled, waving my hands in front of his face. "I'm still standing here, and I have a shitload of schoolwork to do, so if you're going to stand here and flirt right in front of my face I'm going to catch a train back to New Jersey." And with that, I turned on my heel. Suddenly, out of the wall came a flood of flashing bulbs and a white-hot spotlight camera a man held on his shoulder. I was blinded, and when my vision swam back into focus, I realized the "hostess" was dangling a crisp one-hundred-dollar bill in her orange hand like a worm to a fish. A sheepish Brian pushed his hair off his forehead and smiled at me nervously.

"Hey, Harper, I'm Amanda and you're on MTV's *Boiling Points!*" the woman said. My hearing seemed to have left me, and her words came at me like she was shouting from the end of a long tunnel. "If you can just sign your name on this contract and take the money, you'll appear on MTV in a few weeks!"

I looked down at her perfectly applied French-manicure-tipped nails and took the money. Then, I crumpled it and threw it at her feet. "Take your money and shove it up your ass," I said in my deadliest scary whisper (at least I hoped it sounded that way), and walked out the door. I felt like Rocky in *Rocky II* when he beats Apollo Creed. Sure, I'd been triumphant, but at what cost? Brian chased me for blocks. I just kept running. I was Forrest Gump. I ran all the way to Penn Station, where I finally whipped around. Brian, of course, had been keeping pace with me the whole time, not even breaking a sweat, but whenever he yelled, "Harper, just wait!" I ignored him and pressed on. I leaned against a wall, panting.

"Harper, it's a stupid show," he said. "I didn't think you'd get so upset."

"Really, Brian?" I asked. "You think I'd want to be humiliated on national television? Look, I hate to break it to you, but you're never going to be Robert De Niro. Even if you packed on sixty pounds for a role and wore a fake nose you'd still be a bad actor. You can wrestle and you can fuck and that's about all you can do. You want to try and embarrass me? On TV? I don't think so. Now if you don't mind, I'd like to go home. Alone."

I turned then from Brian's gobsmacked face and ran down the escalator, past the big black signboard, and caught the train to New Brunswick a minute before it pulled out of the station.

I cried all the way to New Jersey, big boo-hoos that had the businesswoman sitting across from me shooting me nervous glances. Who was going to pick me up one-handed now?

Brian called me for weeks, but I never spoke to him again. I'd never heard of *Boiling Points,* but when it came on as I was getting dressed in my dorm room one day, my eyes were glued to the screen. I watched another victim get humiliated, and all I could think was . . . she took the money!

So, when I met Andy two years ago at MoCCA, the Museum of Comic and Cartoon Art, I was twenty-one and ready to meet someone who was interested in print, and smart. *Thrash* had really given me great experience interviewing musicians. We'd profile any punk band that swept through Jersey on tour, and by my senior year there was a grand total of three staff members, including myself. My two colleagues still had a year left at Rutgers, and asked if they could keep printing it after I graduated. I said yes, praying there was still a niche readership for *Thrash,* even as the Internet threatened to obliterate the entire notion of do-it-yourself zines.

After graduation, I sent out my résumé to a dozen magazines and newspapers, looking for a job as a music editor. Being a girl it was hard getting male editors to take me seriously, but once I opened my mouth and blurted out every single tiny morsel of knowledge about the music scene of the last thirty years, I landed a few good interviews; one at *Rolling Stone* looked promising. But once I arrived I was informed it was only an informational interview—would I be interested in working down the hallway in an unpaid internship at *Us Weekly* until something opened at *RS*? I was. I'd take anything at that point, even if it meant putting off writing about music for a few years. I held the hope that eventually I'd have the opportunity to do what I loved again.

The night I went to MoCCA, a few friends from my internship at *Us* had invited me along, and when I got there I parted from the group to mosey around. The exhibit was a retrospective of illustrations by Todd McFarlane, the creator of *Spawn.* The turnout that night looked like a cliché of Generation X; guys with dirty hair and combat boots strolled past chubby Goth chicks wearing funky tights. Andy was working as a music writer for *New York*. It was 2008; an optimistic time in New York before the recession, when you could still graduate college and announce you picked journalism as a career without making your parents cry.

It was hard not to notice Andy. His skinny, six-three frame leaned against a doorway as he hunched over a tiny notebook into which he was furiously scribbling. He had a frown in the middle of his eyebrows that made the letter V. He stood in front of lovingly framed illustrations of a muted red Spider-Man swinging through the night past the rubble of dilapidated buildings. I remember smiling, recognizing Andy's journalist stance. I spent a few minutes studying his curly black hair, handsome against his mustard seed–colored smoker's jacket. Here's to hoping this guy doesn't quote lines from *Old School,* I thought, walking over to him. "Are you covering this event?" I asked, and the relationship lasted two years and two months, until one day I realized we'd become roommates, not partners. By the time I moved out we hadn't slept together in six months.

Things about him bothered me. There was no yin and yang with us, probably because we were both writers, and therefore too much alike. I got hired full-time at *Us Weekly* as an editorial assistant. A year later, *New York* had layoffs and Andy lost his job. The healthy competition that once fueled our relationship soured. When men lose their jobs it's like they've been castrated and Andy was no different. He accused me of becoming a writer just to mimic him. He stopped letting me use his laptop. His personality changed. I quit telling him about my day, for fear he'd be jealous. He'd shrug on a rumpled brown suit and head out on interviews. Once, while reading *Us Weekly* in the bathroom, he called out:

"I can't believe you work for a magazine that uses the word 'like' eleven times on one page!"

He started to shut out friends over trivialities. A gentle teasing by our buddy Josh that Andy had gained weight led to him refusing to attend Josh's annual Fourth of July party, something I greatly looked forward to. Once, my best friend Sarah, a photographer who now lives in Chicago, came over for some red wine and to show prints of her most recent work. Andy, who'd just gotten close to a job offer but lost it over a clash with another editor, was outright rude to her, even asking us both to be quiet after Sarah let out a loud peal of laughter. Too polite to cite Andy as the reason, she turned down a third glass and mentioned she wanted to get home before it got completely dark outside. When she reached the sidewalk, I ran to the living room windows, using my wrist to clear the condensation. I watched her walk down the street, mist from a manhole cover swirling around her head, until she hailed a cab and ducked in. I felt like a prisoner at home. Like I was suffocating.

It's not enough to end a relationship, the things I've described here, but unhappiness slowly creeps up on you, like a shapeshifting monster waiting in the darkness of your hallway, his bulging eyes watching your every move. The breath on his slimy tongue makes the hairs on your neck stand up.

The actual breaking up took two minutes.

He was folding laundry on top of our bed. We did the wash and fold for a dollar a pound down the street, and they'd wrapped our underpants and socks and T-shirts in plastic. Something about ending a relationship with a man who is folding your jeans really is a kick in the stomach.

I touched his arm. "It's not really working out, right? This? You and me?"

"I don't know what you're talking about," he said.

"Andy . . ." I touched his arm. He flinched: It had been so long since we'd touched each other. "Can you please stop folding laundry for a second and look at me?"

"You don't want to try and work things out?" he said now, his voice shaky.

"Do you really think that would help?" I asked. "I think . . . I think it's been over for a while now, Andy. I'm going to go live with my parents until I can find a studio."

I thought Andy hadn't noticed the ebb of my belongings, but when I said I was leaving him, he didn't seem surprised. The look on his face was closer to disgust. I hated myself, then. Just a little bit, but it was enough. I was putting down a two-year relationship. Taking it out to pasture to end its misery with a bullet, and it was hard to be the one holding the gun. I'd once asked my mother what giving birth felt like. "Imagine being ripped in half," she'd responded with her usual matter-of-factness. I felt exactly that way now, like I was being torn in two.

He left the apartment first, with a muttered explanation that he was going around the corner to get some coffee. I wanted to embrace him, push the dark curls off his forehead as I'd done hundreds of times before, but I held back. His hand shook as he grabbed his coat, the lone indication that any emotion brewed beneath his cool exterior. He turned for a moment and looked at me. He opened his mouth as if to say something, to wound me with the wide vocabulary he held deep within his brain after twenty-three years of voracious reading. I braced myself for their impact but he closed it again, reached out, and grabbed his coat. There was nothing left to say, and we hadn't used the tools of honest communication for so long our words would only come out stillborn. The wind helped push the door closed behind him and I jumped; it sounded like a gunshot. A migraine thrummed in the base of my skull. I sat on the futon and didn't do anything for several minutes but stare at the dark screen of the TV, which showed my face's reflection: round, freckled, and sad.

I called my parents (who have an annoying habit of picking up different lines in the house and speaking at the same time) and told them I was leaving Andy. There was silence, and then my mother said: "Don't forget to pack your grandmother's rug." I walked blindly around the apartment, stumbling once over a pink Converse I'd left on the floor and banging my left elbow hard on the kitchen wall.

I stepped outside on the street with my purse and the small orange-and-green Oriental rug rolled under my arm. My grandma Ida's rug had been given to me when she died. It smelled like her Bronx apartment: mothballs and matzo ball soup. The whiny *bleep!* of a taxi horn startled me. The sunlight on my face felt un-natural. Noise and color rushed past me but everything was slowed down and surreal. The October afternoon was so beauti-ful; the sunlight filtering through the trees danced patterns on the sidewalk. A toddler being pushed in a stroller lost his blue slipper. I watched it tumble past the stroller and into the street, his father pushing him hurriedly while glancing at his watch. I found myself unable to shout to him, to collect the abandoned item.

I teetered on the front stoop of my building. The skinny bou-tique store owner next door with an Amy Winehouse beehive smoked a Virginia Slim and gave me the stink eye. I thought about the rest of my possessions two flights up, things that didn't fit in grocery bags, such as my CD collection, which was so large Andy had painstakingly spent an afternoon lugging supplies back from Home Depot and built shelves to hold them all. I'd been halfway through transferring all the music onto my iPod, which lay under the couch where I'd dropped it after jogging yesterday. Shit! My stomach flipped over when I remembered I'd also left my diary in the milk crate used as a makeshift bedside table at Andy's. How could I have forgotten something so important? I could rush upstairs and grab it, but realizing Andy could be returning to the apartment any minute set my legs in motion. I'd come back for both items another day. Leaving them behind was worth avoiding an awkward emotional moment.

Turning up my collar against the chill, I mused over possible places to go. Most of my friends were in relationships, and crashing on their couches didn't seem like the grown-up thing to do. Alas, neither did running home to my parents' house, but that was my only practical option. Thinking I'd left my wallet inside led to a near panic attack, until I reached around in my purse and found it, touching a wad of cloth. I pulled it out and stared, blinking my eyes a few times. In my haste to leave I'd stuffed four pairs of underpants into my purse.

I began to move, ducking my head, staring at the sidewalk. It felt strange to traverse the same block I'd been on a million times, only this time as a single girl. I collected the abandoned blue shoe and put it in my pocket. Andy said we could open a pawnshop from random crap I'd found on the street and placed around our apartment.

I realized I could use a cup of coffee, and walked up Seventh Street, taking a right on First Avenue. I passed St. Mark's Place on my left, and made a pit stop to use the ninety-nine-cent ATM in front of Kim's Video.

On St. Mark's dirty guys wearing skintight black jeans hand out flyers for piercing and tattoo shops. (They flick the paper before handing it to you, making a loud *pop* sound to grab your attention; it's really annoying.) Really, let's face it: When a studio goes for twelve hundred bucks (at least) in this neighborhood, *how* bohemian are its residents? If an artist can't get a below-market studio space in the East Village, there won't *be* any more art being produced here. So many friends that Andy and I knew have up and left these streets, shuffling their possessions to Astoria and Greenpoint.

The young people who flock here, are they badass rebels living downtown, or do their parents pay half their rent just like the kids living on the Upper East Side? If the East Village was once a place artists like Andy Warhol and Allen Ginsberg called home, do their ghosts still linger here? Did they leave fingerprints on doorknobs and walk-ups that one could see if they squinted hard enough?

Recently as I was walking down Tenth Street toward Avenue B, a bus pulled up next to me. It looked cartoonishly humongous next to the small walk-up buildings and tiny city cars. A flood of Japanese tourists swarmed onto the sidewalk. They stood in a huddle, speaking rapidly and gesturing toward Life Café, the restaurant where Jonathan Larson wrote *Rent,* and where the last scene in act 1 takes place.

Certainly everyone can see (by the influx of stores such as Starbucks, American Apparel, and Urban Outfitters) that the hood has changed significantly since the days Debbie Harry waitressed at Max's Kansas City. Or, even much later, when The Young and the Useless and Minor Threat opened for Bad Brains at CBGB.

I hit Ninth Street and took a left, crossing over just after Local

Clothing, a vintage store I used to shop in that's gotten so expensive it's cheaper to buy new. As I stepped into Mud Café, a wave of calm rushed over me. I've been coming here so long I know the names of its owners, Nina and Greg, and that they named it Mud because Greg's grandmother used the word to describe her coffee. They don't serve decaf here; the East Village doesn't believe in it.

Mud is where I go to think, write, and brood into my chipped orange mug. I hide from the beast that is New York here. It's my favorite place to be in the whole city. Up the street on Second Avenue is a Starbucks. Starbucks is evil. They wipe out mom-and-pop coffee shops. If I am at Mud and have to poop, I'll go and use the Starbucks bathroom.

The Dirty Projectors were playing overhead as I walked through Mud's narrow door, where inside it hummed with activity. Orders for coffee were shouted over the din of conversation. After the bright sunshine from the street, it took my eyes a few moments to adjust to the dark room. A sense of home washed over me, and I couldn't help but feel that it was the opposite of what I'd been experiencing lately when entering the apartment with Andy in it. That reaction was more akin to panic.

I ordered a mug with lots of cream and sugar from Fiona, whom I recognized from being such a regular. "Is this for here or to go?" she asked, interrupting my thoughts. She had dyed her hair silver. Two buns on either side of her head were woven through with black velvet ribbons. She looked like a cross between Frida Kahlo and a fairy. She was short and somewhat plump; a friendly round layer of pudge stuck out the top of her purple corduroys. She didn't know my name, but I have always been amused with her surly attitude toward the customers. If you ordered anything but regular coffee she stared at you until you ordered a plain coffee. She didn't do cappuccinos, Frappuccinos, mochaccinos. She just did coffee. She hated tourists. When she spoke she often pulled at the whimsical soft blond fuzz that lined her upper lip, and her voice was a deep Kathleen Turner. She wore funny shirts. Today's read: WISH IN ONE HAND, SHIT IN THE OTHER. When she turned I read the back: SEE WHICH FILLS UP FIRST.

There was an empty table in the back room and when I set down my mug the legs wobbled. I slid Grandma's rug under the table to steady it. Pretty purple lights were strung around the door leading to the small eating area which had a thin glass ceiling painted orange. It was cracked in places, and there you could glimpse swatches of blue sky.

Something was making a rattling sound. After looking around I saw it was my right leg, shaking. A little puddle of brown coffee had sloshed over the side of my mug and onto the wooden table. Everything felt just slightly off, like I was looking at this little quaint coffee-shop scene through a piece of broken glass.

Had Andy returned to our apartment? I'd spent two months combing through craigslist to find it, visiting railroad-style rat nests with sketchy real estate agents until I came across the one-bedroom with arched doorways and tin ceilings and fell in love with it. I'd wasted at least two hundred bucks at the Container Store, buying those trivial domestic items such as plastic spring dividers for our sock drawers, a toothbrush holder, a shoe rack that hangs in the closet, a million wooden hangers. I'd moved six times since my freshman year of college, each time buying a ton of crap one thinks one needs and then losing it all from move to move. I tried not to think about the apartment. At nine hundred bucks a month each, Andy and I'd leaped into each other's arms, thrilled.

The steam from my mug floated over my face. A couple next to me was arguing; she kept jabbing her finger into the center of her palm to add violence to her words. She was tall and olive skinned with silver hoop earrings that swayed as she talked and he was short with red hair and glasses. I wondered how he had landed such a beautiful woman, whether he was a famous artist, or witty writer. Andy always said people who fought in public wanted attention. I tuned them out and looked around the room. Could anyone sense how panicked I felt? Surely my face was red. A dated-looking television was perched in the corner. *Kill Bill* was playing.

Clackety-clack. Clackety-clack. Where the *hell* was that tapping sound coming from? My legs were now still. The Oohlas switched off overhead and a new song by Gossip came on. Beth Ditto's operatic voice told me it was a cruel, cruel world to face on my own. As if I didn't know that already. The tapping continued.

To the left of me was a guy with a laptop set on the table in front of him, his large frame bent over the screen, its blue light illuminating his face. He was drumming a huge silver skull ring against the top of the table. I recognized him immediately as Nick Cavallaro, guitarist for New Jersey seminal punk band Hitchhiker's Revenge.

Oh my god! For a second I totally had a fan freakout moment, and had to restrain myself from running over to him and flinging myself across his lap and licking his face. These guys are *huge* in Jersey. They released their first record in high school, called *We Love Beavers.* I have all eight of their albums in vinyl, CD, on my iPod, and even possibly on cassette somewhere at my parents' house. We profiled them several times in *Thrash,* but our tiny staff of three took turns when it came to interviewing famous bands and I got the shit end of the stick when it came to Hitch-hiker's Revenge.

When I moved to New York after college and met Andy, I discovered he was a huge fan too, and we'd see them play in the city at Webster Hall (worst venue *ever*) or the Bowery Ballroom (best venue *ever*) when they came through town. One of my biggest fights with Andy was when *New York* asked him to write a two-hundred-word review of Hitchhiker's last CD, *Bite the Bullet*. I'd read it and thought he'd been way too lenient. The album was good, but Andy had given it five stars out of five, when it was more like a three. When I told him this, he overreacted. "You should stick to writing about celebrities." And then he didn't speak to me for the rest of the day. Whatever. Maybe I was just jealous he was the music writer, and not me. I don't know.

I watched Nick peck at his laptop, each knuckle tattooed with lettering I couldn't make out. Last summer Andy and I stood around at Corner Billiards after Hitchhiker's played Webster Hall. He had gotten word of an afterparty and we waited around for an hour so he could say hello. I found it kind of . . . dorky, and stuck by the bar, sipping a Coke until the band showed up. It was late and I was tired. I watched Andy awkwardly introduce himself; from across the room I could tell he was trying not to overdo his reverence.

Now, I looked around Mud, at the oil painting over the fake fireplace, the tattered American flag that hung on the wall. The poster of a topless mermaid giving the finger. There was a fine layer of dust covering everything, but it evoked a cozy barn. The tables were close and the warmth from everyone's bodies mingled together. Though I didn't feel like talking to anyone, I had an urge to introduce myself to Nick. I wasn't Andy, and I didn't want to act like a typical fan and therefore be uncool, but maybe meeting

Nick now, on the day I walked out—maybe it was the perfect coda.

So I touched Nick's shoulder, all at once surprised to feel solid muscle underneath. He was built like one of my old friends from the Rutgers wrestling team: not very tall, but compact. His head was a perfectly round shape, covered in fine blond fuzz, and buzzed with a razor. He had a faint recession at the hairline that worked for him.

He whipped around, almost violent in his surprise. His eyes sliced through me. Having never seen them up close before, it was shocking. They were the blue that you see when you're at the bottom of a pool and look up at the sky from underwater. Then, the strangest thing: I had a brief image of myself naked and wet, dancing happily in the rain. I dragged myself back to reality. He had a smirk on his face, and for a second I felt the bizarre sensation he knew exactly the image that had flitted into my head.

"You're Nick, right?"

His face went slack, most likely thinking I was a groupie. But to his credit, he caught himself, a quick recovery, and smiled, closing his laptop.

"Yeah, hey, what's your name?"

His voice was deep and hoarse, like stones rubbing against one another. I spoke quickly, a rush of words.

"Oh, I'm Harper?" I stated this as a question. I was nervous, though I'm not sure why. I'd met *much* more famous people while working at *Us Weekly*. I saw him relax a little.

"Well, Ms. Harper. It has been mighty fine meeting you."

He grinned at me, revealing huge piano-key-white teeth that I suspected he'd had bleached at one time or another. It was a detail that didn't quite jibe with the rest of his look: worn-in green sweater with leather elbow patches, like one you'd borrow from a boyfriend and never give back, faded blue Levi's, black Dr. Martens, and a chunky chain connecting his wallet with his back pocket. His sweater was loose around the neck and shoulders. When he moved I caught a glimpse of inked shoulder. He wore a short piece of rope around his neck with a silver anchor dangling from it.

"You too," I said. I wanted him to keep talking to me. "That sweater isn't very punk rock, you know." Crap! Why do I always say the first thing that pops into my brain when I'm nervous?

He looked down, surprised. "My mom gave me this sweater, and she passed away this year."

"Oh. I'm so sorry," I said, a flush creeping up my neck.

"I'm totally fucking with you," he said, tipping his chair back and laughing. What flashed through my mind was: Grandma, what big teeth you have.

"My mom is at home right now in Jersey, probably nagging my dad to mow the front yard," he said. Before his laughter turned cruel he squeezed my arm in a strangely familiar way.

I know it sounds lame, but right then, while the high-maintenance girl argued with her boyfriend next to us, and Fiona came by with a tray full of orange mugs, the world seemed to . . . shimmer. For one terrible moment, I thought I was going to barf. I was like Garth from *Wayne's World,* who throws up every time he sees his crush, Dreamwoman. And then a very different sensation shot through me. It might have been that I was desperate to feel anything other than guilt for leaving Andy, but when Nick touched me it was like a thrilling jolt flew to my crotch, leaving me tingly.

Ahem. Must stop staring. Must stop thinking dirty thoughts. Tucking a lock of flyaway jet-black hair behind my ear, I asked Nick what he was working on with the laptop. Instead of answering my question, he went off on a completely different track.

"You have a really interesting name, you know that?" he said.

I rolled my eyes and took a sip of coffee. Compliments make me feel awkward. "Thanks, I guess."

"No, I mean, are you named Harper, like *To Kill a Mockingbird*'s Nelle Harper Lee?"

"I'm impressed you know that," I said, leaning closer to him in my chair. It's usually people several generations older who catch the reference to my mother's favorite novel.

"I read a lot while on tour." He stretched out his legs near mine.

"Oh yeah, like what? Comic books?"

His eyes widened. "You know, Ms. Harper, when you *assume* something you make an ass out of 'u' and 'me.' "

I giggled. "Reading is rad. I'm halfway through *The World According to Garp*. It's like the quazillionth time I've read it. It belongs to my ex-boyfriend but I'm not giving it back because I just left him this afternoon. We were living together around the corner from here."

"Wow," Nick said, not shaken by my verbal diarrhea. "I'm actually on leave from my old lady too."

"Right on." I had nothing else better to say.

"Hey, is quazillion more than a billion?"

I laughed. "Don't get fresh. You know what I meant."

"So what's your last name, Ms. Harper?"

"It's Rostov and it's made up."

"Ah, like an alias." He winked.

"No," I said, laughing. "Our last name was Rubin, but my grandparents changed it to Rostov in the forties so my uncle could get into medical school. Imagine that! No love for us Jews back then. It's actually a Russian name my grandfather read in a book."

"Jewish women are the best in bed. Hands down."

"I totally agree," I said. "Feisty as hell, man. And we don't put up with any shit. If you think you're getting away with two minutes of foreplay, you've got another thing coming." My words were bold but I had to look down at the floor, away from his gaze, which was curious. I was enjoying our verbal match. It felt like walking along a roof's edge, blindfolded.

"I sometimes consider changing my last name back to Rubin," I said. "You know, just to be, like, super-Jew." It was a small detail, but one I'd never told anyone.

I can't tell you how jealous I am when I meet a Cohen, or a Berkowitz. Without saying a word, those people outwardly tell the world they're Big Heebs. With my mother's Irish coloring, freckles all over my body, I don't even *look* Jewish. I've always longed for olive skin like my father's. Even his large, characteristic nose instead of my tiny snout. Some indication that I'm one of the Chosen Peeps! I got the loud gene, and I'm outgoing and warm, so at least I received some of the traditional Jewish woman characteristics. I've always longed for darker skin, darker eyes. Instead, I was the only kid in my Hebrew school class that looked like they just walked off the boat from Ireland. You can see all of the blue veins making their ways through my arms, and after a few minutes in the sun my nose and cheeks are scattered with tiny brown freckles.

Nick was staring at me again, which made me nervous. Which in turn, made me not be able to stop talking: "Like I'm at the DMV, and I'm filling out paperwork, and I'm putting down 'Rubin,' and the DMV lady is thinking to herself, 'What a nice Jewish girl I have here on my line . . .'"

"I'm not sure people who work at the DMV are ever thinking

nice thoughts," he said. He laughed, and the sound was infectious. It was an impish laugh. I imagined him as a child; he was probably a naughty little boy.

From the corner of my eye, I caught a glimpse of a tall guy with curly black hair walking into Mud and at once I found my chest constricting. But it wasn't Andy. I let out my breath in one short poof. My eyesight had been getting blurry recently. I'd made an eye doctor appointment for this week to have my vision checked out. I could still see things right in front of me, but couldn't read the words on faraway billboards or street signs.

Suddenly, there was a spoon stuck in front of my face.

"Harper, are you ready to move on to the next phase of your life?" Nick was speaking in a strange, booming voice, like a reporter.

"What are you doing?" I slapped his hand away.

"Now that you've left your boyfriend whose name I already forget, are you ready to stop feeling guilty and enjoy this beautiful fall day?" He was still shouting. The couple from the next table stopped fighting and stared.

"You are insane," I told him. "Stop interviewing me with a spoon." He laughed, rocking backward in his chair. He was so weird I started giggling, despite myself.

What a strange day this was turning out to be. I wished witty, brazen words could roll off my tongue like they do in the movies. Speaking to Nick felt like boxing; I had to dodge and weave his sentences. Had to watch his left hook. So I said, "I'd better go," throwing three dollars on the table and standing.

"Where does a woman with no home go?" he asked, raising an eyebrow.

I blushed, remembering my situation, Andy's shaking hand.

"My folks' house in Jersey," I said. I was avoiding his gaze, which didn't leave my face.

"No way! Where in Jersey?"

"Madison," I said.

"I'm from Morristown, right nearby!" he said.

"Oh, really?" I pretended I didn't know, not wanting to sound stalkerish.

I grabbed my purse.

"Hey, is this your rug?" he asked, reaching down.

"Um . . ." I wanted to say no. "Yes."

"Well, don't forget it." He picked up one side of my table with ease and rolled it out from underneath.

"Great carpet," he said, handing it to me.

"Thanks. I don't really feel like going into why I have it with me."

He threw his hands up. "Hey, they get all types in here."

Then, he said something that surprised me.

"Wanna hang out, same time tomorrow?"

The rug had bumpy pink flowers that stood up. The wool it was made from itched against my arm. I looked down and there was a red rash forming already, on the inside of my elbow. "Look, it's been nice talking to you, but I just broke up with my boyfriend an hour ago."

"I can dig that," he said. "Sounds like you've had a bad day."

I'd been enjoying time with this stranger way too much, and I felt guilty, remembering Andy's face when I said I was leaving.

"Well, yeah, that's an understatement. I have to carry this rug home, I'm tired, and I have four pairs of underpants stuffed in my purse. My life is *not* okay right now!" For one horrible second, I thought I might burst out laughing.

"You seemed like the kind of girl who carries underpants in

her purse," he said. There was a ghost of a smile playing around that big mouth, but it was warm. On TV, Uma Thurman was calmly saying: "Bitch, you can stop right there. Just because I have no wish to murder you before the eyes of your daughter does not mean parading her around in front of me is going to inspire sympathy. You and I have unfinished business." Nick and I watched the movie for a second, both transfixed by Uma's steely dialogue. I wished I had the balls (or ovaries) to talk like that.

I stopped watching the movie and discovered Nick looking at me. "Well, see you around," I said.

As I turned, the twinkling purple lights strung along the wall swerved into my vision and I stumbled. His arm shot out and grabbed my sleeve. Steadying me. I took a deep breath. Looked at him squarely. Saw nothing hidden in his gaze. Real kindness behind his hard exterior. "Guess what I saw today?" he asked.

"Um . . . what?" His gaze bored into me. I felt rooted to the spot, staring back at him.

"A monarch butterfly. I didn't think they would be in Manhattan this time of year, you know? A group of us walking on the sidewalk stopped just to watch it fly. It was beautiful, really." I glanced at him sideways, trying to gauge if he was fucking with me. Who talks like that? But he was back to typing something on his laptop, and I realized he was serious, and that made me feel even *more* confused. How could he live in New York and still be so uncynical? It threw me. And then a memory swam into my consciousness from when I was a kid:

It was my first day of summer camp in Bangor, Maine. I was ten and my sister Lauren, seven. We were sent there every summer for a week, to get out of our parents' hair. Coming out of an art class, I watched three boys capture a butterfly and slowly peel off its wings as I sobbed hysterically, begging them to stop. I wondered if any of those boys grew up to be school shooters. Don't psychopaths always start out bedwetting and then graduate to animal torture?

The memory made a sick taste in my mouth and I swallowed, focusing back on Nick. The laptop screen's glow lit the inside of his right ear, coloring it pink like a conch shell.

I couldn't come up with a good reason to accept his offer. But I wanted to be near him again. I hadn't felt this charged in forever. "Okay, I'll come here tomorrow around this time," I said. "But you'd better be wearing a cooler shirt if I'm going to be seen with you." I punched him lightly in the arm. Masked bravado.

"It's a date." He grinned.

"Or a nondate," I said.

"Okay, a nondate," he agreed.

As I pushed open the door of Mud, the early evening air hit me like a slap. The outlines of buildings lining the street were pen-and-ink drawings. The setting sun behind them cast burnt orange and red rays on the sidewalk, like a bruise, and the irony was not lost on me. The wind caught the tops of the few trees lining the street. I imagined everyone rushing past me had rain on their mind. Twin little girls argued with each other, each shaking a snow globe as they walked and shouted. They wore matching outfits, a freakish mirroring that pleases only the parents.

I saw an advertisement for Halloween costumes at Ricky's hung up in a grocery store window. The choices of girl costumes were: slutty cop, slutty firefighter, slutty cavewoman, slutty tomb raider, slutty nurse, slutty doctor. Maybe I'd skip getting dressed up this year. I was probably too old for it, anyway.

I finally caught a cab and spent the next twenty minutes being shown photographs of the driver's six children who lived back in

Egypt. One had a large brown mole on his cheek. "They're beautiful," I lied.

I hate Penn Station. It's filthy dirty, for one thing, and gray steel walls meet the eye everywhere you turn. The only beauty to be found is in the multitudes of languages being spoken; one Hassidic woman walking next to me chastised her small child to stop dragging his heels or they'd miss their train in what sounded to my ears like Yiddish. Hassidic women wear wigs. (Only their husbands are allowed to see their real hair.) I know it's sexist and horrible, but the idea has always enthralled me. I imagine these women coming home, ripping off that uncomfortable wig, their real hair cascading down their backs like mermaids. It seems so *theatrical.*

On the train the girl in front of me had streaked blond hair, which appeared gray under the harsh lighting. I could see her pink scalp peeking through; it looked delicate, like a baby's skull. As our silver train shot out of the tunnel underneath Penn Station, the churning sound of the wheels on tracks rocked me. I pressed my cheek against the cool glass window, looking out into the plush blackness of the sky. There's a mental stretch that takes place when you leave the city, a softening of one's features, an unclenching of one's fists. It takes so much self-reliance to live among so many people, to push your way through crowds. Manhattan can act as a giant suction cup, sucking you into its folds. The city breeds no wimps and makes no apologies.

With a new landscape, my thoughts changed. There's no weirder land than that which lies between New York and North Jersey. It's a gritty backdrop; overturned electric poles lying in former marshland with depressed-looking birds circling overhead, the DRIVE SAFELY white tank from the opening credits of *The So-pranos,* trucks backed into warehouses with no names on their fronts, abandoned bridges with trees growing out of them and graffiti scrawled in what seems like impossible-to-reach places. Giant cranes from the shipyard in Elizabeth stood against the gray clouds like dinosaurs. The sky seemed to stretch on forever and formed a dark line where it blurred the steel landscape. Every-one's voices on the train were hushed.

I hadn't called my parents to tell them I was coming so I'd have to walk the few blocks from the train. Both of my parents work from home. Well, when it comes to the subject of my fa-ther, "work" is a relative word. My mother is a sex therapist and sees patients in a small room in our nineteenth-century house with bay windows. You would think her choice of profession would be awesome, what with the free condoms and all that, but having the birds and the bees explained to you when you're three years old doesn't always work out for the best. She brought out a model of a woman's reproductive organs, and plopped it onto the kitchen table. She was pregnant with Lauren at the time, and spent an hour or so explaining the heroic role my father's sperm played in this event.

When it was my show-and-tell day at school, I proudly brought in the model and showed it off to my class. I even took it apart like a Ford engine and sang the "Have a Look" song while passing different parts around to each child so they would have a turn holding them. When I pointed out the clitoris and called it "God's greatest invention," my teacher quickly asked me to put it away. "Why do the parents *tell* her these things?" I heard her whispering behind a cupped hand to another teacher in the hall-way.

When we were little, Lauren and I would stick our faces

through the banister spindles in our front hallway and watch patients coming and going for therapy. I'd felt superior to my classmates, as my mom knew everyone's secrets in the whole town. In the fourth grade, our neighbor Austin Olivo asked me if he could come over after school to get a look at the "psychos." He seemed to be under the impression my mother treated psychopathic killers. I'd invited him but all he'd done upon arrival was light one of my Barbies' hair on fire.

My dad's position in our family is somewhat harder to explain. In the late seventies, he wrote a memoir called *Dead Head,* about his travels with the Grateful Dead. That book went on to become a bestseller, and sold millions of copies. He has a Ph.D. from Princeton, which, aside from teaching an occasional freshman comp class there, he's never really used. ("Short for piled high and deep," he says.) He never published another book, although ever since I can remember, he's spent hours upstairs in his study, apparently typing out his next great masterpiece. *Dead Head* was made into a movie starring Jack Nicholson and Meryl Streep, and he's received large royalty checks throughout the years that have enabled him to never really work again. He's always loved figuring out how machines work, and became the unofficial mechanic of our neighborhood, constantly tinkering in our driveway with his head under the hood of a car, emerging covered in black oil.

No one has seen any of his writing, and my mother says she's had nightmares where she walks upstairs to his office and every page has the word "REDRUM" written on it. For fun, he reads depressing history books.

Dad is constantly coming up with new careers for himself, the most notable one being when I was twelve and Lauren was nine, he started raising mice. He would sell them to local pet stores as well as to people in New Jersey who owned snakes, which would devour these little white creatures as meals. Only, the problem came when my dad would fall in love with certain mice, training them to do tricks, and then be unable to give them away. At one point we had fifteen mice living in the intricate mazes and pipes Dad built in our living room out of paper towel rolls and masking tape. My mother finally stepped in, said enough was enough, and asked him to choose a less-furry hobby. The older I get, the more tolerant I am of my parents' eccentricities. I've even begun appreciating them. I find myself drawn to neurotic people.

When I was a teenager, I was constantly embarrassed that he stayed home, when my friends' dads all had jobs as lawyers, firemen, architects, and businessmen. They wore proper ties with sailboats on them. They golfed. My dad wore the same jeans with holes in the knees every day, and T-shirts with silly slogans like I'M WITH STUPID with an arrow, or tie-dyed shirts that said LEGALIZE IT. He was always so eager to drive me and my friends to dance class, the movies, the mall. He turned school lunches into an art form, making sure every sandwich represented the ole well-balanced food pyramid. Now that I'm older, and I realize how many absent fathers there are, I see how lucky I am that I grew up with one so present in my life.

As I walked down my street, I noticed all the changes. I got home to see the fam about once every three months. One neighbor had painted her house a peppermint green. A fat gray-and-white-striped cat ran across the street and hid under my mother's Volvo, her belly low to the ground.

"What are you doing home?" Lauren asked as I walked through the doorway. She is taller than me, and leaner. She's also blond, which remains a mystery in our dark-haired family, often inspiring my father to make "your mother and the mailman" jokes. Anna

Freud, our Labrador, happily pranced around me, licking the backs of my knees.

"Mom didn't tell you?" I asked, putting down my purse.

"Did you leave Andy and now you're moving back here to Weirdville?"

"Yep," I said, trudging upstairs. Lauren and I are not super close, but lately we'd been talking on the phone more. I'd told her all about my unhappiness with Andy.

"Did he cry?"

I paused, one foot in midair. My sister has suffered from depression most of her life, yet she's always had an uncanny sense of one's inmost state of being. My dad calls it her "emotional antennae." Had Andy cried?

"More like he acted really passive-aggressive," I said, walking the rest of the way up the stairs. Then, I turned on the carpeted step. "What are you doing home yourself?"

"Dad asked if I'd go to temple with him tomorrow night so he drove down and picked me up at school. I don't have classes on Fridays. You have to come too, you know."

"We'll see," I said.

Lauren laughed. "Just because you're older doesn't mean you get out of going to synagogue. You're not, like, a total adult just because you live in New York. You still have to listen to Mom and Dad."

"Whatever! I'll go to temple. You don't have to be so annoying," I shot back.

How can I describe the relationship I have with Lauren? Twenty years old and born so beautiful neighbors used to stop on the street and reach inside her stroller to pinch her cheeks, she's been in and out of therapy for as long as I can remember; prescription bottles line the counters of all three bathrooms in my house. She has a specialist who deals with depression and manages her medications. We once had a goldfish named Paxil.

If you don't have anyone in your family with depression, it might be hard to understand the love/hate relationship Lauren and I have. I feel sorry her life has been so screwed up by her disease, but at times she can sulk around the house and not speak to anyone for days. Before she went on medication, she was filled with rage; you never knew when she'd turn on you. If you met Lauren for the first time, you might not notice anything "off" about her at all; she got very good at ignoring the demons that haunt her.

She is now a sophomore at Princeton, something we never would have expected a few years ago, when she was at her lowest point, nearly suicidal. It's hard to find the right medication for someone who is depressed, but once you do it's a miracle. They get back the person you knew before their body became a shell to the chemical imbalance. That's why Tom Cruise and his anti-medication rants piss me off. I'd like to see him live with someone who refuses to get out of bed or bathe, as Lauren did two years ago. That summer, I briefly complained to my mother when she canceled our annual Cape Cod vacation; my parents were afraid to take Lauren too far from her therapists. "You could have just as easily gotten her disease," she reminded me quietly. "Depression can be genetic." Then, she'd uttered the phrase I'd been hearing forever: "You have to take care of your sister." We snipped at each other all the time, but recently I've been wishing we were closer. I made a mental note to try and get along with her better tomorrow, to ask her about her classes.

"Night, Harper," Lauren called out from the bottom of the stairs. "I hate you less lately."

I smiled. "Night. Hate you less too." I walked to my room and closed the door. Soon after, there came a light tapping.

"Is that my firstborn?" my mom said, walking into the room. I felt the usual jerk deep in my belly I always experience when visiting my parents. How much longer did I have with them? Would my mother die first, even though my father was several years older? I don't come home very often, and it's not because I don't love my parents. It's the dark corners of the house, the veins in the back of my mother's hand teeming with fragile life. My dad stopping to catch his breath at the top of the stairs. Asking my mother for a tampon and being told she stopped having her period for good two years ago. That she'd quietly gone through menopause. Whenever I think this dread has left me for good, swum deep to the parts of the ocean where it is so dark fish have lights that come out of their heads, it takes only one trip home and the fear of my parents' deaths bursts to the surface, everpresent and suffocating.

When my mother hugged me I inhaled her smell: a mix of earth from gardening and a peppermint patty. I love my mom. Her name is Leanne but everyone calls her Lulu. She was a bra burner in the sixties. Her hair is long and black, just like mine. She always has a fresh pedicure, wears movie-star Chanel sunglasses, and when she sees her daughters her face lights up. "Get into your pj's," she ordered. She's always felt getting into one's pajamas can cure anything.

"Where's Dad?" I asked.

"Oh, he's working on one of his projects. Taking down the play set, I think."

"What? You mean Lauren's and my play set? From when we were little?"

I must have had a horrified look on my face, because my

mother smiled and reached out her arm to move my hair out of
my face and tuck it behind my ear. "You're twenty-three now,
honey. The same age I was when I had you. I don't think you and
Lauren have touched that slide or swings for a good ten years."

"I know, but . . ." How could I explain that this one simple
act bothered me more than I could say? That it felt like everything was changing, shifting, churning, and I just wanted to hold
up a big red stop sign and make it all halt? It turned out I didn't
have to explain.

"Growing up is hard, right?" Mom said. She kissed me on the
cheek and softly walked out of the room. I listened to the sound
of her footsteps on the stairs, the creaking of the screen as she
walked out the back door and into our small backyard. I walked
over to my window, brushed aside the lace curtain, and pressed
my forehead against the glass.

Dad had put down his tools. The slide remained, but the
black rubber swings were lying on the grass dismantled, looking
like sad jellyfish with their frayed yellow strings in the dark grass.
They were hugging, and I slowly lifted the window and knelt
down, pressing my ear against the screen. Dad was crying big wet
tears.

"Our babies are all grown up," I faintly heard him say to my
mother.

"You're such a sap," she said, swatting him on the arm. Laughing, he bent down to kiss her. She was wearing a pretty white
nightgown and in the moonlight it glowed. She looked so beautiful there in the grass, my mother. I was invading their privacy.
I eased down the window and padded over to my bed. Anna
Freud nosed her way into the room, then leaped onto my bed
and quickly turned around three times before settling down.
There was a faint outline of gold hair surrounding where she lay

and I realized she'd been sleeping on my bed probably every night and now was looking me over as if she was debating allowing me to crawl in beside her. When I got under the covers and felt the familiar softness of my rose-covered comforter, Anna Freud let out a long doggie sigh and put her paw on top of my hand and we both fell asleep, holding each other, skin to fur.

Friday

Waking up completely disoriented the next morning, I reached out for Andy only to remember we broke up. Anna Freud had moved too, hopped off the bed in the middle of the night, and I was alone. It felt disconcerting not to see Andy's curly dark head on the pillow next to me. I felt a panicky fluttering; maybe I'd made a mistake. I heard spoons scraping against bowls in the kitchen, the waves of domestic sound a family makes. The sun stabbed underneath my window shade. I stared at the ceiling for a few minutes, the events of yesterday swirling around. I thought of Nick, his stubbly chin, sea-glass eyes, tattooed knuckles . . . The possibility of *him* made the day feel fresh; it had been a long time since I had that warm feeling in my belly, like anything could happen. Would I see him tonight? In the morning light, the idea of returning to the city for this guy seemed ridiculous.

I walked down the hallway, the wooden boards creaking and cold beneath my bare feet. I had to pee, and felt pathetically happy that my parents had the supersoft, luxury toilet paper Andy always said we couldn't afford. (He's not a skinflint. We were just broke most of the time.) Have you ever tried wiping with recycled TP? It feels like scratching your vagina with a dried leaf. It sucks.

I dug around in my dresser until I found a worn pair of sweats, Madison High School's logo stamped on the leg. I daydreamed of a life with Nick. Surely I'd dye my hair hot pink à la Gwen Stefani during her *Tragic Kingdom* days, or get a Hitchhiker's Revenge tattoo on my hip. We'd get married barefoot on the sand like Tommy Lee and Pamela Anderson (though I'd swap the trashy string bikini for a cute white sundress). Green Day would play at our wedding and Billie Joe and I would bond over a mutual love for Lifetime's *Somewhere in the Swamps of Jersey* album. I would live a carefree punk-rock lifestyle, writing about bands and producing babies born with mohawks, who would come on tour with us, learning how to ride BMX bikes from other celebrity spawn.

I reluctantly swung my thoughts back to reality and padded down to the kitchen. My father had plants and potting soil set up along the counter. He clips baby shoots from his large family of spider plants and puts them into water glasses along the shelf in the kitchen, encouraging root growth. He tenderly held out a spider plant stalk in his palm to show me: "This little guy is ready for a much larger pot, wouldn't you say?"

"Indeed it is," I agreed.

He took his glasses off and put them on the counter. It was a well-worn-in gesture, one that reminded me of being a child, when he would take them off to read the small print in one of my children's books. It made me want to cry. What the hell was wrong with me? My emotions were all on edge.

I walked over to the fridge to check out a birth announcement for a cousin's baby that someone had hung askew with a SHOP LOCAL: SHOP MADISON magnet. They'd named the tyke Ashley, after the *Gone with the Wind* dude. He wore blue-and-white-striped pajamas and had a tuft of black hair that stuck straight up. His eyes were spaced an unfortunate width apart. Mom came and stood next to me, shoulder to shoulder. "Hideous looking, isn't he?" she asked, scrunching up her nose. "He's inherited his mother's huge forehead."

"Mom, you can't say that."

"Why not?" she asked, genuinely confused.

"Because it's a *baby.* You're supposed to only say sweet things about babies. Like how cute their chubby cheeks are, or that they have a button nose." My mother, much as I love her, had never been one for sentimentality.

"Well, you and Lauren were some of the cutest kids I've ever seen, but *this* one's parents should have waited a few months before sending out photographs."

I rolled my eyes. Then I noticed my parents exchanging nervous glances. It appeared they were looking for a chance to bring up my current jobless, boyfriendless, and homeless situation. I let out a deep sigh. "Look, I know everyone wants to know what happened with Andy so let's have a family meeting."

With my mom being a therapist, a family meeting to her is like porn to a pervert. When I was a kid we'd all gather around the kitchen table once a week or so to meet, discussing any problems that came up in our little four-person world. The way these things went was only one person was allowed to have the floor at a time, and would get out all their frustrations at once, the three of us listening and dying to jump in. I realize now they were useful when we were teenagers and driving my parents crazy, but there was nothing worse than being hungover, trying to hide it, and being woken up at 8 A.M. on a Saturday to have one of these meetings. Like the Spanish Inquisition, in New Jersey. The Jersey Inquisition. What were we feeling? Why were we mad at them? Why was I stealing Lauren's shoes? Why was Lauren taking mushrooms? Why was I sneaking out of the house at night and meeting boyfriends in their cars down the street? Why were we refusing to visit Grandma this week? You know, typical teenager stuff.

"I liked Andy," Lauren began. "But he definitely had man boobs." She carried her bowl over to the sink and ran water over it, washing out leftover cereal with her hand.

"I think you mean 'moobs,' the male equivalent," said my mother. I glared at both of them.

"Andy was a great guy," my father said tentatively. "Highly intelligent."

Everyone was looking at me.

"I *know* he's a great guy, but he wasn't right for me. He carried a chip on his shoulder the size of a mountain and he wasn't supportive enough of my career." I crossed my arms like a petulant teenager. My mom did her slow shrink nod that drives me bananas. "He also just didn't have a good sense of himself as a man," I blurted out dramatically. Lauren snorted. How could I put into words how his insecurities overwhelmed me? Andy was raised in Minnesota and had this stoic Midwestern persona, never expressing himself about anything. I come from a family where no one ever shuts up. Enough said.

My father put his hand on my shoulder. I thought he was going to say something profound. "Did you remember to grab your grandmother's rug on the way out?"

"Yeah, I dragged it around the East Village and then took a cab with it sitting next to me like a passenger." I let out a strangled laugh. "The whole situation was ridiculous."

"And you've quit your job?" my mother asked, pushing her

glasses onto the top of her head. The concern on her face sent a surge of guilt through me.

Right, I'd promised to dish on what happened with my gig at *Us Weekly*. I'd quit only a week ago but the time that had passed felt like much longer. I was the assistant to a guy who was going through a divorce and subsequently took his anger out on me. I used to look up from my cubicle to find him glaring at me, for no reason discernible, through the glass doors of his office. It gave me the creeps. The only positive thing about the situation was that I made friends with another editor who let me cover the red carpet at a few A-list events. Sounds glamorous, right? If you ever want to feel like a turd, try getting pushed and shoved by other post-English-majors-turned-celebrity-reporters every time someone sparkly and skinny starts strutting toward you. I simply wasn't born with a competitive bone in my body.

The event that ended my career at the magazine was a charity party thrown by the supermodel Petra Nemcova, famous for clinging with all her might to a palm tree during the 2004 tsunami in Thailand. It was held on a foggy Tuesday evening at Cipriani restaurant in the Financial District two months ago. It was a warm September night and the red carpet seemed to pulse with anticipation. I'd gone to Bumble and bumble's salon, where the students do your hair for free, and had a blowout. My hair looked like freshly spun cotton candy. My attempt to look fashionable was a ten-dollar H&M top and gold hoops I'd bought on the street in Chinatown. After sticking my minirecorder in Petra's smooth face, who should walk by but Bruce Willis! He glared at all us reporters as he strolled past us and into the restaurant. Making like I was taking a bathroom break, I eased my way inside after him. I would beat out all the other reporters and get quotes from Bruce! I would become an ace reporter and get promoted and then get hired at *Rolling Stone*!

Giant chandeliers hung from the ceiling, their crystals spitting light all over the room. There were so many shiny, beautiful people I was nearly blinded, but after a minute I spotted ole Bruce at a nearby table and saw he didn't have a drink. I craftily grabbed a cocktail from the tray of a passing bartender. A little purple umbrella spilled out of the drink and I kicked it under a chair. Heart racing, I approached him.

Only, he sniffed me out right away. "You've got a recorder in your hand; you probably want to ask me some questions, right?" The two models on his lap tittered; one eyed me curiously over the rim of her champagne glass. I reached up and realized one of my hoops was missing; I looked like a member of Salt-N-Pepa.

"I brought you a drink," I said, boldly setting it down on the table. Bruce said nothing, sizing me up. Suddenly, he grabbed my arm and steered me away from the table. His grip was so strong that I was instantly reminded of the fifth grade, when a policeman came to our class. I forget the purpose of his visit, probably a remnant of that whole eighties "This Is Your Brain on Drugs" campaign, which, rather than divert me from narcotics, forever ruined eggs over easy for me. Whatever his purpose, the cop asked for a volunteer from the audience to get "arrested," I suppose as a message to any potential eleven-year-old drug dealers. My arm shot up. "Turn around and put your hands on your head," the cop said. Grinning to my class and rolling my eyes, I did as he asked. Suddenly, and without warning, he grabbed my skinny wrists, roughly twisting them behind my back, handcuffing me. The metal dug into my skin. I came home with bruises on my wrists, causing my father to rant for weeks about how police in this country are the Gestapo. He spent hours at his computer, painstakingly typing out a complaint to President Bush Senior. One day a response arrived, strangely containing only a single autographed picture of Dan Quayle.

Bruce was still grabbing my arm, though less hard now. Heads swiveled in our direction. "Look, you seem like a nice girl; I don't know why you're doing this," he said, staring at me with those intense eyes. He's really much more handsome up close, I thought, wondering when he'd let go of me. "You can find a better job than stalking celebrities," he whispered, breath tickling my ear. After finally loosening his grip, he surprised me by kissing me on the cheek. His freshly shaved cheek scraped against my smooth one. He then turned on his heel and walked briskly away. I wanted to shout after him, "I'm not a celebrity reporter! I am a fabulous music journalist! I started *Thrash*!" But he was gone, back to his table and his models.

I stumbled toward the bathroom, the models' laughter following me. I sat on the toilet, peeing and crying at the same time. I called Andy. I remember he took a cab downtown and picked me up even though we'd just paid the month's rent and he really couldn't afford the cab ride. Even though it was midnight and he was exhausted from going on various job interviews all day, he made bean-and-shredded-cheese enchiladas. We stayed up late on the futon and ordered *The Whole Nine Yards* on Cinemax, cracking up at all the bad lines. Andy cheered me up so much I almost stayed with him. After the movie he'd turned to me and said, "Maybe things aren't that bad. You know, with us?" We'd been fighting so much that I'd forgotten how sweet he was. How kind he'd always been to me, even though we hadn't gotten along lately. A brief flicker of hope lit my heart that night, but it turned out it was merely a last gasp. After that everything went downhill, the fighting continued, we drifted further apart.

Now, I looked up and saw three faces looking at me. "Well?"

"So you quit your job because Bruce Willis manhandled you?" Lauren said.

"No, not exactly," I said defensively, chipping at the table with one purple fingernail. "It's more like I realized I was wasting my life obsessing over celebrities when what I *really* want to do is write about music."

Silence, and then from my mother, "I wish Bruce Willis would manhandle *me*." Lauren and I exchanged a look and she started to giggle. My family is weird, but sometimes weird can be good.

"I remember that independent zine you had in college, *Thrash*," Lauren said. "I used to love reading it. It came out every other Wednesday, right?"

I stared at her, amazed. "I didn't know you read it!"

"Oh, totally. Dad would drive down to New Brunswick and pick it up for me. I loved your interviews with bands, I'd tack them up on my wall."

All I can remember from my relationship with Lauren when I was in college was worrying about her mental health and fighting with her all the time. I had no idea she'd read *Thrash* or even cared about what I was writing about. I felt sad that we hadn't connected then, she'd just always seemed so *angry* to me, like she hated my guts. It was hard to differentiate between what her real feelings toward me were and what her disease was forcing her to act out. I think deep down I always knew she loved me, looked up to me even, but our relationship had never come easily, like the one we both had with our parents. She and I always had friction, though if asked why, I wouldn't be able to formulate an exact cause.

"I think you should try and be a music editor. That's what you've always said you wanted to be, even when we were little," Lauren said now. "That celebrity magazine wasn't really going to make you happy."

My parents were watching our exchange in states of shock, not saying a word. They'd always hoped we would get along. I felt like I'd been pushing Lauren away for so many years because I was afraid, in a way, of losing her. When she was in a bad place and threatening to kill herself I would bury my head in my studies at Rutgers or my relationship with Andy. If I were honest with myself I hadn't listened to my mother, hadn't watched over my little sister like she'd always been telling me to do.

"Thank you," I said to Lauren. I reached out and squeezed her skinny wrist. She squeezed me back, but before it could get too corny she jumped up and went to the window.

"By the way, if anyone cares, the Tan Lady is naked in our bushes again," she said, putting one hand over her mouth to stifle a yawn. I ran to the kitchen window to look.

"How'd you know she was here? I didn't see a thing," I called out over my shoulder.

"I heard the jangling of her bracelets," Lauren said, walking back to the table, picking up the newspaper and flipping over a page. My parents walked to either side of me and gazed out the window. My mother sighed.

"Better go upstairs, Aaron," she said to my father.

For as long as I can remember, the Tan Lady has been our town witch. Our bogeywoman, if you will. Though Caucasian, she was given her moniker due to the thick beige makeup she constantly applies to her face, and over her body. (One neighbor claims to have seen her putting it in her butt crack!) She is a homeless woman with an eerie past. The story goes that she was once a fashion model, and lived with a husband and kids in Short Hills. Given her height (she is six feet tall) it could easily be true. As an adult, I now recognize the signs of schizophrenia, but when I was a child, she both terrified and enthralled me. Once, at my ninth birthday party (a sleepover in a tent my father pitched in the backyard) one of my friends said the Tan Lady might be lurking outside our tent, ready to eat us for supper. Phone calls were made, the party disbanded, and my friends returned to the safe warm arms of their parents.

The notion of the Tan Lady prowling around proved not to be far off the mark when, three years later, my mother came across her camped out behind Lauren's and my old jungle gym. If anyone else had found her, surely the police would have been summoned. But, being that it was my bleeding-heart mom, she offered her services for free, hoping to coax her into medication and therapy. I wasn't home when this happened, I heard it later from Lauren, but the story goes that once inside, the Tan Lady took one look at my father and attacked him, kicking and punching, screaming her head off. This reaction happened again a few years later in town, while my father was walking to the post office. This time, she leaped onto his back and knocked his glasses to the ground. He begged my mother to let him get a restraining order, but she'd have none of it. "They'll just arrest her and put her in some godforsaken jail instead of a mental institution because they won't understand her needs," she would shout.

Mom tried for years to help the Tan Lady, even when she took to streaking in our neighborhood, often mistaking our next-door neighbors' flower bed for her personal toilet. "It's good for the soil," Mom would plead when they threatened to call the police. It came out awhile later that the Tan Lady had mistaken my father for a past lover who had scorned her. Apparently, he too was short and balding with thick black eyeglasses. Nothing much else came of the Tan Lady, but my dad always looked around frantically before setting off from the house. I heard she disappeared during one of the years I was in college, and no one had mentioned her to me since.

That's why I was surprised to see her, nude, sitting on a green plastic lawn chair in our backyard. My father had planted hemlock bushes back there, and it was hard to make out the Tan Lady against their darkness, due to the leathery cast her skin had. Whether it was from sunbathing nude or the makeup, I couldn't say. She wore nothing but rows of silver bracelets up to her elbows on both arms. I could hear their clacking as she applied the foundation.

"That woman should invest in drugstore makeup stock," my father said, though he had a somewhat nervous look on his face.

"Seriously, Dad, get your tuchis upstairs," Lauren said. She and I both started giggling.

"Yeah, she's onto you, Dad," I said. "You don't want none of that Tan Lady crazy love."

"Very funny, both of you," he said, but he was walking upstairs quickly now, Anna Freud barking at his heels.

"Mom, it's ridiculous that you don't call the police," I told her. She sighed. "She's never harmed anyone."

"She, like, *assaulted* Dad," Lauren said. "Twice!" My mom didn't say anything, and the three of us stared out the window. I noticed our profiles all shared the same shape nose: tiny, with freckles across the bridge. The Tan Lady was sitting on the chair, legs spread, brushing her long hair. With her other hand, she held what looked like a well-used M.A.C. foundation compact.

"Shit, she stepped it up," I said. "It used to be drugstore brand, remember, Lauren?"

"I think she got a bikini wax too," she said, squinting.

"It's very sad," my mother said. "Her disease could have happened to either of you." She was always saying things like that. When I came home from the first day of fifth grade and told my mother one of the kids had an eleventh finger that he was, God bless him, proudly showing off to everyone in the room, she only shook her head and said, "Let's not judge, Harper. That could have easily happened to you."

"How?" I'd asked, truly puzzled.

I grew bored of watching the Tan Lady brush her hair. I walked up the stairs to my father's office. A funny thing that is, calling it an office. That would suggest actual work going on. My dad was reading a book titled *America's Forgotten Pandemic: The Influenza of 1918,* and I decided not to interrupt him. Lauren scattered to the attic to work on a painting for school. I wrapped a salami-and-American-cheese sandwich in a paper towel and drove off to Morristown in my old car, a six-year-old Honda my dad now uses. One bonus of city living was I no longer needed a car. I passed the old Sweet Dreams Café, now turned into a restaurant. I smiled, remembering how much time I'd spent there as a teenager with my best friend Sarah, listening to awful singer/songwriters and chain smoking. It was the only place around the area that let you smoke. It was probably the least healthy way to spend our evenings, stuck inside a smoke box, but we'd loved it there. At one point Sarah wanted to be an artist, and they'd kindly hung her oil paintings. She even sold one of them for fifty bucks.

Though we grew up next door to each other, Sarah got married to Marc Esposito, a guy we both knew at Madison High but she didn't start dating until college, and moved to Chicago a little over a month ago. For work, Marc does something with consulting that he's explained to me five times and I still don't understand. I don't have a lot of close girlfriends and Sarah leaving dealt more of a blow to me than I've let on. We've been friends nine years. Who else would be willing to watch *Pretty in Pink* with me while sitting in their old prom dress?

Driving on Madison Avenue now reminded me of my father teaching Sarah and me how to drive on this very road. Sarah's parents were both doctors and had a practice in Chatham, so they were never home. He'd been either especially dedicated or especially nutty, as he taught us on his old Honda Accord stick shift. I'd picked it up quickly, but Sarah kept stalling out and the three of us would jerk forward. "Sorry!" she'd say. "I'm so sorry!"

I put down the visor to avoid the sun's glare and suddenly was struck on the forehead by a flying object that landed on my lap. Trying not to crash, I reached down and grabbed what turned out to be a dusty CD. I'd written in Sharpie on it HARPER'S CD YOU TOUCH YOU DIE. It was Hitchhiker's Revenge's second album, *Suits Fucking Suck,* and I turned it up way loud. My thoughts turned to Nick and I picked out the guitar solos, listening intensely. I wondered if he'd shopped here at Quick Check, scaring customers with his tattoos and slinking around the aisles like a wild leopard. He was just so . . . unique. I found it hard to picture him in suburbia between Doritos bags and frozen dinners.

As I drove, I passed a dead deer on the side of the road, a sight as common in New Jersey as diners and McMansions. One hoof was poised in midair; the white gleam of a rib bone shone in the midday sun. I felt the deer should have a proper burial. I imagined this buck, bravely trying to run across the highway that had perhaps once been forest and therefore its home. The car in front of me leaned on its brakes and I slowed down. I closed my eyes and imagined that, instead of a deer by the side of the road, it was a human body. White flesh torn from bones, red guts spilled out on the highway. One eye open but staring at nothing at all.

I passed a WELCOME TO MORRISTOWN sign and took a left on Miller Road. The sun was high in the sky as I parked and walked the pebble stone driveway to Macculloch Hall. The mansion in front functions as a local museum during the week, but it's their garden around the back where I spent most of my angsty adolescent days reading.

After strolling among the flowers, most of which were now fading in color as autumn marched toward winter, I lay down and watched the sky through tree branches for an hour, until the wind grew too fierce. I watched hundreds of orange and yellow leaves swish back and forth as the wind gently nudged them.

It was time to head home.

I drove a car only when I visited my parents. I don't love driving, so living in the city and getting around via public transportation was a true pleasure. Therefore, I hadn't kept my eye on the gas gauge, and it was now flashing a bright red E at me.

New Jersey being the only state that doesn't allow you to pump your own gas, I drove to the nearby station and fiddled with the radio until the attendant brought me the bill, then spent a full minute staring at it. Twenty-five dollars? How could that be? Gas must have risen in price since the last time I'd come home.

Back home, I found Lauren's bedroom door cracked open and her behind her easel, a streak of red paint in her blond hair that looked like spun gold in the fading sunlight. Baby wisps came down from the ponytail she'd fastened, and she was frowning, the lines around her mouth making her heart-shaped face look older. She was wearing a plain black T-shirt, jeans, and brown leather moccasins with white paint splattered across, like she'd dripped her brush on them. She'd painted a face with similar features to her own, slightly blurred, with an arrow coming in one ear and sticking out the other. I felt uneasy looking at it.

"Um . . . everything okay?" I asked.

"Yup."

"You sure? That painting is a little . . . I mean, it's really good work, it's just a little dark."

"What's that supposed to mean?" She thrust her brush into a water solution. I could see a flush on her cheeks.

"I just worry about you, that's all," I stammered.

"Well, you *ought* to be worrying about Dad, who is making another sign for the molester's house."

Okay, so we have a child molester living around the corner from us. I know, I know. It's weird. His name is Martin Peterson and he's really old and has crinkly eyes and snow-white hair and drives a Cadillac. He also molested six boys while he was headmaster of an all-boys boarding school. He spent fifteen years in jail and moved to our neighborhood when I was five. This was before Megan's Law, so no one knew about his dark past until 2004, when the law went into effect and everyone who lives in our neighborhood went down to the police station to sign a piece of paper stating they were aware they were living near a felon. Since then, my father has been holding monthly protests in front of Peterson's house, or as he's better known in my house, the Molester. In the beginning, people were outraged. "He swims at our pool!" "He borrowed my leaf blower once!" "My children cut through his backyard!" But, as the years went by, and the Molester stayed mainly indoors and didn't interact with anyone, people forgot about him.

Not Dad. Ridding the neighborhood of the Molester became an obsession for him, resulting in the Molester filing a complaint, citing harassment. He'd had his bushes ripped from the ground in his front and side yards, rocks thrown through his windows, his Cadillac keyed. My father was never caught for these crimes,

but when he first made a sign that read MOLEST SOMEWHERE
ELSE! and marched it up and down the Molester's front yard, this
turned out to be illegal and now my father marches twenty feet
back, on the street, which is apparently public property and therefore legal.

"Do you think it's too late to stop him?" I asked Lauren, trying
to ease the tension between us with an injection of humor. "Maybe
we could tell him Mr. Peterson's out of town at a conference for
molesters or something?" She turned toward the window to hide
her smile.

Dad was in the basement, wielding a paintbrush. I came around
his tool bench to read his new sign. DIG A HOLE AND LIE IN IT AND
DIE!

"Er, Dad?" I said.

"What, honey? This baby is almost ready to go. Just a few
more dashes of paint, and back to the streets I go. I really think he's
ready to crack. Your mother said Mrs. DeLuca from around
the corner was told by her sister Marjorie's oldest son that the
Molester was seen coming out of a shrink's office on Main Street.
I think I'm really getting to him. He's going to have a 'For Sale'
sign up any day now. I won't have that sicko living around the
corner from my little babies. I'll go to hell and back before he's
allowed to stay here one more day."

"Dad, Mr. Peterson is pushing ninety. If he tried to touch me,
I'd kick him in the balls so hard I'd probably kill him."

"It's not just about you and Lauren; I have to protect all the
other neighborhood kids. Besides raising you girls, it's my life's
calling."

It's hard to argue with my father when he gets on one of
his rants. After all, who wants a molester living nearby? No
one.

I sighed. "Okay, I'll come with you."

His face lit up. "Really? 'Cause I can make you your own sign and everything."

"What about this one here, that says 'Give it a rest, Madison is not a place to molest'?"

He placed a proud hand on the wooden handle and smoothed down his beard with his other hand. "That's an oldie but a goodie. No, I'm thinking for you I'll make something a little more serious."

I walked around the basement, finding old Ping-Pong balls on a shelf inside a dusty goldfish bowl that had held at least five Paxils over the years. (I knew my parents kept buying different fish, but I didn't let on as not to upset Lauren.) I pulled a tarp off our old foosball table, and idly knocked the hard wooden ball around the field, thinking how it was freakish every one of the little wooden soccer players looked just like Bill Gates without his glasses.

With my sign reading DIE MOLESTER SCUM and my father in tow, we skulked around the corner and spent a half hour marching up and down the street, quitting when it got dark and we were hungry for dinner. We didn't talk much, but there was an exciting moment where we thought we saw a second-floor curtain twitch.

Lauren cooked spaghetti and we all took a little quiz my mother concocted where you write down how many presidents' first and last names you know. She'd read something about people in their twenties knowing more *American Idol* contestants' names than presidents'.

"That quiz is so prejudiced against young people!" I said. "Some smug guy thinking he's the cat's ass came up with that whole 'count presidents' idea."

My father won with forty-one, my mother came in second with twenty-nine, Lauren had six. I had four.

"How many present and former *American Idol* contestants can you name?" Lauren asked.

"Um . . ." I counted on both hands. Then, both hands again. "Nineteen. Shit!" We all laughed.

Later, I went with Lauren and my parents to temple. It was neat to see Rabbi Levi looking exactly the same: short and cheerily pudgy. The last time I'd come here was for a Shabbat service two weeks after September 11, 2001. I was seeking answers for the most tragic event of my lifetime. As the calm service proceeded, I'd imagined terrorists bursting through the doors strapped with bombs, the delicate wooden ceilings caving in, the screams, a rush to the doors. Violence felt so much more tangible after 9/11; I no longer felt safe.

Rabbi Levi's round face brought back my childhood. At thirteen, my main concerns were losing my virginity and watching Eric Nies shake his tush on MTV's *The Grind* after school. "I don't even want to *have* a bat mitzvah," I'd haughtily told the rabbi during a particularly tough practice session. He'd leaned in so closely I could see my reflection in his glasses; one single nose hair curled over the lip of his nostril. A smirk played on his lips, or at least I think it did; he had quite a bushy beard.

"Do you have any idea how many presents you're going to get?" he asked. "Now shut up and let's hear you read that Torah portion one more time."

Tonight, we sat in the back row, as usual. My mother had several patients who attended our temple and she was sensitive to the fact that they'd feel awkward running into their therapist. Our seating also worked well for me, as I was able to slip *Time Out New*

York into the prayer book. I don't believe in God, only the long history of my people. As John Goodman says in *The Big Lebowski*: "Three thousand years of beautiful tradition, from Moses to Sandy Koufax."

Barukh atah Adonai, Eloheinu, melekh ha'olam. I knew these prayers by heart like I knew the lyrics to the Ramones' "I Wanna Be Sedated," and spoke the difficult Hebrew only two beats behind Rabbi Levi. My dad sang unabashedly in his booming voice, causing several people to glance over at us. Overcome with emotion and feeling happy among other Jews, I leaned over and whispered to him that I wanted to get my Jewish name inked in Hebrew on my wrist.

"Haven't our people been tattooed enough?" he whispered back, deadpan.

When we got back home Dad said he had some good pot and we climbed out the second-floor window onto the little rooftop there and passed the joint back and forth, watching the sun begin its heavy descent into the back porches of our neighbors. Cars up and down our block pulled into driveways; mothers and fathers coming home from a hard day's work. This was somewhat of a tradition between my father and me: to smoke and talk and talk and smoke. I don't know when it started; I guess sometime in high school. I can see how to some people it might seem strange, but in my family strange is relative. I never graduated on to serious drugs, never had any interest. It's a bonding experience for us, something we both enjoy and an instrument that opens long hours of deep philosophical discussion. My mom had long ago given it up and Lauren had no interest; besides, it would interfere with her medication. Last Thanksgiving my dad had offered to take Andy into the backyard and smoke him up. He'd declined, saying he didn't like feeling "out of control."

After, I sank into the white claw-foot tub in my old bathroom. I'd found an ancient dusty peach bath gel in the cabinet and poured it in, creating huge bubbles that felt slippery and delicious beneath and around me.

I always think of Frida Kahlo's *What the Water Gave Me* while taking baths; I like to line up my toes with the faucets as she did in the painting, sticking my big toe inside the spout to feel the cold trickle of water still filling the tub. At the time of the painting, Frida was fed up with living in Detroit; she felt the United States' art scene was run by a bunch of pompous jerks. I thought back to Bruce Willis grabbing my arm, whispering "You can do better than this" in my ear. I too felt fed up with the industry I was in, only, I needed a plan.

For the first time, I felt the pressure of what I had done churning inside me. I finally lay still, tilted back my head, and stared at the ceiling, which had white paint that was chipped in several places. I allowed myself to think about my future. Was I moving home to Jersey? And why did I still call my parents' house "home"? Could I afford to rent a studio anywhere in New York? How would I get all my stuff from the apartment without running into Andy? I lay back in the tub, my breasts peeking up like lemons. I felt like Ophelia (minus the dead part), my skin luminescent and shiny under the light on the ceiling. I could almost feel the soft petals of lotus flowers floating by, the scrapings of willow branches underneath me. My mother walked by in the hallway and I smiled at the familiar swishing sound of her slippers.

After getting out of the tub I threw on a Pogues T-shirt I found buried in my dresser and walked back to my room, stopping to look at some photographs lining the wall. It was always such a jolt to see Dad's beard a dark brown instead of the snow white it is now, photos where my mother's hair reaches to her waist. There were funny ones of her in a tiny brass bathtub during a trip to France. She's pregnant with me and her stomach sticks up high above the tub, like a mountain. My father must have been saying something to make her laugh, as she's just turned away from the camera and is pretending to look disapproving. I loved the photos of me at three, sitting on our old floral sofa that Lauren has in her dorm room now, my tiny screaming sister placed in my arms looking like an angry squid.

Should I go into the city tonight? Back in my room, I sat down on the purple velvet chair I'd bought in college and kept here because it was too wide to fit in my New York apartment. Something sharp poked me in the thigh and I stood, reaching under the soft pillow. Out came my old Sony Walkman, circa 1994. It was dusty and one headphone was missing its fuzzy ear cover. It was half blue, half silver. I'd decorated it with little rainbow stickers that, now, made me smile. I popped the headphones on my ears and discovered only one side worked. Play and Pause shared a button. Stop/Eject was a long green bar. I hit Play, and a high, unnaturally whiny voice sang Alvin and the Chipmunks–style, too fast. Opening it, I discovered the tape's plastic guts had come out, and I fished around for a pencil in my bedside table. I stuck the pencil through the spokes eraser side first, and wound the reel until it felt tight. It was an act I'd done hundreds of times before. It felt archaic and yet somehow comforting. Seeing a relic from my childhood reminded me nothing changed here in Madison. I could go away and change and morph in all my beliefs and boyfriends and grow up and my Sony Walkman had been here all along, collecting dust.

I hit Play again and Duran Duran's "Rio" came streaming out, still a little high and whiny, but clear. I felt an absurd sense of accomplishment, and sat there happily listening until the sounds of raised voices coming from downstairs reached my ears and blocked out Simon Le Bon's voice. I heard murmured voices, then a loud "No!" More speech I couldn't make out, then "You can't make me!"

Looking at the time on my cell phone I realized it was only five, though it felt much later because it was so dark outside. If I left now, I could probably make it to Mud around seven. I laughed out loud, the sound startling Anna Freud, who was lying nearby. She let out a tentative *Woof?* Was I seriously considering going back there? I changed into my favorite T-shirt, which says I'M FROM NJ BUT I DON'T LIKE BON JOVI: I LOVE HIM. I'm partial to Springsteen shirts, but I don't mind throwing my man Bon Jovi a little love now and then.

I walked into the kitchen tentatively. My parents were sitting at the table; my father's head was in his hands. Lauren cried loudly, her face folded over and crumpled. She sat on the floor, her back against the cupboards. "What's going on?" I asked, though there weren't always concrete reasons for Lauren's breakdowns.

"Your sister feels she doesn't need to take her antidepressants," my mother said. Her tone held both anger and bewilderment. "She has been lying to us for six months while at Princeton, throwing her medicine down the drain." It had taken my parents close to ten years and five different shrinks to figure out which medications were right for Lauren. They'd taken out a loan from the bank because their health insurance doesn't cover Lauren's current psychiatrist. I felt a surge of anger.

"How could you be that fucking selfish?" I asked her.

"I don't like your language," Mom said in a defeated voice.

"Mind your own business, Harper," Lauren said, scowling at me.

"If anyone needs me call my cell. I'm going into the city. It's too crazy around here." I ran upstairs, grabbed the Walkman, and went out the front door, slamming it, and spent the train ride to the city looking out the window, brooding. I got off at Penn Station, feeling like I was repeating yesterday in some kind of *Groundhog Day* daze. The E took me to Fourteenth Street; then I walked up the subway steps and into a busy New York evening. The sweet smell of roasted peanuts from a street vendor wafted over to me. I eyed the overpriced clothing in the window of Urban Outfitters as I waited for the M14 bus. I got a kick out of their overpriced tank tops with sparkly scarves wrapped around the skinny necks of mannequins in their windows. It depressed me that my generation was so gullible as to not only spend good money on a flimsy tank top, but to be sold the idea of wearing it in October. With a stupid scarf that costs twenty bucks.

What the fuck was I doing going to Mud? What if Andy saw me? He lived only two blocks away from there, after all, even though he rarely went to Mud and preferred the Starbucks around the corner. I had no clue what he'd be up to on a Friday night; it was the first weekend we weren't spending together in two years. It felt like my whole world was caving in; everything I knew was changing, shifting. When the bus pulled up I almost missed it, I was so deep in thought. I smiled at a beautiful black woman with a bright purple head wrap sitting across from me, hoping I looked like a nice person and not someone who had walked out on her boyfriend the day before and was now going to possibly meet up with another guy.

Nick wasn't there, of course.

I earned a few glares from people sitting at the bright orange plastic counter. I realized I'd left the door open, and quickly shut it against the evening's chill. Someone had spilled gold glitter all over the entryway floor. It brought about an ethereal quality, like I was in someone else's dream. Fiona had dyed a pink stripe into the front of her hair, curling and pinning it into a roll like the inside of a surfer's wave. The rest of her hair was pulled back in a bun, with a bright yellow birthday candle stuck through it. "Nice shirt," she said when I walked in the door.

I spent the next half hour people-watching, one of my absolute favorite activities second to taking baths. Mud gets quite the cast of characters, all united by their love of a good cup of coffee. I recognized James Iha from the Smashing Pumpkins in the corner, but that's no biggie because on any given day he can be found around here. He's an East Village staple, like Mud itself. I flipped the Walkman on, the coverless headphone scratching the lobe of my ear. "Hungry Like the Wolf" was coming on.

I didn't realize he was standing in front of me until he thrust his thick finger into my face and touched my neck. When I looked down he ducked me on the chin, that old trick. I whipped off the headphones. "You're a brat," I said. He was wearing a Dead Kennedys *Fresh Fruit for Rotting Vegetables* T-shirt. It was one of the first albums I'd ever bought.

"Is this seat taken, madam?" Nick asked, mock bowing at me.

"Yeah, this isn't a square dance."

He looked surprised, then threw his head back and laughed. It came to me then, what being near Nick felt like. When Lauren and I were little, my father would speed up on hills, taking his foot off the pedal just as he drove over the steepest part. Lauren and I would shriek in the backseat, our stomachs feeling like they'd fall right out of our bodies. Nick had intensity like that, and I had to admit I liked it; after being so bored and listless in my relationship with Andy, it felt good to be around someone who excited me.

"James Iha is here," I told him.

He rolled his eyes.

"When is that guy *not* here?"

"Whatever, like when are *you* not here," I said. I was flirting, something I can't recall ever truly doing before. I've always been bold, but never really much of an instigator. I'd never really cared enough, seeming to prefer just falling in and out of relationships like the tides on sand.

"Usually never," he said, eyes bright. "I just heard some crazy chick from Jersey who may or may not be carrying a rug might be lurking around here, so I rode my bike over to see."

"Wow, where'd you get this old Walkman?" he asked, picking it up off the table and turning it over in his hands. "This baby is *ancient!*"

"Oh, it was at my parents' house. Isn't it awesome? And guess what I was listening to the last time I used it, which had to be back in the nineties because I remember I got a CD Walkman after this, then an iPod."

"What? Let me guess. Debbie Gibson."

"No!" I laughed. "Duran Duran. How cool was I when I was ten?"

"You were ahead of your time, oh wise one," he said, doing a little bow.

Before I could think of a clever retort Fiona brought the cup of coffee I'd ordered. "Hey, darlin'," Nick said, standing up to wrap her in a hug.

"How have you been, man?" she asked him, punching his arm and sitting in the third chair at our table. I resented her intrusion, just a little.

"Fiona, let me introduce you to the magnificent Harper Rostov," Nick said. They were both staring at me.

"I know her already, she's in here all the time," Fiona said. "Three cups of coffee with lots of sugar and milk, right, honey?"

I blushed.

A friendly-looking guy wearing a Greenpeace T-shirt and holding a clipboard walked into Mud and approached us with an open face but Fiona impatiently waved him away. "Fuck off, I have enough of my own problems to worry about," she said. Nick shrugged at him apologetically before he slunk off.

"How do you and Nick know each other?" I asked her, sipping my coffee.

"I used to know him in the biblical sense," Fiona said, laughing.

Jealousy coursed through me; I tried not to let it show on my face. Nick threw his head back and laughed.

"Fiona was too much woman for me. Actually, she does our sound when we play New York. She's also some crazy kind of taxidermist," Nick said.

"I'm a crypto-taxidermist," Fiona said, glaring at Nick. "If you're going to tease me, at least get it right."

"Excuse me?" I asked. "What's that?"

Nick was crossing his eyes behind her back and I had to bite my lip not to laugh.

"I re-create mythological animals using parts of real deceased animals, and also carve some additional things like horns out of plaster and later paint them."

"Like unicorns?" I asked. She seemed pleased that I was interested.

"Yes, I've done two unicorns. I got a job to make a griffin next. Do you know what that is?" Her skin was lit from the nearby holiday lights, and I saw pockmark scars on her cheeks from old acne.

Nick jumped in. "Part lion, part eagle, right?"

I shot him a surprised look.

"There's one in *Alice in Wonderland*," he said, shrugging.

"I'll have to come check out your animals," I said to Fiona.

"Please do," she said warmly.

A nearby table signaled to Fiona. "Hold your horses!" she shouted at them. Then, "Watch out for that one," she said, pointing at Nick. Over her shoulder, she sang out: "He's our resident lothario."

Nick made the international sign for crazy, twirling a finger near his ear.

"So how's the situation with your man?" he asked, kicking his boots up on the chair Fiona had vacated. He put his hands behind his head, like someone on a hammock. I almost spit out my coffee. I didn't expect him to bring up Andy. I instantaneously flashed back to the look on Andy's face when I said I was leaving him. My mood dropped.

"Um . . . it's kind of hard to say. I left the apartment yesterday and went home to Madison. I don't really know what my next step is going to be." Voicing it out loud to Nick felt more final somehow than when I'd told my parents and Lauren. "I'm feeling very emo-like," I told him.

"Don't be emo," he said. "Then we'd have to go listen to Morrissey in my hearse and drive around all sad-like."

"Um . . . did you say hearse?"

"Yeah. Bought it on craigslist a few years ago. It gets great gas mileage and the wide back is great for holding all our equipment."

"I'd like to see this hearse sometime," I said.

"Absolutely. Yes, ma'am. Until then, what do you say we go out and cheer you up?" he asked, standing up.

I stared at him.

"Come on, the night is young! We're both single! Let's go have a drink. What's a little alcohol between friends?"

I started shaking my head up and down before the yes came out of my mouth. Then, "Okay."

He grinned.

I collected my Walkman, left money on the table, waved to Fiona, and walked out into the night. I wasn't sure what I was doing, but there was a tiny thrill developing in the very pit of my stomach, like a lick of fire. A spark of life in a body that felt left behind, ignored, unused. If a camera had followed me these past few months, silently trailing behind my gait, it would have depicted the slumped shoulders of a young woman, dulled to the electric environment that is New York City surrounding her, bored, alone. No, not alone. Lonely.

His skateboard was leaning against a tree outside. Shockingly, no one had stolen it. We walked toward First Avenue with no particular destination in mind, my eyes focused only on the shadows our bodies made on the sidewalk as the last sip of light from the day slipped behind buildings, all in a row and slightly crooked like teeth. Because our figures were so long and stretched out on the pavement, it gave the illusion we morphed into each other; where his shoulder ended mine began, like one giant Rorschach test. It was cold and Nick walked near me, a presence. It started to lightly drizzle. We passed many four-story buildings, walk-ups. One thing I love best about the Village is the absence of high-rises. In a city that's so hectic, living in an area where things are low makes everyone calmer. I began to notice men *and* women checking him out. A tiny black-and-white dog followed us for several blocks, staring up at Nick adoringly. Farther along, a man rushing home from work on a bicycle wore a brown leather backpack with a huge bouquet of pink roses sticking out of the top. "You know what, I hate roses," I said in a jocular tone. "I'd much rather a guy gave me a plant."

Nick smiled. "Right. You strike me as the kind of girl who *pretends* she doesn't like roses, when really, you'd, like, go apeshit if I gave you them."

"Whatever. That guy probably cheated on his wife and feels guilty about it." I gestured toward the man, now obscured by an MTA bus. "Thus, the flowers."

He laughed. "Harper the pessimist."

I scowled at him.

He stopped in front of Coyote Ugly, the dive bar that spawned the flick about nice girls from New Jersey "making it" once they writhed on the bar countertop. He found a nearby gate and leaned his skateboard. The board was starting to annoy me—couldn't he just walk everywhere like a normal person? And what was with the means of transportation, anyway? It reminded me of the dopey stoner guys from high school. I'd watch them spinning around in the courtyard of our school, while I sat, bored, in Algebra 2 class.

"You so can't be serious," I said. "This is where sailors go to meet skanky girls during fleet week. This bar is lame."

"I like the way you just said *sooooo*," he said, mimicking my squeaky voice. "Besides, I like skanky girls."

"Well, I like sailors, so there!" I stuck out my tongue at him.

He raised an eyebrow at me.

I thrust open the door. What the hell, I'd have one drink. Besides, I'm from New Jersey; I can dance on top of a bar better than anybody! In the Garden State we do that just after exiting the womb.

We entered a room so dark it took my eyes a few minutes to adjust. I tried to swing my leg over the bar stool in a sexy way and almost fell off. Nick caught me in one swift motion and pushed my butt up on the seat, as if we'd known each other for years.

"Watch it, buddy," I said. "You're cruising for a bruising. Not just anybody gets to touch my ass."

Throwing his hands up mock innocently, he sat down next to me, his knee touching mine, and pushed up one sleeve. His arms were covered completely in tattoos, which I remembered vaguely from seeing him play Webster Hall in a cut-off T-shirt, but it was still a shock up close. Koi fish decorated his forearms, and there were military tanks with large, wide orange stripes in the background; a sunset. Living in this neighborhood I'd seen enough bad tattoo jobs to know that Nick's was expertly done. He had a full sleeve with little color; the artist appeared to have mostly used navy blues, so they didn't appear cheesy or amateur. I touched three squiggly lines, woven in with the fish. "Nice Hot Water Music tattoo," I said, proud I knew what the symbol meant.

"Best band in the world," he replied, motioning to the waitress for a beer.

"I interviewed Chuck Ragan a couple years ago, for this zine I started in college called *Thrash*," I said, immediately feeling young and silly; I'd just aged myself.

"Oh, we know *Thrash*," Nick said. "The whole band reads it. You started that? You're, like, a legend! I always ask my parents to pick a copy of it up whenever I'm going to be home from tour. Isn't it still being put out?"

I felt my chest rise. He reads *Thrash*! "Yeah," I said proudly. "They kept it up after I graduated."

"That is awesome," Nick said. "I feel like I'm meeting a celebrity! So many of my buddies in bands read that zine. Is it something you could do for a job?"

"Nah," I said. "It just barely stays afloat with donations from Rutgers. It has a very small circulation. But I loved working on it. I have to figure out how I can write about music but actually get paid to do it. That's the name of the game, brother."

"How old are you, anyway?" he asked, squinting hard at me while taking a sip of beer.

"I'm twenty-three," I said. "Afraid of getting arrested for soliciting a minor?" Hitchhiker's Revenge had been together roughly fifteen years, so Nick had to be about thirty-five, thirty-six, though he seemed more like guys my own age.

" 'Soliciting' makes it sound like I showed up at your doorstep and tried to sell you Tupperware," he said.

"Do you think they have white wine here?" I asked.

"Are you serious?"

I laughed, and, like him, ordered a beer. I noticed the bartender had been staring at Nick since we got there, so I wasn't surprised when she came over to us. Nick was a guy everyone eventually wound up speaking to. She looked about twenty-one, with red hair to her waist, and was wearing what you'd expect someone who works at Coyote Ugly to wear: a black corset and skinny leather pants. I weigh 135, which is no fatty patty, but I would have a hell of a time trying to squeeze into those pants. She leaned over the bar, her breasts nearly skimming the bottom of her chin. I tried not to be jealous. "You're Nick, from Hitchhiker's Revenge." It was a statement, not a question. He managed to look surprised she'd noticed, like this was the first time he'd been recognized. He'd done the same thing with me when I approached him in Mud yesterday; it must be something he'd perfected, that element of looking humble when someone recognized him. Like a cheap parlor trick. "My ex-boyfriend was way into you guys, I've seen you like a hundred times," she said, speaking only to him.

"They're awesome, right?" I said a little too loudly. She eyed me up and down, taking in my messy hair and Bon Jovi T-shirt.

"I'm Daniela," she said, and promptly leaned across the bar and gave me a huge bear hug. I was surprised by the gesture.

The three of us spent the next two hours talking about music, the ever-gentrifying East Village, and whether the death of CBGB was good or bad for rock 'n' roll. (I thought it was bad to lose a historic place; Nick and Daniela insisted it gave smaller music venues a shot.)

The room started to get that soft-edged glow, and I realized I was drunk. Nick and I had long ago stopped paying for the booze; Daniela was hooking it up for free and even drinking along with us. Finding myself getting a tad jealous when the two of them started arm wrestling (so cliché), I wandered over to the jukebox. It held a lot of my favorite Jersey bands. Hitchhiker's Revenge's first CD, *We Love Beavers,* was even in there. I only had a buck on me, which earned me one song, so I shoved it into the machine and went back to my bar stool. Daniela had left to serve a few dodgy-looking old guys who were ogling her. Her laughter sounded out over the din of the bar. "She's sexy," I said, nodding my head toward Daniela.

"*You're* the sexy one," Nick said. I rolled my eyes at him, but then he put his hand on my leg and everything seemed to stop. His hand was so large, it nearly wrapped around my thigh. "I'm serious," he said. "You're a beautiful girl, and smart to boot."

"I didn't know people actually said 'to boot' in real-life conversations," I said nervously. It had been a long, long time since I'd been appreciated. Andy, while not a bad guy, felt doling out compliments was "fake." He also had never said he loved me, stating that I should just "understand it is so."

Dillinger Escape Plan's "Sunshine the Werewolf" started playing in the background.

"Nice," he said. "And the lady makes a good choice."

"You thought I'd play angry vagina music, didn't you?" I asked him. He was in the middle of downing the last of his beer, which he spit out, laughing. I handed him a napkin and we sat there comfortably.

"My ex has that red hair too," he said, nodding toward Daniela. "Like fire."

"She must be really pretty, I love red hair," I said, trying to figure out how we went from him complimenting me to talking about his ex-girlfriend.

"I always told her how fucking drop-dead she is, but she doesn't believe me."

"What's the situation with you guys anyway?"

"I just needed a break," he said, scuffing the steel toe of his boot on the side of the bar. "I'm working on the cover art for our next album, trying to keep the band together, and scouting for a new rental space for us to practice. We've been using the basement of our drummer John's house for years and I think his wife is ready to kill us."

He turned and looked straight at me, abruptly switching back to speaking of his ex. "She'd been acting jealous, on my back for the last few months about getting married . . ." He trailed off. "I needed some time for myself, just to see if she and I are even going to make it. I'm fucking thirty-six years old; my friends are all married with kids, or about to get divorced. I'm just not sure if she's the right person for me to marry, is all I'm saying, though she's so goddamn pretty and I miss being in bed with her, like I wish I was there right now. I love her so much, but she's a pain in the ass." He reached out then, and stuck his finger through a snarl in my hair, playing with it absentmindedly. "I guess the problem is that I just love women."

I rolled my eyes and yanked my hair out of his grasp, arranging it into a messy ponytail so I had something to do with my hands. His touch had jump-started something inside me, but I didn't want to show it.

"I don't mean it in a sexual way," he said, raising his eyebrows. "Though there's that too. I just love the way women move, their voices, their practical and more gentle way of thinking and existing in the world." He stopped talking to take a sip of my beer, and I watched his Adam's apple bob up and down. "I just get into trouble these days when I try to make something last." He ducked his head. "Don't get involved with me, Harper Rostov, I'm a fucking mess. Had my heart ripped in half a long time ago, been shitty at relationships ever since. Every time I write a song, complete an album . . . It's like, I think I've got it all worked out, you know?" He spread his large hands on the bar. "I've gotten all the rats out of my basement, see, and I go down the stairs to check and there's hundreds of the fuckers, squinting at the light, burrowing into the walls."

"Sometimes I feel like relationships consist of telling your same life stories to different people until someone finally appreciates them," I said. "Until someone finally appreciates *me*," I said quietly.

Nick peered at me, like he was summing me up. Figuring me out. I squirmed a little in my seat. His gaze was so *intense*. "I know what you mean, fuck. It's like the same shit over and over again. Everyone I meet is nice, smart, funny. They just don't make me want to tear my heart out, you know? So what's the point?"

Daniela skipped over to us then before I could come up with

an answer and said she was getting off work—did we want to keep drinking together? I looked at my watch, it was 9:15. I just wanted to spend time with Nick, but before I could say anything he'd said "hell yeah" to her and the three of us were skipping down First Avenue, arm in arm. I thought about the cast of the *Wizard of Oz* on the yellow brick road and wondered which character I was. Perhaps the Tin Man, in search of a red, pulsating heart. Or at least someone to give it to.

We ended up at Bua Bar on St. Mark's, one of those bar-in-a-box places that hangs an Irish flag out front, serves shots of Jameson, and calls itself an Irish pub. Andy had taken me here last Saint Patrick's Day. The bar hired several little people dressed as leprechauns, which felt terribly un–politically correct, and everyone had bought them beers and shots all night.

I quickly ordered three whiskeys, deciding it was that delightful time in the night to switch to hard alcohol. "Have you guys been to Ireland?" I shouted over the noise. Daniela shook her head, but Nick said he'd toured through there last summer for three weeks with Bad Religion. "I was there last summer too!" I exclaimed. "My aunt and uncle got married in a tiny town outside Galway, it was gorgeous."

"Did you get a chance to go out to the Aran Islands?" Nick asked. "I took a boat out there by myself a few years ago when we were playing a few shows in Galway."

"I did!" I said. "I rented a bike and pedaled around for a full day; it was gorgeous. At one point I almost fell off the edge of a cliff, but other than that I loved it!" As we spoke, I noticed Daniela out of the corner of my eye pulling her leather jacket tighter around her body as if she were cold, and drumming her fingers on the countertop. She looked different suddenly, out of her element when away from Coyote Ugly.

"I don't know what the hell y'all are talking about," she said, smiling. I was struck unexpectedly by how pretty she would be without makeup. "I've only been two places: Tennessee, where I was born and lived until I was eighteen, and New York City, where I live now."

"That's okay," I said, putting my hand on her arm, which was very thin. I could feel the bone beneath her skin. "I'm sure you'll get to travel at some point."

"I'm totally scared to fly though," she said, flipping her bright red hair over one shoulder. It was very pretty and fell in waves, like a tide coming in. "I think I'm just gonna stay put."

"We're leaving for Japan next week on tour. If you can scrape the money together, you would be welcome to come with us," Nick said. She let out a happy squeal, and jumped up to hug Nick, flashing me some side boob through her corset.

"Oh my god, Harper, we should both go, wouldn't that just be awesome?"

I recovered fast. "Yeah, we'd have a great time." In my drunken state, it actually seemed like a good plan. "Besides, I'm pretty much homeless anyway these days, so traveling could be fun."

Daniela frowned. "Why are you homeless?"

I sighed. And then, it all spilled out of me. At one point, she reached over and held my hand. Nick put one meaty arm around me, and signaled to the waitress for another round with the other. I saw the bartender reach under the counter and flip a switch and the lights turned way down. A woman wearing a pretty blue-and-yellow dress and brown clogs went around setting out candles on tables, which threw everyone's profiles into a mixture of golden light and shadow. The words just spilled out of me, the breakup, the closeness I wanted so badly with Lauren but didn't know how to make happen, the music writing I yearned to do. The alcohol had made me weepy, and Daniela decided this meant it was an opportune time for a bathroom break. Nick was looking vaguely freaked out. He kept patting my arm in this weird, older-brother kind of way.

"Girl time!" Daniela yelled as she and I excused ourselves to pee, pushing through the crowd. The bathroom had humongous barnlike doors that took the two of us to slide shut. Daniela collapsed in giggles from her perch on the sink while I tried hovering over the toilet. "Why don't you just sit down?" she said.

"No way, man," I said, starting to laugh. She was such a sweet girl. I was starting to cheer up. Hanging out with Daniela made me miss Sarah. I wondered what she was doing in Chicago. They were an hour behind us, so she was probably getting ready for bed. "I've developed thigh muscles of steel from squatting in various bars over the years," I told her. When it was her turn, I winced when she plopped right down on the toilet. She was even thinner without clothes, and I noticed a Chinese letter tattoo right above her crotch. She'd shaved off all her pubic hair. "What's that mean?" I asked, pointing to her tattoo.

"I got this on my eighteenth birthday," she said, and stood, nude, pointing to it. "My older brother's friend raped me and this symbol stands for courage. I was really screwed up when it happened, so I made the guy give me two hundred bucks not to call the cops and took a train to New York. I was on that train for a million zillion hours! I had no idea how far away New York was, only that I had to get here."

"I'm so sorry that happened to you," I said, horrified.

Daniela was doing a drunken swaying motion, and didn't seem keen on leaving the bathroom anytime soon, so I bent down and pulled up her pants for her. She suddenly grabbed my shirt in her fist and pulled me to her, kissing me openly on the mouth. My first thought was how soft her lips were. I'd never kissed another girl before. It wasn't half bad, like kissing a guy without the scratchy-face element. I didn't know what to say when she pulled away, but she started trying to pry the bathroom door open as if nothing had just transpired, so I grabbed her arm. "Daniela, what are you kissing me for? You should be kissing Nick." It was part truth, part insecurity on my part. I wanted Nick to like me, but I was feeling very loving toward everyone, as one does after three consecutive hours of boozing.

"Oh my god, Harper, get a clue!" she said, shaking one French-manicured finger at me. "He is totally into you."

"He's totally *not,* he's into you," I said, blushing.

"Well, he'd probably like to *fuck* me," she said in my ear as we made our way back to the table, "but he's falling for *you.*" The thought struck me as ridiculous. Nick certainly wasn't "falling for me," I'd just met him yesterday! Besides, his openness about talking about his ex unnerved me.

After three more rounds of shots I was flying. Nick and I started arguing over whether Henry Rollins of Black Flag had started out in a band called D.O.A. or S.O.A., and Daniela was deep in conversation with a table of post-work Wall Street types next to us, stealing one of their ties to fasten as a headband. I couldn't believe it when I checked my cell phone and the neon letters blinked 11:14 P.M. at me. Daniela blew Nick and me kisses; she was going home with one of the bankers. "Take care of her!" we yelled at them. Daniela's giggles rang out on the street as she was carried fireman-style out of the bar.

We decided to leave too.

After the heat of bodies pressed against one another in Bua Bar, the cool evening let the flush in my cheeks die down. It had rained, and the black streets reflected the light coming from the bar. Nick grabbed his skateboard, which once again was miraculously still there.

It was a Friday night in the Village, and drunken kids in the streets called to one another. Groups of smokers forced outside to get their fix huddled together like ostrasized lepers near entryways to bars. "Too many hipsters here these days," Nick said. "I miss when Alphabet City was a crack den."

"Ugh, you do not," I said. "Besides, I think you're very hip. Next thing I know you'll be moving to Williamsburg."

"Nah, no thanks," Nick said, smiling. "I don't think I'd fit in. I don't, like, throw dinner parties with little 'ironic' gun napkins or hang out at McCarren pool. I don't need a watch that looks like shit but cost a thousand bucks. Not my thing. Besides, how do hipsters pedal their bikes wearing such tight jeans? It defies logic. It boggles the mind."

"And how do they get their mustaches so thick?" I started giggling. "Maybe you, me, and Daniela are the only nonhipsters left in the East Village," I told him. Nick surprised me by laughing hard.

"She had the hots for you," Nick said as we walked along St. Mark's.

I rolled my eyes. "She kissed me in the bathroom!"

I thought he'd be shocked, but he looked strangely sad, and didn't respond. His moods seemed to switch without warning. We entered Tompkins Square Park, and I took his hand.

He flinched.

"What's wrong?"

"I just haven't held anyone's hand but my ex's in such a long time," he said.

"Well, there's change in the air for both of us," I told him. I

was drunk, and made wide gestures at the sky. My mood was organic; I felt close to the earth. The night. Nick. The air whispering
through my hair. It felt like I held the future in my fist, and I could
scatter it like the gold on the floor of Mud in any direction I chose.
"Can't you feel it?" I tripped then, over a stray branch on the path,
and would have fallen flat on my face if Nick didn't catch me.

"I think what you feel is that good ol' whiskey working its
magic in your system," he said mildly.

There went my hippie idealism. "Anyway, you don't have any
reason to feel bad. Both of us are single, right? So what's the big
deal? Who are we hurting?"

He still looked uneasy. "Maybe you're right. I'm just feeling
guilty all of a sudden," he said. "Like I'm doing something I'm
not supposed to be doing."

"Well, that's not very romantic," I told him, sullen. I started
to feel a bit foolish, thinking about my warm bed a few blocks
over and my other warm bed a train ride away. Maybe it was time
to go home, wherever that was. Nick could go be moody alone.

He grinned, and relief coursed through me. It felt like the sun
had come back out.

"You're probably right," he said, and leaned over to kiss me.
His big lips were wet, his kisses violent.

Nick slipped his hand into the back of my hair and tugged on
a knot, hard.

"Ow!" I said, pulling away. "That hurts."

"You like it," he said.

I did.

My arms slowly left the comfort of my pockets and I put one
finger into his belt loop, pulling him closer. I was surprised how
narrow his hips felt, given his broad chest. When he pulled away
I touched my lower lip. It felt bruised. Kisses of years past flashed

through my mind. Boys in middle school with their braces clacking against mine, a high school boyfriend whose teeth felt slimy. College guys with beer on their breath. I thought about Daniela kissing me in the bathroom and how it had made me sad. Andy had always kissed me so softly, like I was fragile and he was afraid of breaking me. I missed him, suddenly.

When we broke it off it was as though he'd made some kind of decision within himself, and this time he grabbed my hand without hesitation. I could see tons of stars in the sky, rare for New York. They glistened like gel in a Mohawk.

We passed a man squatting down in the bushes. He was swaying back and forth, a long piece of shit dangling between his legs. My stomach lurched and I stopped walking, but Nick tugged on my arm. "That was disgusting," I said, embarrassed. I thought I might be sick.

He was looking away from me, up to the sky. I wanted to reach out and rub my hand along the stubble on his chin so badly I stuck my hands in my pockets. "When I first moved to New York, I was homeless. We had a record deal but split four ways my take-home was about a hundred bucks a week. I literally slept on a piece of cardboard outside the building on Avenue C where Sunburnt Cow restaurant is now."

Though he said this with no emotion, I felt awful about my reaction to the homeless guy. Naïve.

"Well, did you poop on the sidewalk?"

"No, I definitely didn't."

We both laughed.

"Sometimes life is a shit-flavored Popsicle," I told him, having read the expression somewhere days ago and been waiting for an excuse to use it.

A man operating a mechanical wheelchair whirled past us,

the buzzing sound getting softer and softer as he moved farther away.

"If you couldn't afford housing, why didn't you just crash at your parents' house?" I asked.

He shook his head. I waited a few seconds for him to respond, but it seemed he wasn't going to.

Nick having been homeless triggered something in my mind, but I was too drunk to put my finger on what it was. He lit a cigarette, handing it to me and reaching into his pack of Marlboro Reds to shake out another.

"I don't smoke cigarettes," I told him.

"Now is a good time to start," he said, his voice an amused growl.

We arrived at Nick's place and stomped out our cigs. He lived above Zum Schneider, the beerhouse on Avenue C, in a five-story walk-up that looked like it was about to fall apart any second. The staircase curved gently around as we ascended. The walls were chipping off paint—gray and white speckled like a quail egg.

"I love buildings with a little bit of history to them," Nick said, trailing his big fingers along the banister.

I walked in front of him, and he pinched me lightly on the butt. I swatted at his hand.

"Me too," I said. "My parents' house in Madison is nineteenth century. When I was little, I used to think that if I dug around in the attic, I'd find a diary of a girl who once lived there."

"Did you?" he asked, unlocking his front door. There was a NO REPUBLICANS ALLOWED sticker across the peephole.

"No, but I did manage to tear down some plaster and piss my mom off."

"What a creepy little kid you were!"

"Shut up," I said, laughing and turning to swat his shoulder.

"That would have been nice, a present from a ghost," he whispered in my ear, pushing me gently inside the apartment. My arms broke out in goose bumps. The apartment spread out before us as Nick walked farther into the kitchen—a blue room so bright it was almost purple with colorful concert posters pinned to the walls with thumbtacks.

"Do you want something to eat?" he asked, opening his freezer door. I peeked over his shoulder to see several boxes of veggie burgers. One random packet of ketchup was stuck to the door. "I could cook you a veggie burger. Or, um . . . a veggie burger."

"Are you a vegetarian?" I asked.

"Yeah. Total punk rocker cliché, right?"

He shut the door.

"A lot of my friends are vegan, but I'd go crazy. I love my scrambled eggs. I just won't eat anything that has four feet or dreams."

I got a chill down my left side. What kinds of dreams do cows and chickens have? Should I give up meat for a little while, just to see if I could do it? Nick could help me quit meat cold turkey. We'd go on dates to the Indian restaurants on Sixth Street for vegetarian meals, talking and laughing over samosas. How cliché am I?

"Thanks, but I'm not hungry," I told him.

I thought we'd watch a movie, or maybe drink wine together, but I guess that stuff is just done in the movies, because he got a condom on right away, and we fell into bed seconds later—he was rough and gentle at the same time, his big hands encircling my body, his mouth on my breasts. There is something so exciting about being naked in front of another human being for the first time, the electricity in the air before a storm.

"I'm on top," I told him when he tried entering me from behind. "What do I look like, a dog?"

He laughed. "I don't care where you are," he said, squeezing my waist in an intoxicating way I'd never been touched before, pushing lightly on my pelvis and waking up everything below my belly button. "As long as I get you."

"You've got me," I said softly in his ear. I bit him lightly on his earlobe, then immediately thought of the Mike Tyson/Evander Holyfield fight where Holyfield almost lost his ear. I started giggling hysterically.

"Jesus Christ, Harper. What's so funny?"

"I was just thinking about Mike Tyson," I said.

He looked at me. "You are one weird broad."

Suddenly flipping me over, he reached down and started lightly touching me between my legs in soft, feathery circles and I lost all rational thought.

"Are you on the pill?" he breathed into my ear.

"Yeah . . . ," I said warily. I'd gone on the pill when I met Andy.

"So can I not use this condom then?" He was kissing me between talking and it made it hard to concentrate on what he was saying—not to mention the devilish things his fingers were up to. I wanted him to stop talking so much.

"I dunno. Do you have the clap?"

"Like that device that turns the lights off?"

"No. That's the *Clapper*. They sell it on infomercials. I meant do you have any STDs."

I propped myself up onto my elbow and peered at him. Was he less smart than I'd thought? Was I wearing intellectual beer goggles? Crap.

The corner of his mouth dipped. He was amused. "I was kidding, Harper."

"Oh!"

"And no, I don't have any STDs."

Of course I knew he had to wear a condom. Since the lesson my mother gave me at the dinner table as a preteenager with the latex over the banana like some freakish clown trick, I'd been strict with anyone who got to see my vagina: They had to strap one on. End of story. Only a dingbat lets a guy not wear a condom—especially a gorgeous rocker guy who travels with a band, admittedly did drugs, and has women at the ready whenever he enters a bar. I was tipsy, but not stupid.

But I wasn't lying when I said, "There's no time to take it off, I'm about to—" and unsurprisingly didn't need to finish my thought. Somewhere deep inside I knew sex could feel this good, I'd just never experienced it before. Time felt both long and short. He knew exactly what to do. He never hesitated; there were no awkward moments, no fumbling, no mashed kisses. The skin on his back felt smooth under my hands and the smell of him, motorcycle grease mixed with aftershave, gave me an orgasm so strong I grabbed his hand from under my head and squeezed it as hard as I could. He didn't let go, even though I know I must have bent his fingers back.

"Okay, so now I know your superhero power," I threw out into the semidark afterward. My voice came out throaty, like *I* was the one with the Marlboro habit.

He laughed.

"You're beautiful, Harper Rostov," he said. I was lying with my head resting on his stomach, the hair there soft, like down feathers. I hoped the bikini wax I'd gotten two weeks ago was lasting. I crossed my legs just to be safe.

"I'm surprised I was able to come," I told him.

"Why?"

I could see the outline of his large bicep as he propped himself up on one elbow. He was backlit with light from the street and the whites of his eyes were bright spots in the dark.

"I get the equivalent of whiskey dick when I'm drinking. I get whiskey clit!"

"You're a pervert," he said. "And you have a dirty mouth. Which I like. A lot."

"Perhaps. Hey, maybe if you're a good boy I'll even let you come next time."

"You mean, that's it? I don't get a turn?"

"Nah, I'm tired. Maybe in the morning."

"Er, I don't think this has ever happened to me before. Wow!" He laughed. "Good for you."

"What can I say, I'm a girl who knows what she wants."

The sheet was swirling around my body and as I shifted in his arms it fell off my stomach. He touched me lightly on my pelvis.

"This is a cool birthmark," he said.

I have a coffee-colored shape where most girls like to get tattoos.

He ran his finger around it, and the tickling gave me goose bumps. "Oh dude, your birthmark is the shape of New Jersey!"

I sat up. I've always been proud of my birthmark, I don't know why. I don't have tattoos to prove I'm different, just this and I've always liked it. "Really?"

"Yeah, see? Here's Weehawken, here's Morristown, where I'm from. . . ." His finger dipped lower. "Here's Cape May, the Jersey Shore. Wow, that is really rad. I've never met a girl with a Jersey birthmark. You're one of a kind, Harper. You're the real Jersey Girl!"

"I guess I am," I said.

He didn't respond, wrestling me into an embrace. Something about the way he held me, nuzzling my neck, caused an image of

Andy to dart across my mind. We'd play this stupid game called "rabid dog," where we would bite and lick each other like crazy for ten seconds, before laughing hysterically. It was one of those things that is so ridiculous it only makes sense to the couple. I pushed away that memory and looked at Nick's broad back, cuddling into it.

As he slept, I assessed the day. The golden hair Anna Freud had left on my bedsheets. The family meeting around the kitchen table at home. Daniela's tattoo. The taste of whiskey in my throat. The roughness of kissing Nick. I felt neither shame nor guilt. Only a deep sense of disorientation. It was as though the old me, the one who had been called Andy's girlfriend for two long, lonely years, had been kidnapped, only to be released a few hours later, into Nick's colorful arms. Uncertainty about the future flitted about in my consciousness like a pesky gnat. What if I couldn't get hired anywhere? Publishing was breaking down, and there were fewer jobs every day, especially music editor jobs. What would I do if Lauren wouldn't go back on her medication? What if she got seriously depressed again? It would break my parents and end the tiny strides she and I were making in getting closer. What if Andy hated me? I loved sleeping with Nick, but what was I doing? I wasn't even sure he was good for me or not. He seemed very stuck on his ex-girlfriend, and that was a messy situation I wanted no part of. I had my own messy situation.

Feeling restless, I walked over to the window. In the darkness, a green light flickered on and off, on and off, casting an eerie beam into Nick's bedroom. After a few moments I realized it was a neon Heineken sign someone had hung on their wall in the building across the street. Lying back down in the bed, I put my hand inside Nick's. I was startled when, in his sleep, he slid out of my grasp and stuck his hand down the front of his boxers. It now rested comfortably on his penis.

Saturday

When my eyes reluctantly peeled open Nick wasn't in the bed, but I heard rustling nearby. He didn't have curtains on his tall windows and I hadn't slept well, spending hours on my back listening to the sounds outside; noises that seemed so different to my ears, even though his apartment was only a few blocks away from Avenue A where Andy now slept. Andy had been pliable in his sleep, letting me twist and move him into any shape I wanted. Nick fell asleep on his stomach with his face in his pillow as if he was trying to suffocate himself, and remained in that position throughout the night.

There was a fuzziness to the morning, no doubt a result of last night's drinking marathon. I traced my palm along the coolness of the white wall and realized his apartment was set up as a loft, with windows next to the bed making the brick five-story building next door seem close enough to touch. Skylights in the ceiling brought the clouds close. There was a spiral staircase leading to the tiny bedroom. Shimmying out of the bed, I reached back and ran my hand along his green-and-gray-plaid flannel sheets, which were incredibly comfortable but looked like the kind you buy at Target the summer before your first semester of college. I padded naked over to the railing, which looked out onto the living room. A breeze swept over my body, and I felt an unexpected shiver of happiness rush over me. Goosebumps broke out everywhere. Even with the upstairs, the ceilings were high, and my eye traveled up and up into a spiral cone-shaped top. How did he land such a nice pad?

When I descended, I found him eating Cap'n Crunch cereal at a tiny table that had chipped red and blue ceramic tiles on the top of it that matched the colors of the koi fish on his arms. He was wearing a black Meatmen T-shirt, jeans, a backward Dropkick Murphys hat, and black-and-white Sambas.

"Hey," I said, kissing him on the top of his head. I had wrapped a sheet around me like a toga, and sat down in a chair opposite him, immediately feeling sore between my legs. It made me smile. "This is the part where you do the guy thing and act masculine and distant, right?" I asked, pouring myself some chocolate Cap'n Crunch cereal in a bowl he had set out for me. He flashed that toothy grin and my stomach did flips again.

He reached over and poured milk into my bowl. "Yeah, and then you write down your phone number with lipstick and I promise to call you but, of course . . ." He tipped an imaginary hat.

"You're an ass." Then, "What *shade* of lipstick?"

He put his finger to his chin, concentrating. "Mauve."

"Ew!" I threw my spoon at him, hitting him in the chest. It left a white splotch the shape of a question mark. "That is the ugliest adjective I've ever heard."

"I mauve you," he said, coming around the table and making vacuum cleaner–like sucking noises on my neck.

"I mauve you too," I said, laughing. "So how'd you land this place? Aren't you kind of a starving artist like the rest of us?"

"I bought it in the early nineties, before everyone and their grandmother fucking moved to Alphabet City. Literally, you could buy any drug right outside, or even in the hallway. I was the only white dude in the whole building. It was awesome."

"Oh yeah. I forgot you're so old." I blew him a kiss.

"Old and crotchety," he said. "Hey, can I make you a cup of tea?"

I watched the shape of him as he walked over to his stove. He was broad throughout the shoulders, tiny in the waist.

"Ugh, are you serious?" I said. "Do you have any coffee?"

"You know, green tea is really good for you, Harper. Just try it," he said, almost as a challenge.

"Fine. But make sure it's not the kind with the staple in the bag. I hate drinking staple water."

Walking over to his adorned fridge, I ran my fingers over the bumps in a skateboard shop's logo, and several pictures. It was like a scrapbook, all the connecting photographs and glued-on guitar picks and Harley stickers. No one had ever made me tea before. It seemed such a delicate gesture from such a macho guy, and it endeared him to me. I felt a buzzing, like picking up a frequency out of the airwaves. I'd had one-night stands before, and I was always in a rush to leave the next day, mortified at my own carelessness. I touched a picture of Nick with his arm slung around Johnny Cash. Nick's face was lit up like a child's. They were on a wooden stage, its floor covered in a frayed Oriental carpet. Gleaming black speakers were fuzzy in the background.

"Great photo," I said.

He looked up from the stove and smiled. When he set down my steaming mug he looked distracted, as though seeing the picture had taken him elsewhere. I imagined what it felt like to brush against the stiff lapels on Johnny's black shirt, hear the boom in his famously deep voice. Smell the tobacco on his skin. What a legend he was. This was the man, after all, who recorded at Folsom Prison in '68. This was the guy who, when invited to play for President Nixon at the White House, refused Nixon's requested songs and played "What Is Truth" and "Man in Black." Instead of hanging a poster on his dormitory wall like I'd had at Rutgers or downloading his songs on iTunes like millions of kids do, Nick had actually *shared a stage* with Johnny Cash. It blew my mind.

Nick tipped his head toward the photo. "That was taken right before he died. The Rock and Roll Hall of Fame had a tribute where various bands covered his songs."

"They asked you guys to play? That's awesome!"

His eyebrows shot up, a gesture I was beginning to realize he did constantly, as though whoever was speaking was saying the most fascinating thing he'd ever heard.

"Every punk kid in a band looks up to the Man in Black, you know? It's like we're all writing our songs for him. I felt lucky just to shake his hand."

"See? I liked *Walk the Line*," I said. "With Joaquin Phoenix?"

"Eh, didn't catch it," he said. "I do love movies, but in this case I'd rather keep my memory of the real thing."

I sipped the tea slowly, my hands cupped around the sides, the warmth of the mug like a lullaby. "This isn't bad," I said.

"See? It's better for you than coffee," he said.

He gathered a pile of his discarded clothing from last night that I'd torn off him, opened a drawer next to his sink, and shoved them in.

"Um . . . have you ever heard of a dresser?" I asked him.

He turned, sheepish. "I know. This place is really messy. I'm only home for short periods of time, so it kind of remains like this. I thought I'd just clean up a little bit since I have a guest."

"Oh. Well, that was nice," I said, smiling at him. The word "guest" seemed an odd choice.

I noticed a mousetrap on the floor, not an uncommon sight around the city. It's the rat traps that are *really* disgusting. They're the size of a cereal box. They are so large they look like they'd break your whole hand if you weren't careful. The first time I saw one in a hardware store I thought it was a joke. "Do you have a mouse in your house?" I asked him.

"Sure do. It's a long story. I had ordered the PETA humane mousetrap for eleven bucks off their Web site. So I catch this cute little guy, release him in Tompkins Park. Everything goes fine for about a week, then I catch another mouse, and I swear the fucker is the *same exact* mouse I'd caught a week ago! Same gray spot on his head and everything. This happens two more times, so I finally gave up and bought this wooden death guillotine you see before you. I'd almost like to keep the little guy as a pet, though."

"Really? I wonder if it really was the same mouse?"

Nick shrugged, continuing to eat his cereal. My messy bun was hurting my head. Ouch! As I struggled to pull my hair free of the ponytail I'd slept in, I smiled, remembering how it got so tangled last night when Nick was throwing me around in the bed. My hair is a huge rat's nest that sometimes has the capability to look awesome if I take the time to wash it, blow dry, and also run a straightener through it. This level of effort happens about once a year. I actually take pride in my unique do. I think it sets me apart from every other black-haired girl walking down the street. Nick walked over and gently eased the ponytail through the loop, letting loose my cascade of hair. He smiled at me.

"So, what's your plan for today?" I asked. I felt a sudden surge of vulnerability. I stood up, so we were the same height.

"I'm pretty charged up actually," he said, rubbing his hands together. "Driving the shovel over to Brooklyn to work on some songs with the guys."

"What's the shovel?" I asked.

"A motorcycle, lady! Specifically a Harley-Davidson. No other kind of bike counts, really. Remember that." I tried not to let the disappointment that he was leaving show in my face, but I must have failed.

"Listen, you should totally stay here," he said, turning to put his dish in the sink and wiping his mouth on a paper towel. "*Mi casa es su casa.* It's a beautiful day. Go back to sleep, watch some movies, order food. There are cigarettes in the top drawer of my dresser. I'm afraid I'm always on tour and not here so there's not a lot of food, but you're welcome to hang out."

"I don't smoke," I started to remind him, but he was already headed toward the door. He grabbed his keys off the counter and slipped his cell phone into the back pocket of his jeans. "Wait, Nick? Aren't you forgetting something?" I said in a mock tragic heroine voice.

"Oh yeah," he said sheepishly. He jogged back over to me and gave me a kiss. "Listen, what are you doing tonight?" he asked. I thought about all of the fascinating things I could make up, ran through them in my mind, abandoned all of them.

"I'm going to call you when I get back, not sure what time that will be but I'll find you."

"Okay," I said, feeling instantly better. "It will just be me and the mouse." He swooped down and bit me on my thigh, which made me laugh.

After he slammed the door behind him with a loud *bang!* the silence crept up the walls and washed over the ceiling, spreading like a wave around the room. I tapped my fingernail against the cereal bowl, making a *ping* sound.

I looked at the clock on his microwave. It was nine o'clock on Saturday morning, and I had nothing to do. My parents might be freaking out. I found my cell phone on Nick's floor and called to reassure them I'd slept at a friend's house. I thought that sounded better than "Hey, I'm not home. Slept at this guy's house who I met at a coffee shop and who gave me an orgasm and plays in a semifamous band and has tattoos on all his knuckles and most of his body, for that matter."

"We're worried about your sister," Dad said. "She hasn't left her room since yesterday." We spoke for a long time and I hung up after promising to come home by tomorrow afternoon to spend time with her. I was worried about Lauren, but also banking on spending another night with Nick.

i care about u

I texted Lauren, the best I could come up with, and spent ten minutes walking around the apartment trying to get a signal. I finally had service in the little living room area. Nick had a sunken-in brown couch with a depressed-looking jade tree hovering next to it. I filled a water glass under the tap in the kitchen and poured it into the base. The plant must suffer when he's on tour. God help any future pets he might own.

"Hello?" I called out, just to hear the resulting echo. I wandered back upstairs. Nick had set up a makeshift office, a tiny corner of his bedroom that held a beat-up desk with a loose handle dangling from a drawer. Atop, a Mickey Mouse ashtray overflowed with dead cigarettes, which I dumped into the garbage. His laptop was running, and was open to his iTunes list, which seemed to hold songs in the thousands; many were bands I'd never even heard of, a rarity. Held by a thumbtack and hanging askew on the wall next to his desk was an article printed out from Wikipedia. A black-and-white photo of a lobster was at the beginning of the article. It read:

The most common way of killing a lobster is by placing it, live, in boiling water. This is controversial because some people believe the lobster suffers. The practice is illegal in some places. The quickest way to kill a lobster may be to insert a knife into its head and cleave the head in two, thereby destroying two of the most important nerve clusters of the lobster. Some feel that this is more humane than placing the live lobster into boiling water. Some stores will kill a lobster upon purchase by microwaving it. Whether or not death occurs more quickly when the lobster is dropped in boiling water is not clear.

I reeled backward, catching a glimpse of my face in his dresser mirror. It looked blotchy. From the drinking, the hard kissing, or from the crying? I wasn't sure. I smoothed back some hair that was sticking up around my face. And why would Nick tack up such a disturbing passage about lobsters? Did it have something to do with his vegetarianism? I'd have to ask him.

Downstairs, he had a little white bookshelf—always a good sign in a man. My fingers skimmed over some of his titles. Stephen King's *The Stand* impressed me—I'd read that book again and again as a pimple-faced twelve-year-old. There was an entire shelf dedicated to motorcycle books, including *Zen and the Art of*

Motorcycle Maintenance. Not a huge number of books, but I was impressed nonetheless; most guys have none.

Looking at Nick's things made me feel like I was getting to know him in a way that being near him didn't allow. He made me a little nervous. He was such an intense *presence.* The temperature in the room changed when he walked into it, the air pressure dropped, I swear. Dust lined the shelf in the shape of fingertips where I picked up books, holding their places.

What Nick lacked in literature he more than made up for with DVD movies. I breathed a sigh of relief when I did a quick glance and saw none were video games. There must have been over one thousand DVDs. If they were in an order, it must be one available only in Nick's brain; they weren't alphabetized. My fingers skimmed titles such as *Enter the Dragon, Annie Hall, Ju-on: The Grudge,* and *The Shaolin Temple.*

Next to Nick's bookshelf was an ugly glass bench, Hitchhiker's Revenge stickers adorning it. The hinges on it squeaked, sounding like a scream. Inside were hundreds of knives. Some were shaped like tomahawks, others like steak knives. I touched one, staring down at the tiny rosebud of blood that formed on the pad of my finger. I closed the lid and made a mental note to ask him about his collection when I saw him later. It might be helpful if we were going to continue seeing each other that I find out if he were a serial killer or not.

His jeans were strewn across the floor from the night before and I held them to my face, inhaling him. His smell brought it all back, what we'd done, the places he'd touched and kissed me, and I pressed my knuckles to my mouth, biting them as hard as I could. I wanted him then. I touched my right nipple, pretending it was him. I thought back to when I first started sleeping with

Andy and tried to remember if I'd felt this . . . electric. I remember very tender times; not animalistic ones. But a little tenderness can be a beautiful thing.

Nick seemed to have some sort of martial arts obsession. An *Enter the Dragon* poster of Bruce Lee was over his bed, his body forever poised to karate-chop the hell out of somebody, and stickers from various New York jujitsu gyms decorated his bureau mirror. There was something bright pink sticking out of the top dresser drawer. Feeling strange about invading his stuff (but not enough to stop), I opened the drawer. It was filled with guys' boxer shorts and several bra-and-underwear sets that must belong to the mysterious redheaded ex-girlfriend. Could her personality be gleaned from her undergarments? She wore blindingly bright thongs, in tangerines and phosphorescent greens. All of my underpants are gray, white, and black, and they cover my butt. The whole thing. She seemed like the kind of girl who would call *her* underwear "panties." The very sound of that word makes me want to clap my hands over my ears. I hate it. Almost as much as I despise the word "moist." I looked in his closet, and, sure enough, mixed in with his collection of Draven and Vans shoes were several pairs of very high heels. It would appear Redhead not only could manage walking around Manhattan with a thong up her butt, she did so in sexy shoes.

Just how much of an "ex" was she if all her shit was still in Nick's apartment? I felt foolish. And, what was I *doing* here, when there was sweet Andy just two alphabet letter blocks away who loved me every hour, every day? Who might even forgive me for walking out on him? I felt fear creeping into my chest. Should I get dressed and walk over there? Would he take me back? After two years of being cared for, the insecurities one faces in single life held little appeal. Walking to my apartment, well, Andy's apartment now, seemed a very close reality. I imagined the scene: He would angrily ask what I was doing there. I'd break down and beg him to take me back. I could even see his face: hurt morphing into joy.

My fantasy of going back to my old apartment bled on. I began to picture myself weeks, then months back with Andy; the old problems would surely resurface. I'd left him for a reason. I wanted a cup of coffee, and the idea of getting dressed and going over to Mud gave me both comfort and a plan. Ah, Mud! It would ease the walk-of-shame aspect of my morning. There were so many oddballs in there; no one would care or notice if I looked disheveled.

I walked to the bathroom, catching my reflection in the framed posters for Scratch Acid and Vaselines shows. The Acid show was in Texas, 1986, the year I was born. Nick would have been about thirteen. I pictured his teenage, un-inked self rocking out at the show and it made me smile.

Disrobing, I stood on the toilet seat, peering into the mirror and surveying my body. I'm always pleased when I see myself naked. It's not because I look like Sienna Miller. Rather, I have full breasts, a round stomach, and curvy hips. I know culture dictates that I'm supposed to hate my body, but really, I don't. Culture can kiss my big round butt.

Above his toilet was a black-and-white photograph of a naked baby who had thrown a shit-filled diaper onto the ground and was grinning. It looked like a photograph Nick had taken and then had enlarged. Whose baby was this? A friend's? There was a small window in here with a ledge. He had a little feng shui action going on, with a bonsai tree in a long yellow plastic planter that reminded me of the kind of cup you get when ordering a banana split. I touched the fern's soft top. I couldn't help but search for remnants of Redhead. Also, Nick was so damn hard to figure out that I craved learning more about him among his stuff.

Walking two feet to the shower, I fiddled with the faucets. I can never tell what to do when it's one of those single round dials—I always seem to either freeze or scald myself. I opened the top of his White Rain Lavender Vanilla shampoo and sniffed. It smelled more cupcake than tropical waterfall. A blue loofah sponge dangled from the spigot and, stepping under the water, I poured a quarter-sized squirt of body wash onto it. I ran its rough surface over my body. Everything was ambiguous; it could belong to Nick or Redhead.

There was a clump of hair in the drain. I squinted, but couldn't tell what color the hair was. It certainly wasn't Nick's. Instinct tugged at me to remove it, but really that was no way for me to behave in someone else's shower. It had always been my job with Andy, removal of the shower drain hair, but this was a whole new frontier. I left the hair where it was and squirted conditioner in my palm, working it through my black locks.

When I got out of the shower I wrote $H + N$ in the steam condensed on the mirror. Continuing my hunt for Redhead relics, I opened the medicine cabinet only to be smacked in the forehead with a tampon! On closer inspection its box had dust on the top, which provided some relief. I shoved it back in and closed the door.

As I walked past the kitchen on my way upstairs to the bedroom to get dressed, there was a distinct rustling sound. A tiny gray mouse sat on top of Nick's stove. I decided she was a girl. She had a pink nose, and it twitched in tune with my footsteps. And Nick was right! She did have a dark gray spot on the top of her head. When my new mouse friend cocked her head to one side I stepped back. We both stood still for a few beats, studying each other until she scurried inside an opening in the top of stove. I wasn't sure what to make of this exchange, but I was left with the solid impression that this mouse had a high level of intelligence. It had something to do with the sparkling gleam in her brown eyes. Nick would probably never catch her in any kind of run-of-the-mill trap. At least I hoped not.

My wrinkled Bon Jovi T-shirt was hiding underneath Nick's bed. It smelled like cheap alcohol, which is probably because at some point last night I'd spilled cheap alcohol on it. I worked at some of the knots in my hair with my fingers, bent forward, and managed to wrestle my hair into a big dollop on top of my head and tie it up with a rubber band. The shower had helped.

When I opened his door, Nick's hallway smelled like piss. How could I not have noticed it last night? It was overwhelming and I held my shirt over my nose and pinched my nostrils shut. I didn't have a way of locking the door so I closed it tightly behind me. There was a silver line of mailboxes in his hallway I hadn't noticed last night and I could tell which one was Nick's because it was so stuffed with mail, it was open and spilling onto the floor. I picked a few envelopes up and shoved them back into the box. One from a bank was addressed to a "Nicholas Cavallaro." Nicholas. Tee hee. How could he not care about checking his mail? The practical move would be to have it held by the post office whenever he went on tour. It's easy; you can even do it online. But then again, maybe Nick didn't *do* practical.

Outside, Hispanic families mingled on the street. As I walked, the sun ducked and dashed behind buildings like a playful child. The older generations sat in plastic lawn chairs decorated with

Puerto Rican flags. Meandering carefully near an open gate, I noticed a smell of rusty pennies permeating the air. I passed the Lower East Side Ecology Garden, stopping to peer through the gates at the odd sculptures resting on its lawn. Made from garbage, mainly cans, they were shaped into dinosaurs, which were slowly rusting in the sun.

An elderly woman in a stark black-and-white nun habit bent over by scoliosis walked out of the Iglesia de Dios. I worked over the church's English translation on my tongue like a sweet. It was either Church of Days or Church of God. I'd received a D in senior-year Spanish, but my bet was on God. Tompkins Square Park gave me a rush in the pit of my belly; Nick and I had walked through here hours before. Though now, the dog parks were full of unhungover people taking advantage of the weather. Two guys with dreads were playing Frisbee and I ducked to avoid getting whacked in the head. A woman walked by with an over-sized pit bull on one leash, a miniature greyhound trotting along on the other. Waiting for the light to change on Ninth Street, I could just glimpse the beginning of the colorful mural of Joe Strummer painted on the side of Niagara bar.

Petunia was tied up outside Mud, a "regular" like me. She's a curvaceous bulldog with a pink spiked collar who came up to me now and sniffed my feet. They used to allow dogs in Mud, which I thought was nice, but someone must have complained, as now it's a no-no. Inside, I scored a seat at the orange Formica bar in the front. I had the whole day in front of me until Nick called. Was I stupid for waiting for him? I tried to remember his exact words about phoning me later but they escaped me.

I felt propelled to be productive, to do something. After ordering and drinking my coffee I paid and split, plopping down outside on the bench used to prop the door open in warmer months. Looking down at my phone to see if I had any missed calls, I realized I hadn't spoken to Sarah in several days. "Hello, daahhhhling," I said when she picked up. Down the street, a mother pulled her toddler in a red Radio Flyer wagon past parked cars.

"Hey, Harper, hold on a second." I heard her yelling to Marc in the background. "Sorry, I'm back! Damn husband and his damn football game. He actually had the balls to ask me to speak in the other room so he could concentrate! What a bunch of crapola."

"You sound happy," I said.

"Yeah. Being married means you can't murder your husband. More important is how *you* are, Harper. I got your e-mail; Marc and I were worried about you." Oops. I forgot I'd e-mailed her in a panic the night before I left Andy.

"Actually, things are looking up," I said.

"Really? Are you guys kissing and making up?"

I thought she was talking about Nick, so the question momentarily confused me.

"Oh, with Andy?" I chewed my lip, thinking about the best way to tell Sarah about the past two days. When I finished, there was a brief silence on the other end.

"Are you sure this Nick guy is a good idea?" she asked. "I don't mean to sound judgmental, but is there a chance you might be rushing into things?"

I assured her I was going into this with eyes wide open, that I was just having some fun.

"I just want you to be happy, that's all," she said.

"I haven't felt this good in two years," I told her. "Plus, I got laid!" It felt strange, speaking of the amazing night I'd spent with Nick in simple terms, when I really didn't feel nonchalant about it at all. I was belittling the experience so as not to get too attached to it. Sarah knew Andy and I hadn't slept together in months before I'd broken up with him; I later heard this is a common indicator a relationship is headed south.

Maybe Andy was depressed. The thought had never occurred to me before. Maybe him not touching me had nothing to do with me.

Sarah talked about the pool she and Marc were thinking about putting in their yard, the hilarity of her elderly next-door neighbor's upcoming fifth marriage. We rang off after promising not to let as much time go by between calls again. Nevertheless, I felt sad she'd moved so far away, and my breakup felt all the much harder to deal with without my best friend.

I spotted a guy down the street from me with a half-shaved, half-bald head and I quickly scanned his arms for tattoos, thinking he might be Nick. The motion took a split second but my body's reaction was incredible: My breath caught, my heart raced, my stomach clenched. Thinking about him made me want him soon.

How long would Nick's practice in Brooklyn take? Three hours? I factored in another hour for his motorcycle ride back to Manhattan. It was nearing noon: If Nick was calling me around three, I might as well enjoy my day in the city. It struck me that I really should pack up the rest of my things from Andy's apartment, but I'd deal with that another day.

I walked all the way west to Sixth Avenue, then took the D train at West Fourth Street to Rockefeller Center. *Us* had offices a few blocks away from here, and when I was suffering my asshole boss I used to take walks during my lunch hour on Fifth Avenue and pretend I was rich. This stretch between Saint Patrick's Cathedral and Central Park is one of the most expensive strips of real estate anywhere in the world. The Short Hills mall in Jersey always reminds me of it, the way the women put on their best suits and dresses just to shop, how image-conscious everyone is. I'd sample makeup at Henri Bendel, then skip over to Tiffany to try on gigantic diamond rings before reluctantly returning to work.

One of my favorite buildings is the Peninsula Hotel, and I stopped there now. I prayed I didn't look skeezy; at least I'd showered this morning. I went to the roof, jabbing the R button in the elevator. The outside section was closed for the season, but there were several groups of people eating lunch inside the glass enclosure of the bar. I heard at least three languages spoken by businesspeople and tourists who were staying at the hotel. I looked at the menu: sixteen dollars for the cheapest alcoholic drink. Having no job, and about thirty dollars combined in checking and savings, I ordered an orange juice and tried not to think about how broke I was. The pulp felt fresh sliding down my throat. Taking out a pen from my purse, I scribbled a crappy poem on a napkin. I wrote each line without stopping to cross anything out. There's nothing better for the restless mind than really awful poetry, I've found. Here it is:

And the only thing that I could take from this
Would be your breath on my back
In the corpse of a night
That punched the sky with stars
and brought your core
A bit closer to mine.
I would risk that
And that too
and a straight face
And a steady hand.

For just
To lie
beside
you.
Belly to belly.
And smile into a closed palm, curled like a comma
in your sheets.

Writing was cathartic as always. I straightened out the napkin to dry the ink before putting it into my purse. I wanted to glue it into my diary whenever I was reunited with it—it still lay abandoned at the moment inside my bedside table I'd found as a throwaway on the sidewalk in front of the Welcome to the Johnsons bar. (Being broke in New York, you pick a lot of stuff off the street. It's kind of gross, I know. But necessary. You just have to pray you don't get bed bugs.) I wandered over to the window, and looked down. I could see all the way to the park as I pressed my forehead against the cool glass. A businessman glanced at me curiously. A car horn sounded; I was surprised I could hear it so many floors up. People walking below on the sidewalk looked like ants. I grew bored and took the elevator back downstairs.

Back on the street the energy was infectious. A hot dog vendor yelled at a bicyclist who had crashed into the side of his cart. A mother and daughter strolled by. The mom wore a fur coat and pearls, whereas the girl had a pierced lip and combat boots. They had nearly identical faces separated by twenty years. They held hands, which made me smile. I wondered if she had accepted her daughter's style straightaway, or if the bond they clearly shared had taken quite a bit longer to develop.

In Henri Bendel women were lining up to have makeup

slathered on their faces. I sat down in a chair and told the sales-woman I was looking to try an outlandish red lipstick, like Debbie Harry or Katy Perry. This would be the post-Andy me. I'd wear fishnet stockings and buy hats off eBay—little black old lady hats with nets in the front. I'd be the Jersey version of Dita Von Teese! I bought a color called Striptease Red and headed outside, my cash flow down to six bucks. If I got thrown in the poor-house, at least I'd look fabulous!

It had grown colder, and I put up the hood of my sweatshirt. Walking past the doors to the MoMA, I heard my mom's voice in my head saying something about purchasing me a membership last Chanukah. People have varying opinions on the museum's new design, and I craned my neck to take in all of its vast white-ness. There was a unique comfort in its modernness; a feeling of efficiency.

I walked through the revolving door, deciding there was a reason I must have strolled this way.

Everywhere I turned, there was a famous painting or photo-graph on the wall; enough to make your breath shallow. I gazed at a few of Cindy Sherman's photographs from her Untitled Film Stills, where she dresses up as different characters in a pretend movie; a fiction wrapped around another fiction. I made a mental note to discuss them with Nick later; her work felt so innovative to me. From what I'd seen around his apartment, the posters on the walls (especially the ones he'd designed), stickers everywhere, photographs haphazardly hung up, I felt Nick was just as inter-ested in design and artistic expression as I was.

The MoMA owns just one Frida Kahlo painting, and it's very tiny. It's titled *Self-Portrait with Cropped Hair*. The description stated that Kahlo painted it to retaliate against Diego Rivera's many infidelities. There is a scroll on the upper portion of the painting that says in Spanish: *Look, if I loved you it was because of your hair. Now that you are without hair, I don't love you anymore.*

Wandering through archways and exhibits, and taking the escalator to various floors, I wanted to stay here forever, camping overnight the way Claudia and Jamie in *From the Mixed-Up Files of Mrs. Basil E. Frankweiler* did in the Metropolitan Museum of Art. The sculpture garden was still open even though it was fall, and I spent a few hours people-watching, sitting on a hard iron bench that felt cold beneath me. I bought a postcard of the Kahlo painting for twenty-five cents in the gift shop, and filled it out to my sister. *Dear Lauren: I'm at the MoMA and I think you'd really like this painting. Let's go here together this year. Harper.* Staring at it, I managed to squeeze the word "love" in right before my signature.

She must have been thinking about me as well. I checked my cell phone for the millionth time and there was a text message that turned out to be from Lauren. It read: **we are ordering sushi. should i try the sea urchin?** I sighed, and exited the building. I caught the subway downtown. It was six o'clock, and I was tired. I still had a slight headache from last night. I felt homesick, though whether for Andy's apartment or my parents' house I wasn't sure. The enormity of the city pressed down on me. I felt as if my journey around Midtown was just filling time, as I waited for Nick to return. The thought depressed me. He still hadn't called and I didn't feel up for trying on diamond rings at Tiffany.

The sun was setting and the whole city took on a bluish tint as I walked down to Thirty-fourth Street and boarded the Dover Express home. Nick never called.

Sunday

W hat's a four-letter word for yellow ball?" I asked aloud. Thank *God* my parents get *The New York Times*, as Sunday is my favorite day of the week to read it. David J. Kahn's crossword puzzles are so rad. My family milled about in the kitchen, finishing breakfast.

"Yolk," Lauren said without looking up from her cereal with soy milk.

Dad was feeding Anna Freud bits of scone under the table, thinking no one could see him. "Hey girls, want to hear something that will blow your socks off?"

Mom rolled her eyes.

"So my favorite Levi's have this rip here on the back pocket and my underpants start peeking through. Your mother tells me these pants are indecent to wear in public and we have to go buy new ones, even though these have lasted me twenty years and are the best jeans I've ever bought."

"They're also the *only* jeans you've ever bought," Mom said. She was wearing black stretch pants and a blue-and-white nautical silk blouse that tied at the waist. On her feet were her signature black flats.

He ignored her. "So the other day I agree to waste a perfectly good afternoon driving to the Short Hills mall, where everyone is wearing an outfit with a little horse on their shirt and looking like they're about to play a polo match."

"Dad, get to the point," Lauren said.

"So we go to some fancy-schmancy men's store, I forget the name, yada yada yada, and lo and behold, what is being displayed in the front window but several pairs of fashionable men's jeans with—now open your ears, girls—*already-made* wear and tear in the pant legs. Turns out your old man was ahead of the curve, more fashionable than your mother gives me credit for. I take a look at the price tag. I fall to the floor. Two hundred dollars. Two hundred smackers, to buy a pair of pants with holes in them exactly the same as my good ol' Levi's! Has this world gone insane, or what?"

"Dad, *Vogue* might call you any second for fashion advice," Lauren said sarcastically.

Last night with her had been rough. Around midnight, I'd heard a sound like a cat meowing, and found Lauren in our basement clutching what appeared at first to be a dishrag. Her face was blotchy, and she was sobbing in a hysterical way that scared me. It sounds cruel, but Lauren's dramatics can make me angry. It's easy to forget that her moods aren't her fault, that they're the result of a chemical imbalance in her brain. I ripped the cloth out of her hands, and instantly recognized it as her old baby blanket. Its name was Wolly, and I hadn't seen it around for at least ten years.

"Stop crying like that," I hissed, not wanting to wake our parents.

"She's making me age," my mother had confessed recently, on an occasion when Lauren admitted she'd skipped an appointment

with her psychologist. It was the first time my mother ever complained about the ways Lauren's depression affected our family.

"I treated Wolly so badly," she said. Lauren went on, sobbing
that she'd "taken Wolly for granted," and "let him get dirty and fall
apart."

It's hard to reason with her when she's in a state like this, but
I persuaded her to get into bed with me, and immediately realized just why I'd hated sharing beds with Lauren growing up. A
soccer player her whole childhood, Lauren woke me up twice by
kicking me in her sleep.

When I got up this morning, I'd asked Mom whether Lauren
would have to go to the hospital if she didn't get better this time.
It seemed like things were starting to slip into how bad they were
the summer we had to cancel our Cape Cod vacation.

"I understand your worry," she said. "But hospitalization is
the last resort. It's for when you think someone is suicidal. They
might strap Lauren down, force tranquilizers into her arms . . .
there's no telling what could happen to her. And she's promised
to go back on her meds. While I was in grad school at Columbia
in the seventies, I worked at a psychiatric hospital in the Bronx,
and I still have nightmares of what I witnessed there. We'll admit
Lauren only after we've tried everything we possibly can with
her psychiatrists."

Over coffee, we also discussed my job situation, or lack thereof.
"What about health insurance?" she'd asked. My parents are obsessed with health insurance. This is completely the fault of our
next-door neighbors, the Gorskis, who are nice enough folks but
not too bright. Mr. Gorski fancied himself some kind of middle-
aged Evel Knievel and would go dirt-biking around Madison on
weekends. Two years ago he broke his back. My father found him
lying in the middle of our street, his four homely children

crowded around him. Turns out he didn't purchase health insurance that year, and, after declaring bankruptcy, he put his house up for sale and they're moving down south. His wife stops by from time to time to sob to my mother, and it's had the effect of making both my parents health insurance fanatics ever since.

The human resources department of *Us Weekly* told me mine was running out at the end of the month so a few weeks ago I figured I'd better start fitting in every doctor's appointment possible. I had booked an eye exam with Dr. Levowitz for today, back when I thought I would be just visiting Jersey, not living there. He keeps weird hours—open seven days a week, and he takes no holidays off but for once a year in March, when his two pet Pomeranians get their portraits taken.

I love the scene at Dr. Levowitz's office. Aside from the Pomeranian portraits, there are cartoon sketches of children in bell-bottoms trying on glasses, and alphabet charts that were once a shiny white, but now had yellowed with age. One framed poster has a pockmarked Lyndon B. Johnson wagging his finger at the camera, a banner underneath reading *If good girls and boys want to do well in your classes, get fitted with the right eyeglasses.*

He has three women who have been working for him forever. *Why* he needs three assistants is anyone's guess; my father thinks it's to flatter him. The women had aged gracefully, in that Jersey Girl way, with tastefully streaked highlights and V-neck sweaters with gold starfish necklaces (to evoke the Jersey Shore, of course.) One of their names is Glinda, and the women look so much alike that Lauren long ago dubbed them the Three Glindas.

"Harper, sweetie, how are you?" Glinda One called to me as I walked in the door. After a kiss on the cheek and talk of how much I'd grown (I stopped growing when I hit five-three in the fifth grade) she flicked through manila folders behind the counter with one long orange fingernail. And on top of the nail, could it be? Yes! A tiny painting of a sparkly black cat on every finger. Tacky *and* festive. As Glinda Two walked me into the exam room, it felt oddly comforting to see that the instruments used to test vision and a variety of other possible eye problems were the same hulking, 1970s-orange machines that had terrified me as a kid. If the only things in life we can count on are death and taxes, Dr. Levowitz's refusal to modernize makes me happy. The glaucoma test always gives me the most grief; I hate that puff of air into my eye.

There is an unrestrained animosity between Dr. Levowitz and the Three Glindas. The women seem to despise Dr. Levowitz, and, if you look closely, you can see one of them glaring behind his back whenever he barks out a command. "Dr. Levowitz is not a charming man," my mother said once, after an eye exam. So it's a mystery why these women continue working here, year after year.

"How are you, Harpie?" the man himself asked in his thunderous voice, after the preliminary exams were completed.

I sighed. "Er, it's Harper? Actually?"

"What'd you say, honey?"

He appeared to be a hundred and twenty years old. When I was young he'd been in his nineties. His jowls hang down like a bulldog's, rendering his expression a permanent frown, and behind his aviator-frame glasses, his eyebrows were two caterpillars. He always calls me Harpie. It's that older-male generational thing of putting an "ie" or "y" on the end of women's names, that easy slip into assuming every woman wants a nickname. I'd once complained about this to Lauren, who had guffawed so hard she spit spaghetti out.

"What's so funny?" I'd asked.

"A harpy is like this weird bird from Greek mythology that used to steal stuff. They were drawn as ugly women with wings, basically."

"What! Oh my god. I'm totally correcting him next time."

"Caw, caw," she said.

But, I decided to drop it. He'd been calling me Harpie since I was a kid and I didn't think he meant I was an ugly bird. At least I hope not. When he put on the heavy metal frames over my eyes and flipped one lid closed, I was able to read only the top two lines out of four. I had a bad feeling about this. I had always teased Lauren, who had worn glasses or contacts since she was eight years old, that I had perfect vision. It now appeared I would hold this position no more. It was unsettling. "Looks like it's spectacles for you, young lady," he said cheerfully, placing the different types of glass pieces back in their slots.

He must be joking.

"Are you serious?" I asked him.

"Like a heart attack," he said. "And I should know; I've had three."

"Just counting the days until the next one," one of the Glindas muttered under her breath as she escorted me into the frame-trying-on room.

What was happening to me? Three days after leaving Andy and my sucky vision was getting worse? I had to wear glasses? Oh well, maybe I could get some cute tortoiseshell ones, or zany fifties-style with the cat eyes. I drove home, thoughts churning like black and silver waves far out at sea. Was I being sucked into a vortex of bad karma, which was kicking off with a newly confirmed loss of vision? It seemed like a biblical plague. What was next? Frickin' locusts and diseased cattle?

"I think God has put a curse on me," I announced dramatically, walking up the front steps of my house. "I'm blind and I have to get glasses." Lauren and my dad were sweeping the porch. Lauren held the dustpan. She'd tied a blue-and-white flowery bandanna into her blond hair to hold it back. She wore tiny pearl earrings in each ear, one of Dad's Grateful Dead T-shirts, jeans, and her usual paint-splattered moccasins. I was glad to see her still out of her room. Often when she's having a bad spell of depression, she won't leave it for days. It was noon, and the wind was making the trees moan. Winter wasn't far off.

"You don't believe in God," Lauren said. My parents call her our "born-again Jew," after she'd embarked on a quest after reading *The Da Vinci Code* to prove that our family was related to Jesus.

"Our family comes from Europe," Dad said after we learned Lauren was making daily research trips to the Morris County Library.

"You won't even tell us which country!" she'd shouted. It was true; my father was oddly vague when it came to Lauren's and my ancestry. We knew my mother's side was Irish, but when we asked Dad where his side came from he just answered that we were Irish and Jewish.

"Jewish isn't a *nationality*," we would protest. The mystery had something to do with my father refusing to say we were definitely Polish or Russian, since the boundary line kept changing between the countries, and because Poland executed so many Jews during the German occupation.

"Well, if it's not a curse, then it is definitely bad karma coming back to bite me in the ass," I said. I had put in an order for five-hundred-dollar tortoiseshell glasses, a fact I would delay telling my mother for as long as possible. (Having less than ten dollars in my bank account, I'd had to charge it to my parents' credit card, which was for emergencies only.)

"Watch your language," Dad said. "You know your mother wouldn't like it if she heard you talking like that."

Lauren and I glanced at each other and burst into giggles. My mother reviled curse words, but every once in a while would throw the word "shit" into a random sentence.

" 'Shit' is the only curse word Mom likes," Lauren said, which made me laugh harder. It's times like these when I'm reminded there is only one other person in the world who will remember the oddities and humor in our parents long after they are gone. So I'm grateful I have a sister, problematic as she may be.

Suddenly, a glint of sun hitting silver caught my eye.

"What's that metal thing under the porch?" I asked. I peered closer. "Is that some kind of trap?"

Lauren rolled her eyes. "We have a groundhog living under the house. Dad called the town rescue patrol, and the woman brought over a trap. Of course he asked her to stay for lunch, and now they're the best of friends. She played with Anna Freud for a while, so she seems to really love animals, which is important if you are the animal control officer, I suppose."

"You mean they don't trap it *for* you?" I asked.

"No, they suggest foods to put in there and you just have to wait. I've been watching from my room and I saw it walk by the trap six times, nose in the air. There's a whole jar of peanut butter in there, as well as some carrots and lettuce. Dad had to go food shopping just for the groundhog. Guess what else I learned from this experience?"

"What?"

"I found out that a groundhog and a woodchuck are the *same* animal! Never knew!" Ah, the clash of wildlife and suburbia.

"Wow, I didn't know that either, actually."

"So . . ." Lauren put her hands in her pockets. "What's up

with you other than losing your vision and breaking up with Andy and quitting your job?"

My dad whacked her in the shin with his broom.

"Ow! What was that for?" she squealed.

"I thought we decided with Plan B," he said, glancing at me nervously. I realized that my family must think I was slightly off-balance, what with all the sudden changes I'd made lately in my life. Maybe I was. The idea threw me off; Lauren had always been the one my parents worried about, not me.

"What was Plan B?" I asked, putting down my purse and sitting on a wooden porch swing my dad had installed when we first moved into the house. I eased off my shoes and launched the swing with the pads of my feet, feeling the roughness of the wood porch beneath me. A nearby pile of dirt and leaves Dad had swept came slightly undone.

"Plan B was don't ask Harper if she got laid last night," Lauren said wryly, tucking some hair that had sprung loose back underneath her bandanna.

The thing is, sex came up so much in our house that it wasn't even all that weird to be discussing it in front of Dad.

"Both my girls are holy virgins," he said now, setting down his broom. "I won't hear anything otherwise."

"You wish, Dad," Lauren said. Then, turning toward me, she said, "Now spill it, Harper."

I sighed wearily, turning horizontal in the swing and putting my feet up. The momentum rocked me lazily and a small breeze lifted the hair from my brow.

"So I met this guy," I started.

"It always starts that way," Dad said, pushing my legs off the swing so he could sit next to me.

"Well, it happened the same day I left Andy, actually," I said.

"And I don't really want to talk about it because I don't even know what the hell I'm doing."

"Push over," Lauren said to Dad. "It's just getting good."

Why couldn't I have a normal repressed family that had awkward silences and kept all their emotion hidden deep down inside?

"His name is Nick, he sings in this punk band Hitchhiker's Revenge, and that's where I slept last night."

A squeal from Lauren. "I know that band! You used to listen to them in high school, remember? You were the one that got me into them!"

"Yeah, yeah. He's cool. But, cool guy hasn't called me. So that might be the end of that," I said.

"I think you should bring him by the house so your mother and I can meet him," Dad said. "Find out his intentions."

"Dad, this isn't 1912!" Lauren shouted. "And Harper can figure things out on her own. She's smart and mature."

I stared at my sister. Had she always been this loving toward me and I'd just been too wrapped up in my New York life and Andy and getting distance from her depression to realize it?

"Well, then this being the modern age and all, why don't you just call him?" Dad said. "Take the lead."

I smiled at his corny expression. "I don't know if I'm all that interested in him," I said. "He's kind of intense. And full of himself."

"Oh. Well, maybe have some fun and see where it leads you," Lauren said.

"Um . . . thanks, Lauren! That's actually really good advice," I said.

Dad no longer cared what we had been discussing. He was happily watching his two daughters getting along and sharing confidences. He had his hands folded on top of his round belly and his glasses on top of his head and he was smiling.

"Well, I still don't see any harm in bringing him by for your mother and me to meet him," Dad said. "We're not *too* embarrassing."

"Dad, you don't bring someone home you're dating until, like, the fifth date!" Lauren said. "This is why I don't bring anyone home that I date! Because you and Mom would probably ask for his whole sexual history, and then Mom would decide he was a serial killer or something!"

I laughed. "I'm going to go inside and check my e-mail," I said. I squeezed Lauren's shoulder as I walked past her. "Thanks for the advice."

"No problemo," she said. "You need sweeping, groundhog trapping, or love life advice, you come to me and Dad here."

Mom was in with a patient so I tiptoed past her office even though she had a sound machine that emits white noise. I know a bomb could blow away half our house and the patient wouldn't hear a thing. I'd borrowed it once when I was fifteen to sneak a boy into the house after my parents had gone to bed—CJ Finnaway. I'd liked him for two reasons: he bought me turkey-and-cheese subs at Quick Check every day, and he was seventeen and drove a loud Ford truck that was so high off the ground I had to stand on his knee to get in. Our entire three-month relationship consisted of subs, his big-ass truck, and administering piss-poor handjobs on my bed after I'd steal Mom's sound machine and set it up just behind my bedroom door. Being a very shy and quiet boy (I sometimes wondered if he was borderline retarded), CJ never gave me much insight as to how he wanted me to move my hand up and down. I'd never heard of lubrication (sex education in Jersey basically consists of the school nurse one day

walking down to your homeroom and strongly suggesting absti-
nence) and rubbed his poor penis so much that fall that it caused
a raw-looking friction burn on the shaft and we soon after broke
up. I forget why, but it wasn't because of the friction burn. Whatever happened to handjobs, anyway? I feel like they went out of
style around the same time Guns N' Roses broke up.

In my room upstairs, some of the furniture was new. Since
I graduated Rutgers and moved to New York two years ago, it's
been a running commentary between my mother and me that she
was going to turn my room into a library, and I could see she'd
gotten started. The thought of my old bedroom being used for
something else made me feel a little panicky, but I pushed the
thought down. I knew it was immature to want to hold on to it;
I only came home once in a while, but still I felt a resistance to
any change. I plucked the first book off the shelf and smiled at its
dusky blue cover. *The Journals of Sylvia Plath 1950–1962* is an
amazing read. Punk boys can have their Johnny Cash; for a voracious reader like me, Sylvia Plath is my heroine. At any random
part in her journals you can just be blown away. I closed my eyes
and opened the book to page twenty-three. It read:

*I have a lot to give to someone, someday. But I must not be too
Christian. I can only end up with one, and I must leave many
lonely by the wayside. So that is all for now. Perhaps someday
someone will leave me by the wayside. And that will be poetic
justice.*

See? Amazing. Nick could keep the *Zen and the Art of Motorcycle Maintenance* I'd found on his bookshelf yesterday. Plath was
an angsty rock chick way ahead of her time.

My computer from college was on my desk and I turned it on, amused my parents still had dial-up. In the city, I just stole a signal from a neighbor near our apartment, or got a Wi-Fi connection at Mud. Plus it's endearingly amusing to see the crazy names my neighbors gave their signal channels. One is Too Many Margaritas. My favorite is Butt Sex Boy. I smiled, remembering how Andy would always walk in the room wanting to look something up online and call out "Babe, is Butt Sex Boy up and running today?"

The humming of AOL on my parents' dial-up connection sounded like a thousand wasps being slaughtered, and simultaneously made me nostalgic. You must know its "melody" by heart: *A-weee-woooo-chiiii-chiiiii-phhhhfff-ie-ie-prrrrr.* Knowing it was pathetic, I checked my inbox just in case Nick had e-mailed me. I'd written it down for him before he left for Brooklyn. There was one from Sarah and Marc's recent trip to Disneyland (which she had somewhat unsettlingly titled her baby-making vacation). I quickly thumbed through cute photos of the two of them sporting Mickey Mouse hats.

In Google's address bar I typed *Hitchhiker's Revenge.* It took me to Facebook, and I clicked on Photos. It was wild to see press shots of the band, including several of Nick glowering at the camera. They had a shot from the early nineties posted, when Nick sported a spiky purple Mohawk and a hoop through his left nostril. He was riding a longboard, crouching down and grinning. It was weird to see him with hair; it changed the shape of his face. "Such a tough guy," I said aloud, smiling to myself and remembering the tender way he'd traced the outline of my birthmark the other night. I typed *Nick Cavallaro* into Google and was shocked to see there were hundreds of photos taken of Nick in concert, as well as a ton with him signing autographed CDs at last summer's Warped Tour, which Andy and I had caught when it traveled through Asbury Park. My eyes lingered extra long on photos of Nick at shows, the sweat dripping down his white wife-beater, his muscles rippling. Some of them caught him in midair, a look of pure happiness on his face, eyes closed, his mouth wide open while singing. My gaze rested on his lips, wide and plump like a bass's or Mick Jagger's.

There were also three fan sites dedicated to him, and over twenty for the band. I shifted around on my seat. I knew Hitchhiker's Revenge had a loyal New Jersey fanbase, but I hadn't realized they were so big worldwide. One fan site was run by a girl from Beijing, China, and was dedicated to how she wanted to marry Nick. A particular photo gave me the creeps; she'd taken a photo of herself in a wedding dress with a guy, cut out the guy's face, and Photoshopped in Nick's.

I took my phone out of the back pocket of my jeans and looked at the screen. The background showed a picture of me and Andy taken over the summer in my parents' backyard. I'd taken it by holding out my arm so it was fuzzy but we both had huge, cheesy smiles. I was running through the options menu to put a stock sailboat picture onto the background when my phone started vibrating in my hand. It was a 718 area code. Brooklyn.

"Hello?" I said.

"Yo." The word came out in a growl, and I could hear the sharp intake of a cigarette after he spoke.

"Who is this?" I asked, pretending I didn't know.

"This is Nick Cavallaro," he responded, the smirk obvious in his voice.

"Do you always say your whole name?"

"I'm taking a break from practicing and wanted to know how

this Sunday afternoon is treating you, gorgeous. How are you enjoying life?" I wanted to ask him why he never called me yesterday like he said he would, but now he'd caught me off guard. That same instant closeness I'd felt when he touched my arm in Mud.

"Well, I was Internet-stalking you, but don't get all bigheaded about it," I told him.

"Yeah? Find anything good?"

"Did you know there's a girl in China who is in love with you?" I told him. "It's kind of creepy." This didn't seem to unnerve him.

"That's awesome of her," he said. "We have the best fans in the world."

Silence for a few beats.

"Hey, so what's up with that article on microwaving lobsters?" I asked.

"What article?"

I felt silly now, bringing it up. Like he'd think I'd been snooping around. But what did he expect, leaving me alone in the apartment? I'm a curious girl. I have an inquisitive mind.

"You have, like, this printout about how some restaurants microwave lobsters instead of boiling them because they think it's more humane."

"Oh, I just thought it was so insane that they do that, don't you? Microwave a lobster, like that's any less awful than throwing it into hot water? Still, it sure tastes delicious on a summer day, microwaved or boiled, right?"

"What? I thought you don't eat animals?"

"Ah, you've forgotten about my four feet and dreams rule. As far as I know, lobsters don't apply."

It seemed kind of odd to be horrified enough by an article on microwaving lobsters to print it out and tack it to your wall, only to then have no qualms about eating one. I was starting to realize Nick dealt in contradictions, of all shapes and sizes.

"Hey, I met your mouse," I told him.

"No way! What's he like?"

"Well, I think it's a *she,* as we totally had female bonding. She sat right on your stove and looked me over."

"Hmm, interesting. Methinks I might have to just buy a cage and wheel and let her live with me." He sounded distracted. I heard shouting in the background and an out-of-tune merry-go-round melody. Someone was playing a piano.

"Yes, I don't think she is your average mouse," I said, but he wasn't listening.

"So, what's happening over there on the other end of this telephone?" he said.

"I'm with my folks out in Jersey. Where are you?"

"I'm at John and Rose's house in Brooklyn. It's so fucking noisy here that my ADD is acting up."

"I have ADD too!" I exclaimed.

"Diagnosed, or just because it's cool?"

"Diagnosed since I was thirteen," I told him. "I've tried Adderall, Strattrera, and Ritalin. None of them worked so I went off the meds and now I'm like woo-wee-woo at all times!"

"Well, I can respect a woman who's embraced her inner freak," he said. Then, "Listen, we have a show at the Bowery Ballroom tonight, it's a charity thing to raise money for Indian Larry's family. Bring that gorgeous face to the concert and afterward we can frolic."

"Can we frolic à la fresco?" I asked off the cuff.

He laughed.

"You bet."

"Okay, I'll just shower and then I'll get going."

"I hope so, 'cause you stink."

"Whatever! You're like the King of Stink. You don't even wear deodorant."

"You're stink-a-licious."

"You're Sir Stink-a-lot."

"Okay, you win. Doors open at eight, just ask the front door guys where we are and they take care of you, okay?" And he hung up.

"Who the hell is Indian Larry?" I said out loud. "And what front door guys?"

Lauren was walking by. She peeked her head in, curious.

"Indian Larry is only like *the* most famous biker of all time," she said, rolling her eyes. "Your punk guy probably worships him. He's dead, but he used to build motorcycles. Like, sculpt them and stuff."

Lauren always surprised me with how much information she kept lodged in her brain. She always won when we played Trivial Pursuit.

"Thanks," I told her, smiling and stripping off my clothes. I dashed to the bathroom.

"You're welcome, oh naked one," she said, walking back to her room.

Fresh out of the shower, my ass totally jiggled as I ran past the mirror. Andy and I hadn't had a full-length mirror so I hadn't seen my butt in years. It was also so white I was nearly blinded. I ran past it again, this time more slowly, and it didn't jiggle at all. I breathed a sigh of relief, until I realized I had nothing at all to wear. All of my clothes were back at Andy's. Any clothing at my parents' would be items I hadn't worn in forever. Yipes.

I opened up my dresser drawer. Apparently, Dave Matthews

was really cool in 1999 because I found two tie-dyed tour T-shirts.
He'd been a huge favorite of mine, along with some other hippie
bands, before I got so into punk. Mixed among them were a few
tiny hoochie tops from college I wouldn't be caught dead in now.
Or fit in now, for that matter. I spotted a Guess top, with a sexy
lace tie up the back, which made me feel a little sad for my college
self. Was I really trying *that* hard back then to be noticed? Ugh. I
thought of my new bartender friend Daniela, and wondered how
it went with the Wall Street guy she had gone home with. I hope
he was a nice guy, though I wouldn't put money on it.

What if I just waited outside on the street to check if Andy's
light was on? I could be in and out before he ever came home and
caught me. I still had my key, but the thought of running into
him made me too nauseated. My life might be a mess, but my
number-one priority was to find a cool T-shirt. I actually snapped
my fingers. If I'd been a cartoon character, a lightbulb would
have been drawn above my head in this frame. Mom had a Bruce
Springsteen T-shirt from his Born to Run tour, which would
probably go over big with Nick. I streaked into her bedroom and
grabbed it. Lauren was floating by in the hallway humming a
tune I didn't recognize and surprised me with a silver skull necklace. "Where did you get this?" I asked, touched.

"Oh, some kid in my painting class at Princeton was selling
these for fifty bucks and I felt bad for him and bought one."

The skull's eyes were a glittery yellow.

"This looks like a piece of crap," I said.

She rolled her eyes. "He had a limp."

It wasn't funny, and yet we both started giggling somewhat
hysterically. It felt good to laugh with my sister. We'd grown so
distant in recent years. Something about having my guard down,
being knocked in all directions by my screwed-up life, was mak-

ing us closer. I felt like she was looking after me, when it's usually the other way around.

"So that made you buy the necklace?" I asked.

"Would you please just wear the stupid thing? *Gawd,* Harper. You make everything into such a big deal. Besides, if you're going to be punk rock now you should own it."

"I'm not 'punk rock' now," I said, suddenly irritated. "I'm just me."

"And who *is* that?" Lauren threw over her shoulder, as she skipped into her room across the hallway, slamming her door. I didn't have time for Lauren's head trips, but the necklace *did* look great with my faded Springsteen shirt. I ran down the stairs, scribbled a quick note to my parents, threw on my dad's faded green army jacket he'd rescued out of a bin at the Salvation Army, and ran out the door. It was six blocks to the Madison train station and I arrived out of breath, barely making it onboard before the doors closed.

I got off inside Penn Station and took the E train to Fourteenth Street, hopping on the L to First Avenue. I'd rushed around my house in New Jersey, eager to see Nick, and gotten into New York way faster than I'd expected. It was six o'clock and I had two hours to kill, so I walked over to Mud to read. Fiona had a silver fork sticking out of one of her pigtail buns and was wearing a vintage-looking brown dress with orange crosses. She hadn't shaved her legs and her calves were coated in fine blond hair, which I assumed must be her real hair color. A guy sitting at the front counter was belting out Lynyrd Skynyrd's "Sweet Home Alabama" to no one in particular as I pushed by to sit down in the back. Fiona brought my coffee over without me saying a word.

"How are you, Fiona?" I asked as she slammed down my mug.

"Sweating my balls off," she said, pausing to readjust the fork. Her arms were covered in tattoos. She had a series of topless pinup girls with purple lotus flowers blooming around them. One had orange nipples. I hadn't noticed them before.

"Pretty tattoos," I said.

She looked pleased I'd noticed, easing up on her tough attitude just a little to talk to me.

"A friend works part-time at New York Adorned and did these, but it's not finished; I'll eventually have a full sleeve. Next weekend I'm going back for more shading."

"Doesn't it hurt?" I asked, curious, never having had a tattoo myself.

"It feels like a tickle," she said sarcastically. I thought of Nick's colorful body; the fact that I was seeing him later made me jittery, like I'd had too much caffeine already.

I took out *The World According to Garp*. Andy once asked me, "Why do you read the same books over and over again?" It was hard to explain. In a way, it feels like seeing old friends. I think Nick would understand that, as it's similar with music; loving a few great bands all your life, listening to the same albums repeatedly.

Feeling bold as Fiona stopped by and gave me a refill, I remarked that I was going to see Hitchhiker's Revenge tonight.

"I'll be there too," she said, plopping down across from me and putting her feet up on the seat next to her. "I'm doing sound."

I realized Fiona must be close to Nick's age, in her late thirties. I was nervous around her; she'd been a part of the East Village punk scene a lot longer than me.

"Have you fallen madly in love with Nick yet?" she asked, startling me out of my reverie.

"Well, I think he's a great guy," I said cautiously.

"Nick's the one in the band all the girls fall in love with," she said. "But you're probably smarter than that."

I felt uncomfortable.

"I just got out of a long-term relationship, so I'm not looking for anything serious," I said.

She rolled her eyes.

"He's got that bitchy girlfriend he always goes back to, just to give you a heads-up. She'll make the rounds again at some point."

I didn't know what to say. A man at a nearby table had been signaling to her to bring his bill our entire conversation. He'd grown so tired of waving he was now resting his cheek on his bicep, his arm up straight like he was a student. "I'll see you later tonight," she called over her shoulder.

I threw down money and made a hasty exit. What did Fiona mean by saying Nick "always went back" to Redhead? Did that mean they'd broken up before? That this breakup might not be final? I felt more guarded, suddenly. Nick was impossible to read; I couldn't tell if he liked me or was just having some fun. I didn't know what I wanted, either. Surely if he'd called me to meet up with him at the concert, that was showing interest. I'd forgotten how difficult the travails of dating can be. Guys suck and I was rusty. I was at a clear disadvantage. I had to put my game face back on.

St. Mark's was full of outdoor stalls selling cheap Halloween accessories. On the street, a man perched high on a unicycle pedaled by me. I had to quell the urge to give him a little shove. He looked so pompous, there atop his stupid one-wheeled bike. Suddenly, a hot pink wig caught my eye. It was short, with bangs.

"How much?" I asked the Middle Eastern guy running the stand.

"Forty dollars."

"Yeah, right."

"Fine. For you, twenty bucks."

"I don't think so."

He sighed. "All right, ten dollars. No more going down in price."

I paid him and then happily plucked the wig from where it hung and dug around in my purse for a ponytail holder. Putting my hair back in a low bun, I caught my reflection in a parked car window and used light from a street lamp to adjust the wig, tucking strands of shiny black hair underneath. My heart raced at the thought of Nick looking up from his guitar and clapping eyes on my pink hair.

I started walking downtown on Third Avenue until it became Bowery. It took much longer than I thought. Before I'd always shared a cab with Andy, but being solo I couldn't really afford one right now.

Already the Bowery Ballroom's entrance was a hum of activity, with lots of skinny sound guys in tight black jeans looking like janitors with hundreds of keys looped on their belts. They tossed out insults to one another as they tuned guitars and replaced strings. "Sound guys," I said aloud, rolling the words over my tongue. A few eyed me curiously as I made my way over to the stage. I didn't know if it was because of the pink hair or because I was the only person with a vagina within a fifty-foot radius.

I recognized Marty Ferraro, Hitchhiker's lead singer and bassist. Though he must have been about the same age as Nick, his face was more weathered. He had slicked-back black hair like John Travolta in *Grease* and his sideburns were flecked with gray.

He looked like he should be carrying a monkey wrench in his back pocket. He wore black jeans and a black shirt that read BIG KAHUNA MOTORCYCLE RENTALS SHOP, HONOLULU HAWAII. Had he bought it on tour? That would mean Nick had been to Hawaii, a place I've always wanted to visit. What a life he led, traipsing around the world. Never having to work a desk job to buy groceries. I felt jealous.

My wandering mind suddenly came into sharp focus when I realized the short, unassuming guy wearing glasses Marty was talking to looked vaguely familiar. "Sorry to interrupt. I'm looking for Nick?" I rubbed the heel of my sneaker on the floor.

"Nice wig," Marty said, reaching out to stroke it. It felt like a gesture too intimate for a first meeting.

"Thanks. I just bought it." I smiled.

"That motherfucker is around here somewhere; I think I just saw him shooting up in the bathroom," Marty said.

My eyes went wide.

"I'm joking, he's probably just doing his kung-fu warm-up," he said, laughing and stretching out his hand. I smiled at his formality.

"I'm Harper Rostov," I said.

"Nice to meet you, Ms. Harper Rostov. I'm Marty. So, what are you all about, give me a synopsis in five words or less." He reminded me of Nick, the way he verbally sparred with you; only, Nick was way smarter. That I could tell already.

"I'm a wannabe music writer," I said, nervously rubbing my palms together. I realized I was slumped over and tried correcting my posture by pretending I was standing against a wall.

"Hey, hey, hey, there's no such thing as wannabes in this family. Here on out we consider you a full-fledged rock journalist." I smiled. He was kind of cheesy, but nice. He turned to the guy next to him, who I suddenly realized was Rivers Cuomo. "Rivers, Harper. Harper, Rivers."

I nearly choked, then tried to turn it into a cough. I quashed the urge to shout out to him that I spent my sophomore year of high school watching Weezer's video for "Buddy Holly" over and over again on MTV.

Marty lit a cigarette, which I tried not to stare at, as surely it was illegal to smoke in here. He saw me noticing and winked—a gesture that pulled the whole side of his face up toward his eye.

A short, chubby guy with sideburns, purple Chuck Taylors, and a studded belt buried underneath a mountain of a gut stopped by to talk to Marty about the band's guest list. His stomach was covered in black spiky hair and hung out over his studded belt. Marty introduced me and Rivers to him. His name was Bullet and he had a somewhat vacant look in his eye, like he'd done a wee bit too many drugs.

"Why do they call you Bullet?" I asked, my rock journalist hat on.

"I tried to shoot myself in the head with a shotgun ten years ago and missed. The bullet is still in my shoulder."

Marty started to laugh, coughing out smoke. I was sorry I'd asked. Bullet looked me up and down.

"Where'd this little hottie come from?" He reached over to put his arm around me. I shrugged it off.

"Oh, she's feisty!" he said.

I rolled my eyes. "Keep it in yer pants there, Missed Shot, or whatever your name is."

Marty laughed so hard he started choking again. Rivers whacked him on the back.

"No love for the fat man," Bullet said wistfully. "Even when

I was in Catholic school and all my friends got molested, no priest wanted to fiddle the fat kid."

"Was he serious?" I asked Marty when Bullet wandered off.

"Sadly, yes," he said, still laughing. "He's a fucking moron but he's *our* moron."

I watched the hum of setting up for the show unfold around me. I hoped others I would meet tonight would be a little bit less . . . weird. On a positive note, everyone buzzed with excitement and energy. It was like there was an electric current in the air that you could plug in to anytime you wanted.

"Welcome to the jungle," Rivers said softly beside me.

"Hi. I loved *Pinkerton*," I told him, immediately feeling like a dork. Though it was trashed by other music critics when it came out, our teeny-tiny staff of three at *Thrash* loved it. We once did a story reflecting back on the best albums from the nineties, and *Pinkerton* was in the top five.

"Really?" he asked, staring at a spot just over my shoulder. "That album flopped."

Marty rolled his eyes at me. "Rivers is ridiculously hard on himself, as you can see."

"Whatever! I played 'Pink Triangle,' like, a million times over in my room," I told him. "It rocks. Oh! And while we're talking about your music, I love love *loved* the video for 'Buddy Holly.'" He didn't say anything, so I blurted out: "And I also loved to play 'Say It Ain't So' when I felt all emo and melodramatic and would light incense in my bedroom and feel all intense about life and how shitty and beautiful it is all at the same time." Oh, me and my verbal ADD. I had a fight with a friend once in junior high because she asked me if I liked her new headband with a big neon orange bow on it and I said no, and she told me I needed a social filter then didn't speak to me for two weeks. I walked around imagining myself holding up one of those metal grates that go in your air conditioner to trap air pollution.

"I'm glad you didn't burn your house down," Rivers said, bringing me back to reality.

Marty was looking at me, his mouth twitching. I'd been spacing out.

When I'm nervous, I talk a lot. I don't know what came over me, but I started singing out loud: "Ooooh yeaaaah. Aaall right. Feeeels gooood. Insiiiide." Marty joined in with me then, which made me feel less stupid. We might have even harmonized, I'm too tone-deaf to know: "Your drug is a heartbreaker." Rivers smiled politely at us, but I think we were kind of freaking him out.

"I get to do the guitar solo!" I called out.

"It's all yours," Marty said.

I did a kick-ass air guitar, or at least I thought it looked pretty good. I was having a great time.

"Thank you so much for liking my music," Rivers said, smiling almost painfully.

"Gentlemen, I am on a mission, but should you wish to see my air guitar again or hear my amazing vocals, I'll be around after the show to take requests," I said.

Marty bowed to me, looking amused. "Let me take you to your guy," he said, walking me down the dark hallway lined with previous concert posters. We stopped at a door that had orange light flowing from under it.

"There she is," Nick bellowed when I finally found him. He was involved in some complicated-looking stretching in a room set aside for the band. It was tiny, with signed posters of the Ramones and Dolly Parton on the walls. I waited for him to mention the wig but he seemed not to notice it, which was pretty strange since it was neon pink. "Don't you just love Dolly," he said, doing a split on the floor. I tried to do one and fell over, laughing. My wig fell off and I shoved it in my pocket. It seemed kind of dumb, anyway. Lauren was right; I *was* trying too hard to be punk.

"I haven't been able to do a split since gymnastics when I was five," I said.

"No one can ever call you old if you're limber," he said earnestly. "You should really take vitamins. I'll buy some for you at the grocery store. I take lots before shows. It offsets all the drugs I do."

This was the second time in less than an hour that Nick and drugs were mentioned together. It was making me uneasy.

"So you're not straightedge?" I asked.

He made a choking sound I realized was laughter.

"Wow, I haven't heard that term since the nineties," he said.

I felt my face go red.

"Do you really do a lot of drugs?" I asked, sinking into a black pleather chair with stuffing spilling out of a hole in the seat I wouldn't ever hold a black light up to.

"Define 'a lot,'" he said, balancing his body on one arm in a yoga pose. It's funny; I would have thought for a guy to do yoga moves would be somehow emasculating, but with him it was an absolute turn-on. He was wearing regular blue jeans, a Bad Brains T-shirt he'd cut the sleeves off, and his usual black Dr. Martens.

"I dropped acid once when I was fourteen," I said. I'd tried it and hated it so much I never did drugs again, other than pot, which I don't consider a drug. I don't think drugs really do much for people with ADD. We live in our own world most of the time as it is, and drugs just made me feel spaced out times a thousand. Not fun.

"When you were fourteen I was twenty-seven," he said, standing and grunting as he stretched his left arm over his head. Wrapping around his thick bicep were lyrics to a track off *Morristown Is Mean,* their third album.

"Big whoop," I said, which made him laugh. There were creases in the corners of his eyes, which I liked. It's a part of aging I wouldn't mind, getting those laugh lines.

"Hey, I met Marty downstairs. And your friend Bullet."

"Ah, the whole skinny jeans squad. They're a bunch of clowns."

"I can't believe that guy shot himself," I said. "It's so horrible that everyone calls him Bullet! I feel sorry for him."

"I believe he started calling *himself* Bullet," Nick said, standing up so we were eye to eye.

Suddenly, he pushed me up against the wall for a kiss. His breath smelled strongly of cinnamon. The prickles of his facial hair scratched against my bottom lip. His blue eyes shone, and I wondered briefly if he was on anything before he stuck his tongue deep in my ear. Oddly enough no one had ever done that to me before. Had it been anyone but Nick, I totally would have immediately called to mind some gross porn star with a huge dong who sleeps in purple silk boxers on leopard-print sheets, but instead I was surprised by how fast it turned me on. It reminded me of our night together, how he'd been with his hands.

"It's really nice that you came all the way here," he said. He smiled. With him standing very close to me, I noticed absentmindedly how short he was, because most of the time he was such a huge *presence* I forgot he was only about five-six.

I didn't want him to think I was going to be living in Madison *permanently,* or that I'd come just for him, though of course I had. "Well, I got a lot done today beforehand," I lied.

"Oh, did you work things out with your boyfriend?" he asked, rubbing my shoulder.

"What? No!" I stuttered. I took a step away from him. "Why, do you want me to?"

He blinked, confused.

"I thought you guys were trying to work things out," he said, going back to stretching on the floor, not looking at me.

"Where did you get *that*? We broke up, I left him, I moved out."

"Okay then," he said, standing and throwing up his hands defensively. "Guess I misunderstood the situation." He bent forward at the waist, took one step forward, and did a squat like a runner. His hands pressed his hips forward.

"I wouldn't be visiting you here like this if I had a boyfriend," I continued, still upset.

"Okay," he said. He stood up and kissed me with those big wet lips. He was a slow, aggressive kisser, fitting my face in his palm.

"Yummy," I said now, to Nick. Both of us groaned as his bandmates entered the room and loudly started cracking open beers.

"*All right,* Cavallaro," Marty said in a jocular tone. "Love that tongue action."

I turned away, rolling my eyes. What is it with guys always calling each other by their last names? It's as though saying the first name is a gesture simply too intimate.

"You'll have to excuse Marty," Nick said. "He's from Bayonne."

"Hey, if it's from Bayonne, leave it alone," I said.

All the boys laughed. It was deep male laughter, rumbling around inside the small backstage room, touching all the walls.

"Do you want something to eat from our rider?" Nick asked. He made quotation marks in the air when he said "rider." The only food in sight was Twix bars and Pabst beer.

"Gimme a beer," I said. I gestured at the table with the scant food. "Hey, you are so fancy-pants with that rider."

He laughed, rolling his eyes. "What can I say; we're totally big-time rock stars."

As Nick went over the set list with Marty, I started talking with a woman named Rose, who was married to John Fitzgerald, their drummer. She stood only about five feet tall, and had fluffy bleached blond hair to her shoulders, with a fringe of early Deborah Harry bang across her forehead. Her eyes were clearly her best feature. They were very large and a deep, chocolate brown that reflected light from the room. When she smiled, which was often, she had small teeth and showed a lot of pink gums. She also had a bit of a hard look around her eyes; like you could bullshit all you wanted and she wouldn't believe a word because she'd already seen and heard it all.

Rose wore a shirt that had the letters QVC in a circle with a big red slash across like a no-smoking sign. After speaking with her I found out she had a theory that the shopping network preyed on the mentally ill, which stemmed from the recent death of her mother, who suffered from autism and lived in Detroit with a nurse. When Rose went to her house she found nothing but unopened cardboard boxes, shipments of all the loot she'd been buying off QVC.

"You feel injustice more strongly when you have kids," she explained. "I have an eight-month-old, named Miles."

"Oh, cute! How do you like being a mom?" I asked. We were sharing the black pleather chair, our bodies squished together.

She beamed. "I'm head over heels in love with my baby. He finally has enough hair for a Mohawk, so John is psyched." She reached over me and grabbed a beer from the minifridge. "I had to persuade him not to dye it green, because it wouldn't be safe for his skin." Rose's right arm had a tattoo of the Loved Ones logo with doves on either end.

I felt conspicuously undecorated compared to everyone else in Nick's world, and unzipped my army jacket to reveal my Springsteen T-shirt in the hopes that it would make some kind of statement as to who I was. Maybe even that I have good musical taste. I fingered the wig in my pocket.

Rose had been talking to me but I hadn't heard her. She smiled and repeated herself: "Did you know they are coming up on their fifteen-year anniversary? They're going to have a huge party in Asbury Park for it, and release a special disc, kind of a greatest hits even though they don't get played on regular radio."

"No, I didn't know that," I said. "But that's great! Fifteen years is a hell of a long time to be in a band."

"Tell me about it," Rose said.

"It's funny, Nick didn't mention it to me. I'll have to congratulate him."

"It's all due to him, you know."

"What is?" I asked.

"Every band has one genius in it—there's not enough room for more than one brain or ego that size. Nick's our genius."

"What about John?"

"John's the best drummer in this industry, he's my husband and I love him like mad, but Nick is like on a whole other level from the two other guys. You know he writes all their lyrics," she said.

I nodded. I did know that, having proofread the stories on the band in *Thrash* before they went into print. It was part of what attracted me to Nick; their seemingly blasé lyrics about girls and breakups and heartache that actually were quite profound.

She surprised me then by suddenly standing and lifting up her dress. She had hot pink underpants underneath. No one paid her any attention. Maybe flashing was a regular occurrence with this crowd. "Now, tell me the truth," she said. "Can you see the stretch marks on my hips? John says there's nothing there, but I can totally see them. They're like little evil white squiggly lines."

I laughed. "You would get along with my family," I told her. "We are all exhibitionists. And your stretch marks are barely noticeable. They're beautiful, anyway; a sacrifice you've made for your child."

She lowered her dress, pleased. "That's nice, you saying that."

"If I had a baby, I'd be one of those people who get so obese they have to knock down a wall of their house and hoist them onto a whale stretcher," I told her.

She laughed, and slung an arm around me just as Nick walked back over to grab his guitar.

"I like this chick," she told him.

"I do too," he said, grinning at me. My stomach flipped.

"Let's celebrate this new friendship with some booze!" Rose said, grabbing a bottle of whiskey out of John's hand and taking a slug.

"Hey!" he yelled mock-aggressively. "Come back here with that bottle, woman!"

Rose ignored her husband. "I'm not breastfeeding anymore," she confided, passing the bottle to me. "Thank God. My nipples were cracked and hard as walnuts."

"Hey, I wouldn't judge you if you were," I said, taking a slug.

Nick was wrapping black electrical tape around his wrist.

"What's that for?" I whispered to Rose.

She snorted. "Probably just for show. No one primps or preens more before a concert than punk boys."

I saw Fiona then, across the room, and waved. She blew kisses at Rose and me, and we blew some back. She was holding a long black cord.

"Fiona's the shit," Rose said.

I nodded in agreement.

"She used to be in this all-lesbian band in the early nineties called Labia," she said. "When she was at Evergreen, in Washington."

"Fiona's gay?" I tried not to look surprised. One's sexual orientation always has escaped me; I suppose because I never felt like it really mattered all that much. I'm always the last to know when someone was gay. My parents taught Lauren and me that sexuality is life, that it's organic. That every adult went home at the end of the day to someone's embrace, whether it was a person of the opposite gender or not. My freshman year of college my mom sent me a vibrator, with a note on ROSTOV FAMILY stationery that read: *For my oldest daughter: To use in case you don't find a great boyfriend right away.*

"Haven't you seen her 'Proud to Be a Rug Muncher' shirt?" Rose asked, interrupting my thoughts.

I giggled. "What instrument did she play when she was in a band?"

"I don't think she even played anything, she just would take out her tampon and chuck it at people in the audience and do a lot of screaming, mainly." I tried to imagine Fiona at eighteen, angry and pigtailed. I couldn't picture it.

"Didn't Bikini Kill come out of the same school?" I asked Rose.

"Yeah, they did. Fiona was friends with Kathleen Hanna."

"Oh my god, I *loved* Bikini Kill in high school," I said. "Don't you feel like there's no good chick music anymore? We had Ani,

Sarah McLachlan, Indigo Girls, Liz Phair, Courtney Love, Sheryl Crow . . . They kicked ass and took names."

"I know what you mean," Rose said. "It's all prepackaged bullshit. The big labels churn out these groups like machines. I've even settled lately for listening to the fucking *Dixie Chicks*."

We sat there for a few minutes, reminiscing and passing the bottle back and forth, eyeing some groupies huddled in the corner, Hitchhiker's Revenge tank tops tight across their chests. Several wore leather wristlets with spikes on them, and the customary Chuck Taylor pink high-tops. "Gotta love this," Rose said. The corner of her full mouth was turned up in a smirk.

"What do you mean?"

"You know. Young girls who think they're *so* sticking it to the man if they glop on the eyeliner and buy the tight black jeans and get their boob pierced. I've seen Ramones patches *already stitched on* pants you can buy at Trash and Vaudeville. It's so fucking lame. It defeats the whole method of thinking behind wearing patches." She held up her finger like she was a professor delivering a speech to a crowded lecture hall. "In the old days, it took work! You'd go to a great punk show, grab a bunch of free ones from the merch table, and go home to iron them onto your jacket. Also suitable would be to write in to the fan club of your band of choice and collect patches in the mail."

"In high school I thought I was so badass because I asked my dad to help iron on a Green Day patch to my jeans. I'd buy them at Scottie's Record Shop in Morristown, which is still around. I thought I was so unique."

"I know that store, John and I used to hang out there too. I went to Morristown High with the boys a million years ago before my mom moved west. Well, at least you put some effort into it," Rose said. "Kids today! They want their punk handed to them!"

"Do you think these girls use their arm cuff spikes for a specific purpose?" I asked Rose, looking over at the three fans. One was playing with the piercing in her lip. Rose pretended to think about it.

"Maybe to pop balloons at a preppy person's birthday party?"

"I think there has to be a more practical reason," I said, chewing my bottom lip. "Say they're in a gang . . ."

"Harper, they're like twelve years old."

I felt bad for labeling the groupies. If I am being honest here, I'd have probably shit in my pants if I'd been allowed backstage at a Hitchhiker's Revenge show at their age.

"So what's up with Nick's ex-girlfriend?" I asked, when we tired of picking on the fans, now shooting nervous glances at us.

"What about her?"

"Well . . . are you friends with her?"

"She's a real nice girl, sure." Rose looked around the room, nodding her head to Silversun Pickups' song "Lazy Eye," which was playing from loudspeakers as background noise. "Hey, want to get out of here? I think the boys are starting."

"Sure," I said.

We walked out of the tiny room and found a small empty space on the crowded upper balcony. My eyes flew over the massive crowd below, the security who stood, backs to the stage, to assist crowd surfers who would jump onto the stage, scream a few belligerent lines into Marty's microphone, then dive back into the audience, content with their own little way of participating in the concert. I could make out Nick against the large black banner spelling out HITCHHIKER'S REVENGE. He was tuning his guitar, his bald head bent intently to hear the sounds his strings made over the din of the room.

"Are you interested in Nick?" Rose asked into my ear, raising a perfectly shaped eyebrow.

"I've actually been warned against it," I told her, laughing nervously. "By several people. Including Nick himself."

She turned to me, fully listening now. The stage lights were behind her and her face was lit in green and red colors. I suddenly had the sensation we were on a set, with Rose about to deliver lines we'd rehearsed before. I felt déjà vu. I almost expected a director to jump out from behind her and yell, "Cut!"

"Just enjoy yourself, you're only a baby!" she said. And she smiled, which took the edge off her words. "Nick is not boyfriend material," she added. "Just think what we put up with: worrying they're fucking everything that moves while on tour, taking care of Miles by myself for three months at a time . . . My sisters are both married with kids too, and they give me sad eyes whenever I bring up John, like 'Oh, poor Rose, alone again with the baby, how does she manage it, blah blah blah.' Sometimes I worry about John so much I think I'm going completely crazy!"

I nodded encouragingly, trying not to show my stomach was in knots.

"Mae was always showing up at our house, wondering if Nick was there, or calling him three hundred times a day while they were on the road."

She was quiet for a beat.

"You can understand how she'd feel, can't you?"

Her question agitated me. I didn't want to sound bitter, but I was jealous Mae had gotten Nick to commit to her, even if it sounded like he made a shitty boyfriend. I had a name to consider now: Mae. It was my mother's middle name.

"He doesn't really give a shit about Mae, she was basically a replacement girlfriend when Lana left him. Did he tell you about her?"

"He kind of hinted he'd had a girlfriend for a long time," I said. "And I saw her name tattooed on his arm."

"Yeah, he was with Lana for eight years," Rose said. Someone bumped into her, spilling her drink a little. "Yeesh!" she said, readjusting the black headband in her hair.

"Okay, so back to Nick's tale of fucking woe. Lana totally screwed him over and he never got over it. They were engaged, and she left him for Tom, who the guys knew since middle school. He was their guitarist in the band for ten years."

"He played guitar too?" I asked. I'd read about Tom's abrupt departure a few years ago, but the article had been brief and didn't hold many details.

"Yeah, they used to have two guitarists," Rose said. "It was a really bad time when Tom left the band. Tom and Lana ended up getting married and moving to California, so I guess it was worth it to them."

"Wow, that's messed up," I said. "Poor Nick."

"Yeah. I don't think he ever got over that," she said.

As I watched, the colors changed over Rose's milky white face as the lights were turned way down to illuminate the stage. There was a loud gnashing of guitar, followed by excited screaming. The concert was starting.

I recognized the first few chords of "Seaside, Sleazeside," and Rose grabbed my hand. We ran out of the room and up some stairs to a balcony for a better view.

"This crowd is fucking rad!" Nick shouted into the microphone.

They responded with a roar. Kids started moshing below us, their skinny legs and arms jabbing toward the ceiling. I saw the scene like a painter would, a mishmash of solid dark colors: blues, grays, greens. One girl crowd surfed in a yellow cotton dress I recognized as off the racks of American Apparel. I was impressed with her chutzpah, but I truly had no desire to ever be thrown around a room like a Frisbee. It looked dangerous. I'd be afraid someone would cop a feel.

As Rose jumped up and down beside me and hundreds of kids screamed below, my eyes were focused solely on Nick. His energy was infectious, the way he'd run from one end of the stage to the other, or step on top of a speaker and thrust his hips and guitar into the crowd. They loved him. Though Marty was the lead singer, he stood in one place, as he had to sing *and* play bass. It was clearly Nick the crowd came to see, and I realized the experience he gave the audience was akin to what I felt when naked with him: like anything in life was possible, like you were the sexiest person alive. He fucked the entire room, gave himself over completely to his fans. He did an impressive stage dive as the song ended and small lights were set off, like mini fireworks, their crackling sound and silver sparkles bouncing around the room.

Though it was a cool night, it may as well have been Havana inside Bowery. My Springsteen shirt stuck to my ribs as I felt a trickle of sweat slide between my boobs.

"Do you want a drink?" I yelled into Rose's ear.

She couldn't hear me, and shook her head, pointing to her ear to explain. Because she was also jumping around, she had the comical appearance of someone with swimmer's ear.

I mimed throwing back a drink at her and she gave a thumbs-up. The art deco–style bar was directly behind us and it was made of beautiful multicolored stained glass. It looked like someone had salvaged it from a church. A group of girls in front of me had ordered their drinks but were still standing at the bar, chatting. One of them wore a Hitchhiker's Revenge T-shirt from their 1998 Chicks and Bikes tour. I studied her face, totally taken by her eye makeup job, with a Cleopatra-like line at the corner of each eye, and dark navy and gray shadows. The best I can do with eye makeup is do the same rocker chick eyeliner over and under each eye, like a raccoon. It's been my go-to look since high school. I'm always fascinated when I come across women who are able to pull off a really fantastic makeup job.

I briefly entertained the idea of asking how she'd applied her makeup, but before I could walk over to her she plunked a five-dollar bill on the counter and danced back to the balcony, hair swishing, friends pushing her from behind like wind.

The crowd though were mainly young men, wearing shirts advertising other bands I know Nick has toured with in the past. Many had shaved heads, pants tucked into high black boots. A few had that androgynous skinny rocker look, with greasy bangs pushed to one side, but most were the burlier type, fleshy. The guy who would win a fight in a bar. They went up again and again for beers; their intense energy (an emotion close to anger) made the whole room feel as though it were vibrating. The excitement exhausted and titillated me at the same time.

I got two shots of tequila and waded through the crowd back to Rose. The next hour and a half passed mostly the same, with either Rose or myself making pilgrimages to the bar for over-priced shots in plastic cups, and dancing our asses off. At one point I had my arms raised above my head and saw hundreds of people below me doing the same thing, and I felt part of something big. Something beautiful. When the show was over I got a quick sweaty kiss from Nick before he had to do an interview for East Village Radio. I listened in for a while. His eyes never left the woman interviewing the band, and he was gregarious and funny, making her laugh several times. I'd hoped we could make a quick exit, but it wasn't going to happen.

Trying not to slur my words, I called my parents from the downstairs girls' bathroom, telling them I wouldn't be coming back tonight. The images in front of me flashed like rapid snapshots: a girl reapplying bloodred lipstick in the dirty mirror, another holding her friend's sandy blond hair back as she puked in the toilet, my hands glowing white under the lights as I fished for a stick of gum to try and abate my booze breath. I was just drunk enough to realize I had to pretend to be in control of myself. A tremor of worry squeezed my stomach. Andy had always taken care of me when I was drinking, either red-flagging me and taking me home in a cab, or convincing me to eat a slice of pizza at two o'clock in the morning to soak up some of the alcohol. I'd have to watch out for myself now: a daunting undertaking.

Then, it was a lot of waiting around. Rose went off to call her aunt, who was babysitting Miles. I ran into Rivers again and made yet another attempt at nervous conversation with him. Nick, hurrying past us at one point, put his arm around Rivers and pointed at me. "Rivers, tell Harper about going back to Harvard, and you, Harper, my dear, should find the right place to write about it." Then, Marty was calling him; they had to pose for pictures with fans who had won a Sirius radio contest.

"So, what's up with Harvard?" I asked Rivers. "Didn't I read in *Rolling Stone* a few years ago that you dropped out?"

We were sitting outside on the curb. Now people smoked

around us, rings of white surrounding their heads like crowns. A few glanced at Rivers curiously. Guys walked around handing out flyers for future shows. They said things like "Don't miss this one!" Or "Killer opening act."

Rivers had found a lit cigarette in the street and was scraping at it with a stick, putting out its orange flame. "Yeah, I'm kind of just going to finish up my final year, it's not a big deal. I haven't told anybody other than these guys about it."

"I think that's great, that you're completing your degree," I told him.

"Well," he said. He was someone who could say the word "well" with meaning. But I enjoyed talking with him, until Nick finally came out and asked if we wanted to grab food. It was nearly midnight, and I had that kind of dull feeling from too much booze. Everything looked slightly slanted. It had rained while we were inside, and drops clung to Nick's Harley, which was a vintage-looking model with high handlebars. It was a beautiful piece of machinery, and I was terrified of it.

"Here, babe, wear my helmet," he said, throwing it to me. I caught it. It was shiny and black, and I turned it over in my hands.

"Um . . . I think I'll just take a cab and meet you there," I said.

He smiled at me. "A motorcycle virgin, are we? Not to worry, my lady, I will have you to our destination without a scratch."

I smiled nervously at him. Fuck. I'm sure Mae just hopped right on there, fluorescent thong, heels, and all.

"I'll take a cab with you, Harper," Rivers said, next to me.

"I'm sorry, Nick," I said, horrified at my cowardice.

"Don't be silly," he said kindly, starting the motor and edging out of his parking spot with the toe of his boot. He called out over his shoulder: "Everyone should do what makes them happy in this world!"

"I feel like such an idiot," I told Rivers in the cab. I was almost crying, and all the booze I'd drunk tonight while waiting for Nick didn't help. Rivers looked sad, somehow.

"Harper, who cares what Nick thinks?" he said. "You have a right to make decisions for your own safety. Anyway, you know what doctors call those things?"

"What?"

"Donorcycles."

I laughed. "Thank you for being so awesome."

"Glad I could be of service," he said. There was an awkward silence, so I did what I always do when nervous. Talked.

"What does a gay horse eat?" I asked him.

"I give up!"

"Heeeeeeeey," I said, doing a little shoulder shimmy.

He surprised me by shooting one right back at me. "What kind of karate does a pig do?"

I thought about it as the driver made a quick turn, tires squealing. I put on my seat belt. "I give up."

"Pork chop," he said, making a karate chop in the air.

I shrieked. "You are *hilarious!*"

We ate at Veselka on Ninth Street. It was all of Hitchhiker's Revenge, some girls Marty had met at the show, Rose, Fiona, me, Rivers, and a few guys from another band on the same label. About seventeen people in all. Nick was the life of the place, and his energy was exhausting; it made me tired just looking at him. I tried to catch his eye but he spent the meal talking loudly about the show, mercilessly teasing Marty because his voice had cracked during one of their songs.

At one point Marty and Nick got into a fight and started

wrestling, fooling around. John and Rose were having an intense private conversation outside. Rose had mentioned to me she wanted John to start helping her more with Miles when he was home from tour, and I think the alcohol spurred her to want to discuss that issue *right now.*

"I don't like you one *fuck,*" Marty said when he finally sat back down in his chair, hair all sorts of disheveled.

Nick gave him the finger.

"Nice," I said. "*Let It Ride* is a great flick."

Marty's eyes lit up with interest. "Ah, a hot chick who understands movie references. Nick, man, don't let this one go."

I glanced at Nick, who appeared to be text messaging on his phone, his fingers looking clumsy and too big for the small letters. He made a noncommittal nod.

"I'm a huge film guy," Marty said. "Actually, um . . ." He scooted his chair closer to mine. "I was an extra in *Parenthood,*" he said. "Just a weird little factoid for ya."

"No way, that's awesome."

He looked sheepish. "Yeah, don't let that get out. My solid rep as a tough guy will be ruined."

"So did you want to be an actor?" I asked him, crossing my arms. Marty had this way of leaning in a little too close. New Yorkers are very aware of personal space, and I had a feeling Marty was somewhat of a ladies' man.

"Um, no. My mom saw a flyer posted to a tree and forced me to do it. I think she had visions of me becoming this big star but I just wanted to sit in my room and sing show tunes all day."

"Show tunes?" I glanced at his black T-shirt, black jeans, heavy sideburns, and full tattooed arms.

"Yeah. I love anything by Rodgers and Hammerstein."

It was funny. Nick was ignoring me and I was actually having an interesting discussion with Marty, who I'd at first thought was sarcastic and off-putting.

"I guess you can't judge a punk rocker by his cover," I said to Marty, and gave him my real smile, which is unguarded and shows a lot of teeth.

"Yeah, guess not," he said, finishing his omelette—an odd choice for the middle of the night.

John and Rose walked back inside. Rose looked calmer. The issue had been resolved, apparently.

"Okay?" I mouthed to her. She nodded, smiling.

Marty had turned to Rivers and was apparently still talking about Keanu Reeves, the star of *Parenthood*. I caught the tail end of the conversation:

"I totally get what you're saying, Rivers. If he hadn't done *Speed* he wouldn't have a career today at all. I do love that movie, and I used to live right near the 105 freeway in Los Angeles where the whole thing was filmed."

Rivers nodded. "I loved the *Matrix* series, but that may be more due to the Wachowski brothers' talent than Keanu's acting abilities as Neo, you know?"

I jumped in. "Did Larry Wachowski really get a sex-change operation? I mean, good for him and everything, I know he's very open about dating a dominatrix, but it's pretty shocking, no?" I was proud of myself that I could keep up with Marty on pop culture knowledge. Working at *Us Weekly,* it was a job requirement.

"If I got a sex change I'd never get out of my apartment because I would stay in bed all day and play with myself," Marty said, laughing at his own joke.

Okay. Maybe the guy was still off-putting.

Nick was now talking to Rose. I felt proud of myself that I

could hold my own in a discussion among his friends. I didn't need him to pay attention to me in a room full of people I just met. I was smart enough to join in any discussion, to talk about a variety of subjects.

"I heard it's a rumor for publicity, but who the fuck knows," Marty said, still discussing Wachowski.

The band was full of inside jokes and memories of years past. They seemed to speak their own language, finishing each other's sentences, anticipating what the other was about to say. The boys debated for a long time whether to let Fuse do a big profile accompanied by a live set. The channel has been playing their videos, but they tossed the interview idea back and forth. John held strong that he didn't think their fans would see it as "selling out," and Marty agreed, but Nick was still hesitant when we gathered up our things to leave. I was starting to realize that Nick was the least easygoing member of the band. His emotions seemed to brim at the surface, easily accessible at all times. The man didn't seem to know how to relax. Rose, Fiona, and I exchanged phone numbers, and I spent most of the night talking to them and Rivers. I slipped out at one point to call Sarah, but she must have been asleep and I left a slightly slurry message on her home phone.

"Are you coming home with me, pretty lady?" Nick asked after the bill was paid and folks started taking off. I didn't want to leave. The closeness that existed between everyone here was unlike anything I'd ever experienced in my life. I'd always felt alienated among Andy's friends. He'd gone to Brown, and most of the people he hung out with in New York were alumni transplants. They'd always seemed slightly condescending when speaking with me.

I hesitated. Nick watched my face. The thing was, I *wanted* to go home with Nick, and surely the last train back to Madison had already left the station. It was very late. But he didn't call when he said he would. I'd had a wonderful night, but he hadn't exactly looked out for me. I was a fish out of water. I felt like he could have checked in with me a little more at the concert and during dinner, but it didn't seem like Nick's style to do so. It wasn't callousness; he simply believed I was an independent woman and therefore I should be able to manage on my own. Maybe he'd asked Rose to keep me company, I don't know.

I felt his hand on my face as he pushed some stray hairs away and whispered in my ear: "I liked your pink wig, Harper Rostov." His deep, rumbly voice made my stomach flip over. I struggled to not let it show on my face that he was turning me on.

"I didn't think you noticed it!" I breathed.

"Of course I did. When it comes to you, I notice everything." He grinned. "You're so cute. When you blush, your freckles stand out."

I rolled my eyes and shoved him. It was like trying to move a mountain. He kissed my cheek, then leaned over to nudge the kickstand on his Harley and push the bike along the street next to me. Glass broke in the street where his wheels rolled over shards of glass. When we reached Tompkins Park, a late-night basketball game had broken out. A bored-looking pit bull was tied to the fence and glanced up at us as we walked by.

I tried expressing to Nick how much I'd enjoyed tonight as he pushed his bike. I walked next to him, balancing on the curb like a gymnast. Whenever a parked car separated us, I walked around it only to join him on the other side. We made figure eights all the way to Avenue C. "Yeah, we're a family," he said. "I'd die for any one of those guys, and them for me. That's what happens when you tour together for fifteen years, the first ten spent driving around the country in an RV."

"And I love John and Rose's marriage," I said. "He's so nice to her, like how they left the diner when she started feeling tired. I hope to someday have something like they do."

He looked amused. "They're not perfect people, Harper." His face darkened. "Besides, John's been a real pussy lately."

I stopped walking and put my hand up in front of his face. "Okay, first of all, I hate it when men use the word 'pussy' to mean someone is weak. And second, what are you talking about?"

He kissed my palm. "He's trying to shorten our upcoming tour in Japan, which took our tour manager, like, a year to line up. He also wants to start putting an album out every three to four years, not every one or two like we've been doing forever."

I was quiet, thinking. "Yeah, but isn't that kind of understandable now that he has a wife and kid?"

"I guess, but it just sucks that I've put fifteen years and all my blood and guts into this band and now he wants to 'take it down a notch.' When you do that, when you start doing that shit, the fans will notice, believe me. They'll notice and be pissed and that will result in smaller album sales, and less kids coming out to see us play. It's a bad move. We'll lose a shitload of money."

When we passed the Avenue C sign I jumped up and touched it.

"Oh, poor you," I said. "You'll have to get a job like the rest of us." It came out harsher than I'd intended. Like a punch on stage meant to be theatrical, but accidentally striking tender skin.

His eyes widened, but he stayed silent.

He disappeared for a minute to park his bike. We walked up the stairs to his apartment, my thighs groaning in protest.

"I noticed something when the girl from the radio station was interviewing you," I told him hesitantly. We sat down on his couch and he drew my feet into his lap.

"Yeah, what's that?" he asked. He was giving me his wolf grin, teeth and all, but I didn't feel like having sex yet. I was too wound up.

"She asked when you'd have enough songs written to start recording." He slowly placed my foot back on the couch. "You seemed to . . . tense up."

He was quiet for so long I thought he'd chosen to ignore my question.

"The writing is nearly finished, but I'm not progressing much on the cover art," he said. He went into the kitchen to fix our drinks. I noticed he poured very little alcohol into my glass. I wondered if he thought I was drunk. I was touched he cared. "I'm trying to paint it this time in oil, then transfer that to my computer," he said.

"And how's it going?"

"So-so. The label gave me a laptop for this record," he said.

"They must be taking you very seriously."

"Want to see what I have so far?" he asked, taking my hand and leading me over to an easel next to his bed. He was smiling at me. His concerned mood had vanished as quickly as it had come on, and now his smile was infectious. I grinned back at him. The door to his closet was ajar, and the mirror on the front of it gave the impression that there were two images of Nick and me, two of his hands on mine. It was strange; for the first time since I met him, he seemed nervous, almost humble. I looked at his work for a long time. "I still have to fill it in with more paint," he said. "It's just a rough idea."

It was a concert, with kids moshing and crowd surfing. The

main focus was a young kid with shaggy hair, colored like straw. He was poised to leap off the shoulders of security and into the bright lights of the crowd.

"It's . . . neat," I said, peering closer. In the background I could see bowling lanes, and realized the painting was of Asbury Lanes, a popular venue for punk bands in Jersey.

"I wanted an image I could paint that signaled Jersey to me," he said.

"That's a fun venue. I saw Sticks and Stones play there in college," I said. Behind us I heard rain tapping on the outside of his windows.

"So. What do you really think of the painting?"

"Honestly?"

"Yeah."

"I kind of think it sucks. It's way too personal a reference—I don't think anyone outside Jersey is going to recognize the bowling alley. I think you can do way better."

"Wow. Brutal honesty."

"Well, you asked for my opinion," I said.

"I'm having trouble with it, yeah, because so much of the album takes place here in New York. For instance, several of the songs are about a past relationship I had, while living in another apartment here in the East Village in the nineties."

"Oh. I see what you're saying." I was quiet then; talk of his exes upset me. He had an old-fashioned camera slung over the easel, the kind you have to look down into to focus the picture. "Where'd you get that?"

"Oh, I've had that forever. I take pictures with it around the city when I'm home from a tour."

"Let's see them."

"Really? They're pretty lame."

"Give up the goods, Cavallaro."

Most of them were kind of lame. They were blurry sepia shots. We sat on his bed, our thighs touching, and he was quiet as I flipped through them. I could hear the television in the apartment next door. I liked one of Marty and Nick having beers on the back of a bus. Whenever John appeared, he looked incredibly serious; either reading or practicing on his drum kit. There was one of Rose that made me smile; Nick had caught her on the toilet. She was hugely pregnant, and giving the camera the finger. In some, Nick inexplicably wore an eye patch, like a pirate. I paused when I came to a photograph taken in black and white. It was captured just as the band was preparing to start their set. Marty was taking a swig of beer in front of the microphone. John's foot was frozen in midair as he climbed behind his drum kit. Nick's beefy arm was visible, and seemed to be pointing toward the swelling crowd, which was in the thousands. It was a beautiful shot. "Nick, you should make this photo your album cover, not the oil painting."

"Really?" he asked, taking a cigarette out of the pack in his pocket and rolling it between his fingers. He ripped off the filter and lit it, his cheeks sucking in.

"I'm serious," I said. "The painting is nice, but this photo *says* something. It makes you want to keep looking at it. You can still have your title and band name scrawled across it in a cool font, this would just be the background."

We both listened to the rain outside for a few seconds. It was hitting his skylight like a steady drumbeat.

"That's a really good idea, actually," he said, sounding excited. "I'll run it by the guys tomorrow." He leaned over and kissed me then, softly.

He stood and walked over to his desk and turned on his iPod. Mission of Burma's "Academy Fight Song" started to play. I nodded my head along.

"Hey, Nick?"

"Yeah?"

"I don't think it would be selling out if you did the Fuse interview. It's not like it's MTV. Fuse is not really mainstream yet."

"Yeah, it's just that we built this band on the premise that we would keep things somewhat low-key. I even struggled with going on our first European tour back in the nineties."

"Yeah, but I mean, you guys have to make a living *somehow*. Miles needs money for college," I said.

Nick cracked a smile. He flopped down on the bed and leaned over to remove his boots. I took his foot onto my lap and slowly pulled out the laces. My fingers were smaller and I was quicker. "I hear you. We will probably end up doing it. I like the channel, and a lot of bands we're friends with are on there a lot."

"Hey, if you could make the band be like, *famous* famous, would you?"

"Like Yo La Tengo famous or Green Day famous?"

"Green Day famous." I set his foot back on the floor.

"Thanks, babe," he said, referring to the boots. "And nah. I don't want to get up to that level. Then you get into the bigger shark labels trying to get you to agree to their ways of thinking, fucking clothing companies that want you to wear their stupid shoes. You got tour managers who don't give a fuck about putting you in great, smaller rock clubs because they don't make as much money as the bigger venues. No, fuck that."

I lay back against his pillows and put my arms behind my

head. My small breasts stuck out and I noticed Nick noticing them. "I do love Green Day, though. I was just listening to *Dookie* the other day. I feel like every song on that album is golden."

He tore his gaze away from the girls and said something surprising: "Oh totally, I do too. I'm not a music snob. Green Day is kind of like pop music, which goes in a giant circle, with bands imitating one another. A lot of my heroes write pop songs mixed in with other kinds of harder music. Fall Out Boy, Paramore, No Doubt . . . all good bands, all popular bands."

"What makes something pop music, do you think?" I asked him.

He put his head on my thigh. I could feel the warmth of his breath through my jeans. I ran my hand over his shaved head and he snaked his arm around my waist.

"With pop music the response is universal; the lyrics have you trapped inside the warmest, clearest summer day. The harder stuff I write is written only for me."

Now that we were on the subject of music, he talked adamantly. It was like I was the only person on the planet who mattered to him. When I started to speak he sat up and looked me right in the eye, nodding so hard I thought his neck would snap. He was so many things: self-involved, narcissistic. And yet . . . and yet he listened to me more than anyone ever had. I felt like right now, right here tonight, that I was more open with Nick than I ever had been with anyone before in my entire life. Like all the years of loving music and writing about it had come to a head, just to have this conversation with him.

"I feel like pop music cares if it's liked, and punk doesn't," I said. "That's the basic difference."

"Yeah," Nick said. "Yeah! You totally fucking *get* it! There's a song on the new album called 'A Perfect Hour' that definitely has those pop hooks. I'm not afraid to be both, to want to be liked and also not to give a shit. I think you'll like it."

I would have thought Nick would be a strict punk snob.

He had a bag of potato chips on his bedside table. I reached in to grab a bunch. "Mmmm, salty and delicious," I said.

He held a chip up to the little bit of yellow street light coming from the skylight on the ceiling. "Isn't a potato chip just so amazing. This little fellow right here once was part of a big spud, just growing on a farmer's land. And then they slice and fry them in sunflower oil and this is the result. It's frickin' awesome."

I laughed. "I agree. And then we buy a whole bag of 'em for three bucks and eat them!"

"Did you know that the first potato chip was invented by a chef who had some asshole customer sending his fried potatoes back because they tasted thick and too soggy? This was in like, I dunno, the eighteen hundreds. So the chef dude decides to slice them thin and stir-fry them and the customer ends up fucking loving them!"

"Wow, I never knew," I said.

"Yeah, it's a stupid fact to know."

"No, I actually think it's really cool to know stuff like that, the details in life. My sister is like that. She's interested in everything and forgets nothing."

"That's me, the historian of Avenue C," he said. He stood, then put his hand out and pulled me off the bed. He was strong, and I flew right into his chest. I put my hand against his T-shirt, over his heart, and gave him a light kiss on the lips.

"Hey lovely lady, come outside and keep me company," he said. "Soon it will be too cold to sit on the balcony." The thought of still being with Nick inside his apartment when winter swept into New York made me smile. I wore a white long-sleeved waffle shirt of his to keep warm. He carried out two plastic lawn chairs, hoisting them onto both his shoulders. They clapped like butter-fly wings. His balcony was attached to the back of the building and was just big enough for our chairs. There were a few dead potted plants around our feet. Lights switched on in various apart-ments in the building across from Nick's. We were only five flights up and I could see cars driving down Avenue D. When we were settled in the chairs, my feet on his lap, I said: "Let's play a get-to-know-each-other game."

He took a deep drag and raised an eyebrow at me.

"You go first."

"Well, what's your fantasy life soundtrack song?" I asked him.

"Harper, what are you talking about?" He was running his fingers up my leg and I slapped at them.

"Okay, well for instance, when I'm jogging, I like to play Billy Idol's 'Mony, Mony' and pretend I'm in the Olympics for ice-skating and that's the song I do my routine to. It's ridiculous, I know."

"Nah, it just shows how you're a creative-minded person," he said.

"So let's hear it," I said.

"Hear what?"

"Your fantasy life soundtrack song. Give it up, dude."

"Fine. But you can't make fun of it." And then he mumbled something incoherently.

"What? Speak up, I can't hear you."

"I do the 'Thriller' dance sometimes, in my room," he said.

"*What?* You mean the Michael Jackson song?"

"Yes. The Michael Jackson song."

"Do you do the crotch grabs?" I asked.

"Of course I do the crotch grabs. They're the best part."

"Oh my god, that is awesome. Will you teach it to me?" I pleaded, hands under my chin like I was praying.

"Only if you are willing to show me your skating routine," he said. "And wear that little sparkly skirt outfit they wear on the ice."

"Deal," I said. I held out my hand and he shook it and we both burst out laughing. It was a perfect moment.

He lit another cigarette, and I watched the smoke curl up and over the balcony, out into the night. "Tell me something I don't know about you," I said.

He looked up. The moon was full and he was backlit, making it hard to see his face, like when there is an eclipse and you wear the special glasses that protect your eyes. "I was born on this very day," he said. "Around this time of the night."

"What? Do you mean it's your birthday?"

He nodded, his expression flat.

"Well what the hell? Why didn't you tell me? We could have celebrated it!" How weird of him not to mention it!

"We already did," he said. He stood and walked over to the balcony's rail, putting his back against it. "What a night, you know? All those crazy kids, having such a great time." He took a drag, his cheekbones sticking out. The moon shone silver on the side of his face, and he looked a little vampirelike.

"Yeah, but we could have had a cake."

He cocked his head and gave me a thin look that was more grimace than smile. "Harper, would you seriously have done all that? I hate my birthday." And with that, the mood suddenly shifted into something else.

I was flabbergasted. When it's my birthday, I tell people at least two months in advance to give them ample time to shop for a present. Three months is too far ahead; they'll forget.

"No one hates their *birthday*," I said.

I went to punch him lightly in the arm but he caught my fist and kissed it. "Want to know my favorite thing to do out here?" he asked suddenly.

"You mean besides smoke a zillion cigarettes and be cranky?" I said.

"No one likes a smart aleck," he said. I was relieved at his banter; it meant his mood was lifting. "So if I've had a bad day, or had a fight with my old lady, or whatever, I like to come out here and scream things into the night. Things that don't make any sense." He lifted an eyebrow. "Dirty words."

"Oh yeah?"

"'Cause it's like New York is such a big animal, and there's all these people in their little apartments living their little lives. Walking down the street, thinking their little deep thoughts. If I want to scream until my lungs give out I'm not bothering any-one, no one can even hear me. I feel like out here I can get my anger out. Like this." And he leaned over the balcony so far my hand reached out into the air to grab his shirt. "Piss goddamn tits balls!" he screamed into the darkness. I was amazed at how unself-conscious he was.

"I like it," I said. I gave a little laugh, but it wasn't funny, re-ally. I thought of all Nick's fans that were pushing, moving as one to his music tonight, how they looked at him with such *admiration* in their eyes. He'd seemed to fill up the entire room just a few hours ago with his energy. Right now he looked very small against the night.

"Well, I can beat that," I said.

"No way."

"Jersey Girls have the trashiest mouths around, didn't you know that?" The mood had lifted a little more. I put my belly against the cold rail as he had and cupped my hands around my mouth.

"Cunt-licking motherfucker asshole raping slut of a grand-father!" I yelled.

"Whoa. Okay, you win. That was some fucked-up stuff," he said, laughing. "I'm now terrified to let you back into my apartment."

"I thought the 'slut of a grandfather' had a nice ring to it," I said, as he slung a heavy arm around me and we went inside.

I thumbed through an issue of *Alternative Press* on the bed while Nick worked on his painting. The silence was a warm one, punched with the sounds of the scrape of his brush against canvas, the turning of magazine pages. "Nick, what's your take on band names these days?"

"What do you mean?" he asked, peering around his easel at me. He had red paint on his cheek, making him look like a war-rior.

"Okay, well, two things bother me about so-called punk bands these days."

"Oh yeah?" he asked, amused now. He stuck his brush in a jar and joined me, throwing his legs over mine to create a figure eight. He took his shirt off. What was that little line called, that trail of soft hair that men have from belly button to groin? It came to me then. *Happy trail.*

"Okay, one is that they have seriously stupid names. I was just reading an album review for a group that calls themselves Drop Dead, Gorgeous."

"Those are a bunch of nice guys from Denver, you can't rag on them too much," he protested. "We toured with them three summers ago and they're chill. Besides, that's a *very* well-placed comma, and a play on a movie starring Ellen Barkin and Kirsten Dunst. It's a *clever* name, really."

"Yeah? Well, let's see you talk your way out of this one: As I Lay Dying." I saw a smirk start to weave its way onto the corner of his mouth. "Funeral for a Friend? It Dies Today? Scary Kids Scaring Kids? Poison the Well?" We were both laughing by now.

"I *like* Poison the Well!" he shouted. "That song 'Zombies Are Good for Your Health' rocks it." He started to crack my toes, one by one. It hurt a little.

I flipped the magazine closed and swatted his hand with it. "It's all just *so* melodramatic! Just because you didn't make the football team in high school you have to torture my generation with your version of punk rock? Give me a break. Stop imitating the Misfits with your stupid black eyeliner, get those piercings out of your face, and concentrate on writing good rock and roll!"

"Well, what would your band name be?" he asked.

"Leaping Lizards."

"Leaping Lizards?" He started to laugh.

"Dude, Leaping Lizards sounds *totally* rad," I told him. "It's like, my band name is so stupid that I don't even care! We're the Leaping Lizards! We're more punk than any of you fuckers!" I jumped up and down on the bed, sending pillows flying.

"Hitchhiker's Revenge sounds just as over the top as those other bands you were mentioning," Nick mused. "But it's okay because we play better rock 'n' roll than anyone. Plus, I've got the biggest dick on the Warped Tour." I threw my magazine at him, which started a wrestling match, which of course led to sex right there.

"I'm almost there," I told him, concentrating on coming. He'd pinned my hands against his chest as he moved above me.

His collar bone was slick with sweat. A tattoo of giant black wings spread across from nipple to armpit. "Don't fucking stop," I ordered.

A grin spread its way across his face; his eyes were closed. He went slack on top of me.

"Did you just come?" I asked him, incredulous.

"Yup." He rolled over, one arm slung around my middle almost as an afterthought. I sat up in the dark; I had been so close. I pushed his shoulder and drew my arm back when suddenly he emitted a loud snore. I thought about masturbating, but felt too tired. Instead, I snuggled into Nick's back in a reverse spoon. He had no shades on his windows, and the moon outside was pregnant and enormous. It lit the bedroom, making the furniture look like parallels of their day selves. I walked to the window to look for the green neon light across the street—for some reason it gave me comfort—but the building was dark. "Happy birthday," I whispered to Nick, whose body lay still under the covers across the room from me.

Monday

the man is *colorful* when nude. The sheer brightness of the ink on his skin was almost blinding when I woke up beside him Monday morning, like rising to a rainbow. I was finally able to trace all of his tattoos with my pointer finger, something I'd wanted to do since I met him in Mud. His back tattoo was an immediately familiar image; the skyline of Manhattan. Looming over the dark outlines of buildings was an orange tiger. His blue, purple, and gold body took up most of Nick's shoulders and upper back. His tail dipped into the East River. His nails were bloodred and clutching several of the buildings. Below it was a large banner stretching onto the top of his small white butt—one of the few blank spaces left on his body. It read: *9/11/01 Our brothers we will never forget, they will always live on in our hearts.* It was a memorial.

I ran my hand over his butt and down one thigh. It was ridiculous, really. At thirty-six, the signs of aging should have been slowly threading their way through his body, but he had the look of an adolescent boy, with sinewy, taut muscles, and smooth skin brimming with possibility. He had hardly any body hair, and what existed was a light brown. Even his pubic hair was soft, not wiry. He twitched in his sleep, but didn't wake up. His right leg had Katsushika Hokusai's famous painting *The Great Wave,* which I'd proudly presented on my wall in poster form freshman year of college (only to later discover it was in almost every other dorm). Around his calf was written *I Heard They Suck Live,* which puzzled me for a few seconds until I remembered it was the title of a NOFX album. His legs had a multitude of other tattoos. Even his kneecaps hadn't escaped, with Japanese letters decorating them.

"You look pretty when your hair's all messy like that," he said, startling me. I'd been sitting up in bed, and with one quick swoop he grabbed me under my knees and lifted me on top of him, one arm snaked securely over my behind.

"Is that your come-hither look?" I asked him.

"Yeah!" His voice was even gruffer when he woke up, like he'd been smoking since exiting the womb.

"You look like the snake in *The Jungle Book,*" I said. "Like your eyes are trying to hypnotize me." But then his big wet mouth was on top of mine and his hands were doing what they do best, and I couldn't talk any longer.

Afterward, I lay with my head on his chest and he drummed a beat on the nape of my neck with his fingers. With his other hand, he puffed quietly on a cigarette.

"I have to catch up with e-mails from fans on our stupid Facebook page today," he said. "Then go to John and Rose's house in Brooklyn to do a little practicing. I'm not sure what your plans are, but if you're not busy would you like to join me?" It was cute, how he often phrased his sentences so formally. So . . . earnestly.

"Let me think about it," I said. "Aren't you a little old for Facebook?"

"It's just helpful for us to keep in touch with everyone

from other states and countries," he said. "Staying connected to bookers from clubs all over on that site helps us get better tours, bigger venues. Are you on there?"

"No, not yet."

"If you decide to have a page, what picture will you use?"

I groaned.

"I forgot about that part."

"I love the people who have, like, professional portraits taken for their profiles," he said. "Their hair and makeup is perfect and shit." He took a drag of his cigarette, pinching it between his thumb and pointer finger.

"I like the ones where they try and look 'arty,'" I said, making quotation marks in the air above our heads. "Like, they're looking away from the camera as if something caught their rapt attention, and they just *had* to stare intently at it."

"Then again, maybe if you *intentionally* act as if you don't care, and put up a crappy photo, that's actually putting more effort into it than just having a fancy photo, and therefore you're way lamer," he said.

It was fun to talk to Nick. Being with him made me realize all my worlds were coming together. I'd started a music rag that had written about his band, and now I was lying here naked with him. Life is funny.

"I bet you could write a great book," Nick was saying.

"I'm still trying to figure out if I even am a writer."

"You?" he asked, tracing his finger around my belly button. Andy and I used to call my round stomach my little "papoose."

"To the core." He tapped my chest lightly, over my heart.

I sat up suddenly, the blue sheet sliding off me. "Hey, what about that idea of pitching the story of Rivers going back to Harvard to someplace like *The New York Times* Arts section?" I asked him. He took the sheet off me and touched my left breast. He pinched my nipple and it *hurt*. I surprised myself by slapping him.

"What was that for?" he asked, laughing. I was angry. He pulled me back on top of him.

"Don't pinch me like that again," I told him, glaring. "That fucking hurt. You have to be gentle with my breasts. Didn't any of your past girlfriends teach you that?"

"You're cute when you're mad," he said. Then: "I'll have Marty call Rivers today and ask him if he'd be cool with it."

"Thanks, babe." My anger dissipated as quickly as it ignited. Nick's fast-changing moods were catchy.

We listened to folks downstairs at Zum Schneider setting up tables for the afternoon German beer–drinking crowd: bartenders gossiping, chairs scraping, and glasses clinking together as they were set out. It felt weird not to be at work on a Monday. If I were still at *Us Weekly* I'd be fetching coffee for my demonic boss, or looking at mindless gossip on PerezHilton.com. A shiver ran through me; I'd escaped just in time from that awful place. I'd felt like a rat in a cage; my cubicle was miles from any windows. My coworkers and I used to joke that the only fresh air we got came from the plants on our windowsill. If Nick was somehow able to carve out a life by doing what he loved, surely I could find a way to be a music journalist and get paid for it. I thought of all the late nights I'd spent in my rented apartment off-campus at Rutgers poring over photographs and editing stories for *Thrash*. I'd cared more about that shitty little music rag than I did about any class I'd taken during college. Working at *Us Weekly* I'd gotten too far from that. I wanted to return to that feeling of showcasing great new bands.

"I'd better start looking for a job soon," I said aloud. "I'm broke and I don't have any savings."

"I can lend you some money," he said. "I have a shitload of it."

I peered at him. It seemed an oddly arrogant way of phrasing his words, not to mention bizarre coming from someone I barely knew.

"I didn't know you had a lot of money."

"Yeah, I have a ton of it. How much do you need?"

"Um . . ." I knew it was a bad idea to take money from Nick. My mother would be so disappointed—all the lectures she'd given me about making my own money so I'd never have to rely on a man. "That's really sweet, but I'll make do," I told him.

"Okay, my offer still stands whenever you change your mind," he said. "I really mean it. I'm happy to help."

He propped himself up on one elbow. "So you should come to Brooklyn with me."

"Oh yeah? Why's that?"

"Well, we're working on the new album and I'd really like your advice."

"Well in that case, okay. But only because you need my expertise and you're hopeless without me, obviously."

"Obviously." He grinned.

We took a shower together. As he was only an inch or so taller than me, I could lean back into him, my head fitting into the nape of his neck. He put shampoo in my hair and started washing it, his big hands gently cupping both sides of my head. "I feel like Meryl Streep in *Out of Africa*," I murmured.

"What's that about?"

"Oh, a woman and a coffee farm and a plane crash . . . you'll just have to watch it. It's rad."

"Maybe I will," he said, shielding my eyes as he gently dipped me back to wash the shampoo out.

"Hey, by the way, your hard-on is totally poking me in the back," I said.

"Just saying hello," he said. "Just being friendly. Care to engage?"

"Not right now. Can't you tuck it between your legs or something? Like a tail?"

"A tail?" he said. "Yeesh, Harper."

That strong sense of familiarity was back; it seemed as though I'd always started my days this way, with Nick washing my hair. Talking about movies. Teasing him about his hard-on.

I changed the subject. "Do you ever wish you could live forever?"

His hands paused. I felt as if I'd said the wrong thing, but didn't understand the why of it.

"No," he said. "I don't."

"If scientists invented a pill where you would never die you're telling me you wouldn't swallow it?"

"I don't want to live forever," he said. "I would do the same things over and over again, and eventually I'd get so bored I'd probably shoot myself."

"That's horrible!" I spun around, my hair still half full of suds. "I wouldn't let you die."

"Harper the drama queen," he said, smiling at me and gently tilting my head back to rinse off the remaining shampoo. His hands on my scalp were heaven. "You're morbid today. I'm going to start calling you Wednesday Addams."

He turned off the water and pushed aside the curtain. I felt the soft shower mat underneath my feet. I dried him off, carefully running the towel over his hard body. His muscles flexed where my hand touched. He watched me quietly, his eyes a darker blue today.

"Do you have any more towels?"

"What for?" he asked, baring his teeth in the mirror as he squeezed toothpaste onto his brush.

"For the beach. To sit down on."

He chuckled. "I only have the one towel," he said. "Never really needed more than that."

"What? What did your girlfriend use?" I asked. I didn't like talking about Mae, but I was honestly curious. Who only has *one* towel in their entire apartment?

"Er . . . I don't know, actually," he said, turning and laughing. "Maybe we just shared?"

Strange. I decided to drop the subject. I was beginning to learn that Nick wasn't very practical when it came to keeping essentials in his apartment. He seemed to spend most of his life on tour, and not to have made much of a home here in his Avenue C apartment.

When we were ready to leave the apartment I thought I heard the mouse on the stove, but when I took a step back inside she wasn't there.

"Ready?" Nick called from the hallway. "Your chariot awaits. Chariot meaning my shitty car, of course."

The car was a powder blue hearse, and it was parked underneath the building, in a garage. It had little white lace curtains in the back. Next to the car were various parts of motorcycles, dirty rags with grease stains on them, and a few scattered tools on the ground. His Harley had its own spot, nearby. Its silver handlebars glistened like shark gills. I eyed it with apprehension.

"Wow, you weren't kidding when you said you drove a hearse," I said, walking slowly around the car.

"Yeah. We drove this baby all over the East Coast on various tours. She's actually been really good to us," he said, patting the hood affectionately. "She caught on fire once on the George Washington Bridge, but we put it out by spraying it with a can of soda."

I laughed. What a crazy world Nick inhabited.

"Wow! When the hearse is a-rockin', don't come a-knockin," I told him, when I swung open the door. The inside smelled like cedar. His steering wheel had a huge skull in the center, and dangling from the rearview mirror was a silver disco ball. The dashboard had a Buzzcocks sticker on it. "Hey, wouldn't it be funny if someone put a Dashboard Confessional sticker on their dashboard?" I said to him as he pulled out of his parking spot. He had loose speakers in the back, and they rattled around. I spied a rubber chicken, but decided against asking where it came from. His gearshift was a round eight ball.

"That would be cool," he said. "Those guys are a bunch of dorks though. I hate that whiny shit. It's not rock and roll."

I held up my hands in mock surrender.

"Yeah, but Chris Carrabba is *hot,* I wouldn't kick him out of my bed," I said. I'd hoped to make him just a tad jealous but he didn't react at all, only started flipping through channels on his XM satellite radio. The band name DENGUE FEVER sprang up on the digital reading, and a woman's eerie warble came through loud and clear.

"This band is awesome," Nick said, turning it up. "It's five guys from L.A. and their lead singer Ch' hom Nimol is from Cambodia and has the best fucking voice. They're insanely good."

"It's making me want to belly dance," I told him, wiggling my upper torso around in my seat.

He grinned at me. "Belly away," he said, lighting a cigarette. We drove like that, Ch' hom Nimol's voice sounding like a phoenix rising from ash, the speakers in the back of the hearse clanking, the disco ball throwing glittery light onto the side of Nick's handsome face.

At one point I noticed a loud clicking sound. "Do you have a flat tire?" I asked him as we drove over the Manhattan Bridge, Brooklyn's rooftops spreading out in front of us like tin cans.

"Nah. She always starts to make that sound after a few miles. I just turn up the music louder," he said, reaching over my thigh to adjust the knob.

John, Rose, and Miles lived in a tiny one-bedroom in Greenpoint, Brooklyn. The street was barren, but they'd obviously made an attempt at cheeriness. Their house was a pale pink, with dark shutters painted a clashing red. Carefully trimmed boxwood bushes had been planted around the steps leading up to the front door. A bird feeder swung from a young-looking cherry tree in the yard. There was more dirt than grass, with a few determined tufts growing here and there as though in solidarity. Nick found parking on the street.

Rose interrupted my brooding by letting out a squeal when she saw me with Nick. Her head was covered with a red bandanna, and she wore a white cotton dress with colorful stitched flowers along the bottom. Her feet were bare. Her left calf was covered in a purple-and-pink butterfly tattoo. "You brought Harper!" Rose exclaimed. "Finally, I'll have someone to hang out with while you three fuckfaces destroy my basement!" Her energy was infectious, and I smiled when she threw an arm around my neck and hugged me tightly. She put her other arm around Nick and drew us both to her chest. Her large breasts were like two soft pillows.

"Your wife is trying to suffocate me with those bombs," Nick said to John as we walked into their entryway.

What surprised me most about their house was how *domestic* it was. Either Rose or John had a great eye; there were amazing antiques everywhere. A mahogany bentwood rocker showcased a rectangular American flag pillow. Concert posters were tastefully framed on the walls. I recognized a sampling of Nick's work, as he had a small following in the art world after designing and drawing all of Hitchhiker's posters and flyers. Miles sat on top of a Noah's Ark blanket. He was adorable, with an Alfalfa-like sprout of sandy hair shooting straight up on the top of his head. His eyes were the same huge owl-like brown as his mother's. He lifted his tiny arms up and Nick hoisted him on top of his shoulders. "I love this little dude," Nick said as Miles cheerfully slapped the top of his shaved head. Rose was looking at me with a knowing side glance.

"Don't get any ideas," she whispered in my ear. "They're a lot of work."

I blushed.

Rose hung my jacket behind the door. Marty cruised into the living room, a Sixpoint Craft beer in his hand. He set it down on the coffee table and zipped up his fly.

"I just took a shit in the bathroom that was like giving birth to a small child. I should send out fucking birth announcements," he said.

"You're just a class act all around," John said dryly.

All three guys were wearing black. They looked like pall-bearers for a punk-rock funeral. I'd borrowed a Lynyrd Skynyrd shirt from Nick, and tied it in a knot at my waist.

John must have opened a door somewhere in the house because suddenly I was knocked over by what seemed like a hundred dogs. There were small little mutts, all the way up to what appeared to be something mixed with Great Dane. They rubbed against my legs, looking for attention. Nick bent down with Miles, who was making little "oof, woof" sounds. One of the smallest dogs, an ugly-looking creature with bug eyes, stood in front of Miles, growling at Nick. Nick kept reaching his hand out, laughing when the dog snapped at him. *Can he not allow anyone not to like him?* I thought.

"That's Miles's guard dog," John said. "He won't let any of the other dogs near him, it's really funny."

"Where did these dogs come from? Are they all yours?" I asked.

Rose groaned. "I *hope* they don't all end up being ours."

"My wife helps foster dogs for a shelter around the corner," John said, smiling at me. I realized he was the quietest member of the group. He spoke softly, and seemed more mature than Marty and Nick. Maybe fatherhood had mellowed him. He offered me a beer but I declined. My head was still throbbing from last night. I'd been drinking too much lately anyway.

"I'll bring you some tea," Rose said, going into the next room. Marty danced a waltz around the living room with the Great Dane's paws on his shoulders.

"Mae was over here earlier," Rose called out from the next room. I'd been reaching for a bowl of M&M's and my hand froze.

"What did she want?" Nick asked. I saw him roll his eyes at Marty, who laughed, setting down the dog.

"I don't know," Rose said. I could hear her clattering pots and pans around, looking for a teakettle. "She was on a break from the restaurant and wanted to see you, I guess."

"Can't shake that poor girl, can you?" John said, drumming a beat on the coffee table. "I felt sorry for her; she hung around for like an hour playing with Miles. I know you guys didn't work out but she's a sweetheart. I think she wants you back, dude."

"No way, I am split from her for good this time, boys," Nick said. "That's a headache I don't feel like drinking myself to death to avoid anymore. I'm a single man, and that's it." He was smiling, but there was bite behind his words. He dug around in his back pocket and stuck a slim blond toothpick between his teeth. It was like I wasn't in the room. I realized I'd been holding my breath, and let it out in a whoosh. I reached for Nick's hand and just before I made contact he picked up Miles again and stood him up, trying to balance him. "Uncle Nick is taking you to your mom," he said around the toothpick, the little boy's hands curled around two of Nick's big fingers as he tried walking, his body pitching back and forth.

The boys went to the basement to practice. "If any of you even *think* of smoking down there or doing any drugs, I will put your balls in my Cuisinart, is that clear?" Rose shouted downstairs.

"Yes, ma'am," Nick called up to her.

"Do you feel like walking?" she asked me. Perhaps she sensed my mood, which was dark.

"Can I hold Miles?" I asked her.

"Are you sure?" she said. "I don't want you to feel like you have to."

"I've babysat since I was twelve," I told her. "I'd love it!"

"Oh good, now I can reapply my lipstick. My hands are never free."

After lathering sunscreen on him despite the cloudy day, and bundling him in both a zip-up fleece and cute pom-pom hat, she strapped Miles onto my chest in a BabyBjörn, with him facing out. We set forth. A neighbor had swept a large pile of crispy yellow and brown leaves into a pile in front of the house next door and they'd blown part of the way down the road. The buildings on Rose's street looked like they'd been molded out of Play-Doh and slapped together. The tops were a different color from the bottom. The bottom jutted out wider than the top, or vice versa. Their sides were vinyl and one had a BEWARE OF DOG notice in bright red on its metal fence yet there was no sign of a dog. Maybe the dog died but the owners were too sad to take it down.

"Can I ask you something?" I said to Rose.

"Anything you want," she said. "Anything in the whole wide world. I'm an open book, as you literary types like to say." She smiled and I noticed she had pink lipstick on one of her front teeth. I contemplated pointing it out but feared it would embarrass her.

"Do the boys do drugs, like, all the time?" She slowed down her steps to adjust Miles's hat, which had fallen askew.

"It's pretty much just Nick and Marty these days, since we had Miles," she said. "John and I both were major potheads for years, but having a kid kind of gets in the way." She smiled at me playfully. "Why, does it bother you that Nick gets fucked up? Of the three of them, he always seemed the most in control, if that helps. You can pretty much never tell when Nick is high."

I frowned. "It's not that I'm judgmental. I smoke a little pot myself now and then. But what drugs is he into? Like, serious ones? The bad-for-you kinds?"

Rose's brown eyes widened. "Harper, does it really matter? I mean, if you're looking for a guy who doesn't do the shit, is Nick really right for you? Does it matter if it's coke, as opposed to heroin? Or uppers instead of downers? If you are looking for a guy you can count on, Nick Cavallaro is good to sleep with, or as a friend. He's loyal to the core, been amazing to John and me over the years, but yes, he does drugs. Musicians are not exactly the most reliable people."

She bent down to examine an orange leaf on the ground, and then tucked it behind her ear.

"Many different kinds, and often. Trying to gauge how often or what kind is missing the point."

My cheeks felt hot. I looked through my purse for some gum to hide my face from Rose. I looked down at Miles, whose lips had turned a perfect pink color, a shade of raspberry. His skin looked untouched, smooth. One of the six dogs started tugging on the leash and the rest followed, so we started walking again. They were surprisingly well behaved, walking in a pack. "Do you ever wonder about their prior lives?" I asked Rose, eager to change the subject.

"All the time," she said, gazing down at them. "One or two of them won't let you pet them on the head, which scares me into thinking they were abused." We walked in silence for a while. I mused over the fact that most people would probably think Rose and John's lifestyle was odd, what with their tattoos and not having desk jobs, but in reality punk people are usually the gentlest, kindest folks you'll ever know. They're like hippies, only they wear way more black.

The wind was rustling in the trees, which had just a touch of red on some of their leaves, like parts had caught fire. The tip of Rose's nose was red from the cold. "Doesn't it feel like summer went by too fast?"

I told her about Andy then, how I'd moved in with him at the end of August and moved out just four days ago. "It feels like a world away," I said.

"You should have the guys help you move out the rest of your stuff," she said. "Only, good luck getting them to focus on anything else but the new record."

"I don't want Andy to see Nick," I said. "He knows who he

is—he reviewed Hitchhiker's last album. I pretty much got him into them in the first place."

Rose nodded and gave me a knowing look.

We walked into a pretty little bakery on Franklin Street. It was a cute place, and they had a dogwood tree outside where she tied up the six dogs. "Rose! My love!" A very fat old man with a gold pocket watch hanging from his trousers came around the counter and embraced Rose. He had hair more silver than gray, a brown snakeskin belt, and pennyloafers with a shiny penny sticking out from each shoe. "I haven't seen you forever, my dear."

"Antonio, this is Harper. Harper, Antonio." He looked like the Godfather, puffy cheeks and all.

"Hello," I said. He proceeded to kiss me on both cheeks, as Rose looked on, amused. He bent down and kissed Miles.

"Is it the usual wine and French bread?" he asked her, pulling out chairs for us. I unsnapped the Björn and held Miles in my lap.

"That would be divine," Rose told him. She rummaged around in her diaper bag (a purple tote bag with Hitchhiker's Revenge pins all over it) and produced a bottle for Miles, who let me feed him. While he ate, he reached back and stroked my cheek.

"He's so snuggly," I told her, tilting my elbow back farther so he didn't get any air bubbles. The top of his head smelled like powder. As we waited for the bread to heat up, Antonio kept coming by and fussing over the place settings and floral arrangement on the table. After he left, Rose leaned over to me.

"John told me he used to be the head of a New York mob family and he killed over forty people and buried their bodies near Giants Stadium, but I refuse to believe it." She said all of this in a cheery tone, looking at her reflection in a spoon. She wiped the lipstick off her tooth. I peered more closely at Antonio, who was chiding the busboy to hurry up and bring our wine. He looked like someone's grandfather, with his twinkling eyes and tan-lined face. I tried to picture him stuffing a body into a trunk.

We heard the bell tinkle over the front door and looked up at the same time. Fiona walked in then, and our eyes met across the bakery. She'd dyed her hair bright blue, and there were orange gerbera daisies sticking out of both her pigtail braids. She wore dark blue overalls with clown-orange Dr. Martens. "Love the new do," I told her when she walked over to us and plopped down in a chair.

"Fiona, you freak, I thought you said you'd never do blue again!" Rose said, giving her a hug. "Does the memory of turning my bathtub Smurf blue ring a bell?"

"I believe the color was *cerulean*," Fiona said haughtily. "Anyway, I was feeling down. Very Pablo Picasso blue period–ish. My lady friend went on tour this morning with Saves the Day to do their merch and won't be back for two months."

"At least she'll return before the holidays," Rose said. "John leaves for Japan in two days. It will be a whole new *year* by the time he gets back." I felt a wave of panic. I'd forgotten Nick was leaving so soon . . . and for so long. I think he'd mentioned it when we were at Bua Bar with Daniela but I'd been drunk and not really listening. I saw Rose studying me, and changed the subject.

"You're not working today?" I asked Fiona.

"No way, chickie, I worked every day last week. I'm doing my art today."

"Oh, that's right, you do taxidermy, right?"

"Crypto-taxidermy," Rose and Fiona sang in unison, which made me laugh.

"See, Fiona has me trained," Rose said. "I even know how to *pronounce* it correctly now."

A lock of hair had struggled out of her bun and Fiona pulled it down in front of her eyes. "I *dig* this color. I think I'll keep it for a while."

"I like it too," I said. "I've actually never dyed my hair before. I always wonder if I should."

"Are you crazy?" Fiona said. "If I had that color black, I'd never dye it ever. You look like fucking Wonder Woman. It's awesome."

"Thank you!" I said.

Rose growled at me, mimicking Fiona's deep voice. "Don't touch it!"

I smiled at her.

We split a bottle of white wine, a type I'd never tried before. I felt so European and glamorous. Don't they drink wine in the middle of the day, like, every day? Antonio brought over the bread, right out of the oven, doing a little bow at Rose, which cracked up Miles. "You girls should come see my studio," Fiona said to us. Rose and I looked at each other, then down at our laps. Fiona put her hands on her hips. "What else do you two broads have to do today, sit around and stare adoringly at John and Nick while they practice?"

"You have a point, lady," Rose said. "Can I bring the dogs?"

Fiona sighed. "Always with the dogs. *Yes,* you can bring the dogs."

I walked between them, holding three of the hounds. Miles was asleep, his hat askew. His neck seemed so *elastic* as his head drooped. I felt a little bit the same way, slightly buzzed as I squinted and looked up at the sun. I realized my mood was significantly lifted from earlier, as I walked between my two new friends. Sarah and I had been very close until she moved to Chicago, and since then I hadn't had many girlfriends. Maybe it was time to start.

Fiona's studio was housed in a building three blocks away,

which had a sex shop on the sidewalk level. A sign on the door read in scrawled pink lettering: ARE YOU HURTIN' FOR A SQUIRTIN'?

"You should see the guys that go in there," she told me as Rose tied up the dogs. Suddenly, a man in a suit exited the shop, then looked around furtively. He carried an umbrella; the handle was a beautiful soft gold. The three of us (four counting Miles) ducked behind a tree. Rose let out a yelp.

"Jesus, Fiona, where the hell did you bring us?"

"It's totally safe," Fiona said. "My friend Adam runs the place. It's all, like, closeted gay guys who go there to jerk off to porn on their lunch breaks."

"What are those little lights?" I asked her. From my vantage point I could see there were six doors in the back of the shop. Two of the doors had red lights switched on above them.

"Oh, those are so you know someone is in there," Fiona said casually.

"You mean there are guys in there *masturbating* right now?" I whispered.

"Well, they're not watching the fishing channel," she said.

"Yipes," Rose said.

Stepping into Fiona's studio felt like entering a new, secret world—like entering the closet in *The Lion, the Witch and the Wardrobe*. Though the walls and floor were painted white, there were sticks and branches strewn across the ground, and a forestlike earthy smell permeated the air. "I'm having a show in a few weeks, that's why everything is on pedestals," Fiona said. She walked slowly around the room, Rose and I trailing behind her. Miles slept on. There were creatures everywhere. The first I saw was about the size of a fox and had a nameplate beneath it. It was something called a jackalope, and an inscription beneath read:

A jackalope is a folk figure which is a cross between a jackrabbit and an antelope. Legend has it that a jackalope can imitate any sound, including the human voice.

I got chills up my arm, for the second time today.

I looked across the large room at Rose, who was staring up at something towering over her. She seemed as frozen as it was. I didn't have to read the nameplate to recognize a dragon. I thought of Nick's tattoo, the one that wraps around his rib cage. Fiona's dragon had fish gills around its face; it was petrifying. "I made that one out of fake crocodile skin," Fiona said, joining Rose and me at the creature's base. It had to be at least six feet tall. "Its gills are from a real hammerhead shark, and its eyes are from a dead cow. It took me months to figure out how to preserve them."

"The poor cow!" I said.

"I'm a vegan, actually," Fiona said. "All the animal parts I use are from animals that were eaten for food, not hunted. They would have been thrown out otherwise. Everything else is synthetic." And Nick was a vegetarian. I was starting to think that being vegan and vegetarian was a part of being punk. That the world of animal rights and punk music were linked. I thought back to bands I'd interviewed during my days at *Thrash* and counted five off the top of my head where the lead singer was a vegetarian.

Suddenly, I had locked eyes with something that appeared to be a cross between a mermaid and a unicorn. It had shiny silver skin and looked real, her scaly arms reaching out from her pedestal toward me. "These are wild," I told Fiona.

"I'm glad Miles is asleep," Rose said, warily eyeing the mermaid. We spent another half hour there. Fiona had about thirty creatures in all, each with its own plaque explaining its place in folklore history.

Fiona wanted to spend the afternoon working, so Rose and I gathered up the dogs and started the walk back to her apartment. We were both quiet for most of the way. "Pretty far-out art, huh?" she asked me as we neared their street.

"Yeah." I laughed uneasily. "Who knew Fiona was up to that all this time?" I couldn't find the words to express how the creatures had bothered me. The thought of them being hollow on the insides, incomplete animals, well, *disturbed* me. They were unfinished, the color of the mermaid's eyes, the dichotomy of their existences . . . it all felt very wrong.

"I have days like that, where I feel like a woman *and* a dragon, especially when John's too lazy to wake up and feed Miles and I have to do it," Rose joked. It hit me then what felt so off about Fiona's creatures: *I* felt split in two. For the past four days, I'd been living a life unfamiliar to me. I had grown so used to Andy, to living in the East Village, my job at *Us Weekly*. What I was doing now, with Nick and his friends, was new territory. It was off the map. I'd also been fighting on and off with my sister for so many years. I was just starting to realize how important she was to me but I wasn't exactly sure how to get close to her again, the way we were when we were kids.

When we returned to Rose's house she went to put Miles down in his crib. I went into their tiny bathroom on the first floor and stared at myself in the mirror. The change was so minor I almost missed it. My irises expanded and contracted with the changing light emanating into the bathroom from the tiny aqua blue stained-glass window. I'd gone from knowing one existence of living with Andy and working at a job I hated, to quitting my job and meeting Nick. I didn't know where I belonged, whether it was in New Jersey or New York. I'd become a hybrid, like one of Fiona's preserved creatures. Even my thoughts felt scattered, like a waterbug skimming the surface. Making shallow, circular ping indentations. I wasn't sure who I was anymore.

I left the bathroom and traipsed down the steps to the basement, still lost in fragmented thought. Cigarette butts littered an ashtray near Nick, and the sweet smell of pot wafted through the air; I could tell the guys hadn't heeded Rose's request. I was filled with things to tell Nick, about Antonio, the white wine, the six dogs, Fiona's mermaid, but after the guys nodded politely to me and Nick didn't kiss me, I sat down on a nearby plush purple couch and watched them practice. There were blue and pink needlepoint pillows scattered on the floor and I bent down to put one behind my back. One said DREAM. Nick had a pen in his mouth and was crossing out lines on a sheet of paper. He pointed at John. "I think you should just do that da na, da na, da na beat you were doing before." He tapped out a rhythm with his boot on the stool in front of him.

"Okay, man," John said.

"While you're doing that, I've got to make this chord sustain. It can't die down. We've got to get that part right *today*." He lit a cigarette. "That's what the crowd will go wild for on stage, we've got to make that part sound like a crack and then a rumble like the whole world's crashing down on everyone's heads. The whole live show will depend on it, that forty-five–second interval. The whole fucking *album* depends on that forty-five–second interval."

I listened, transfixed. I'd never seen part of a song coming together before. Once, while vacationing in Cape Cod, they'd shut down one of the beaches to allow turtles to bury their eggs in peace. The whole town had parked on top of the hill at night and watched the tiny turtles emerge from their shells and waddle down into the water, writhing and free, their bodies winking in the moonlight like fireflies. Their births had instilled a sense of awe inside me, which I felt again now, watching Hitchhiker's new album come together. Music was such a big part of my life; to be behind the scenes like this was awesome.

Marty was drinking hot tea. He noticed me looking, and pointed to his throat.

"My voice is all fucked up and we go on tour on Wednesday," he said. "I have to get it healthy again by not talking too much." I nodded.

"Well, since that's impossible with your big mouth, you might as well try singing this song Nick wrote," John called out from behind his drum kit.

"Dude, do you even have hair below your belt yet? Settle down." Marty rolled his eyes at me, and I laughed. I could tell Nick was getting annoyed.

"Let's just play this song one more time before we break, this time with the longer interval," he said, grabbing his pick from the floor where it had fallen.

"The man is relentless!" Marty said, putting down his tea. I could see Nick's sheet from where I was sitting. The song was titled "Sad Sad Girl." I couldn't help but wonder if it was written for Mae. But after the conversation he had earlier, I knew he didn't care enough about her to write a song. The words were more likely directed at his long-lost ex, Lana.

After seeing them live twice in big venues, it was a treat to listen to the band play acoustic from three feet away. Nick's fingers found their way up and down the strings so fast! Oh, what those hands could do to me! I shivered. I found a pack of smokes on the coffee table and lit a cigarette, taking a deep drag and blowing smoke Nick's way. Even though I wasn't a regular, I could see why people smoked; it gave me something to do with my hands. It provided a punctuation between moments in time, and settled my nerves. Everybody needs a few dirty habits.

Nick concentrated exclusively on his playing, looking at no one. For a somewhat immature guy, Marty's voice is something of a wonder. It's tough and deep like Nick's but with a strangled vulnerability when he reaches higher notes. While the lyrics look kind of stupid when read off a piece of paper, Hitchhiker's Revenge is famous for having silly lyrics that turn into great songs because of the skill of the instruments and Marty's voice. The lyrics have changed slightly now that the album is out, and the tempo when they play live is very fast punk, but this is what I heard that day:

Sad girl
You're sadder than my dad
(I might like you just a little)
I'm hypnotized
By how brave you are
You're sadder than my cousin
You laugh with others
But I know your inside
Is crying
You're sadder than my mom
A girl
A sad, sad girl
I could love you
I could love you

I didn't want to leave. Rose asked me if I wanted to check on Miles with her and so we walked together to his room. It was adorable really, how they'd made a little nursery for him out of very little space. The room looked like it had once been an office—an abandoned computer sat on the floor in one corner. Above his crib was a diamond-shaped window, the paint around it charmingly chipped.

"I like the mural," I whispered to her.

"Thanks, I painted it when I first found out I was pregnant," Rose said. It was a cow jumping over the moon, yellow stars spilling over the walls onto the ceiling. A silver shooting star streaked across the scene.

Miles was curled in the corner of his crib like a millipede, his tiny fists clenching and unclenching. An air purifier was running and it made a soothing hum. I ran a finger over the baby acne on his forehead. He had a homemade mobile casting shadows across his small shape. They were blue skeletons, hung from gold twine, dancing a jig.

"Sometimes I just stand here and watch his chest rise and fall," Rose said.

She put a hand on his belly. He was wearing a white onesie with a blue anchor stitched on the front of it. Very punk rock. Rose pulled a blanket over him, covering his chubby legs.

"When he was first born I'd sleep in here. John thought I had postpartum. You know, like one of those crazy ladies you read about on the news who sticks her kid in the microwave? But I was just so afraid of everything in life that could get to him. All the assholes out there, earthquakes, schoolyard bullies, fucking chicken pox."

"Well, I think you can rule out earthquakes in Brooklyn," I teased.

"You'll see someday," she said. She put an arm around me. She was right: She never did have her hands free. "Come on. Let's go make sure those stupid boys haven't burned down my house."

When I got downstairs Nick had my purse and was hugging Marty and John. "See you 'round the way," Marty said to me, winking.

"Thank you for having me," I said to John.

Rose laughed. "You're so fucking polite, Harper." She came over and hugged me, landing a huge smooch on my cheek. "I hope we see you really soon."

She punched Nick in the arm. "Be nice to her, Nicholas."

He held up his hands in surrender. "I'm always nice," he said.

On the car ride home the sun was setting in the sky as Nick weaved in and out of traffic. I was full of warm thoughts about Marty, John, Rose, and Miles. I'd enjoyed their company so much; they were smart and inventive in a way that I hadn't encountered with other young people I'd met in New York. These were revolutionaries, people who were *making* the music my children would someday listen to and call classic rock, the way I adored and enjoyed listening to Springsteen, or Fugazi.

Half the sky was filled with the setting sun; the other half was dark and gloomy as Nick chatted away. He was filled with enthusiasm; the songs were coming together, the album was better than he'd expected. They would try out some of the new material on the upcoming tour to get a feel for the crowd's reaction. Each time he remembered something new from rehearsal, he would slam his fist down on the dashboard, excited about something Marty had done with his lyrics, or when he described how good a drummer John was. He spoke in a steady stream but he never asked me about my day with Rose. When I finally brought it up, he reached across the stick shift and squeezed my thigh.

"Tell me all about it."

I tried to describe Fiona's creatures, Antonio's big belly . . . but the details felt hollow in my mouth, trivial now. I couldn't organize my thoughts to express to him the range of emotions I'd felt today. The masturbating businessmen and their naughty red lights no longer seemed funny.

I looked in my purse and saw I'd missed another text message from Lauren: **mom and dad are going to a stupid play tonight. are you coming home?**

not yet I texted back. **soon.** My phone buzzed a few seconds later with another message: **groundhog caught in our trap by accident, dad is releasing in woods driving back to princeton.** I felt a jolt of melancholy that I wasn't home with my family; they always make me feel so safe. An infant floating in an amniotic sac. That New Jersey and New York were connected by the world's largest umbilical cord, and I would only have to follow it, hand over fist, to get to either home.

When we got into Alphabet City the night was full of a prestorm thrill; the sky was heavy with clouds and electricity riding in the air. It seemed like whenever I was with Nick it was either raining or about to. People in the street were dressed up to impress each other. Girls wore leggings with cowboy boots, sweaters to their knees, and oversized silver hoop earrings. They had hair down to their waists or they had blunt, highlighted bobs. Guys wore dark jeans that hung loosely on their hips, studded belts, plaid long-sleeved flannel shirts, and Converse. Some wore fedora-style hats and colorful rubber arm bracelets with one charitable cause or another stamped across them. A few brave souls sat outside at a restaurant, bundled in heavy jackets. Nick suddenly made a turn onto Seventh Street. "Why are we going this way?" I practically shouted. Nick glanced at me sideways.

"Avenue B has some kind of block party going on. We have to go around." My old apartment had the television on; I could see its light from the street. The lace curtains I'd found at the Brooklyn Flea with Andy were pulled aside. I knew without seeing him that Andy was sitting on the couch, alone, watching *Weeds.* We'd watched it together every Monday, and I knew there was a new episode tonight. I felt a pulling in my chest, and didn't realize I was crying until Nick pulled his van over to the curb. A cab behind us honked and Nick reached out the window and gave him the finger as he raced by on our left.

He stared at me like I was an alien that had just flown my spaceship onto his front seat and waved hello with my tentacle. "I'm sorry," I said, wiping my cheeks with the back of my hand. "It's just that we passed my old apartment, where my ex-boyfriend lives, and it made me feel like shit."

"Why?"

"I don't know, maybe because we just broke up four days ago and I'm here. With you. In your car and you've seen me naked."

"Well, we can take another street." He looked clearly uncomfortable at my tears.

"I had to pass by at some point, I guess. All my stuff is still there."

He threw an arm around my shoulders. "How about some food? That always helps, right? What do you feel like eating?"

"I don't know, something really fattening. Cream à la cream à la macaroni and cheese."

He laughed. "I think we can get you something *close* to that."

We parked under his building and walked to Momofuku on First Avenue. Not the fancy reservations-only one, but the real noodle bar with the framed poster of The Band on the wall. We sat around a blond wooden bar on high stools and I scarfed down about a million fried pork dumplings.

Nick had the ginger scallion, feeding me a bite of noodles with his blond-wood chopsticks.

"Ginger Scallion would make a great stripper name," I said, leaning forward on my stool so I didn't fall off. "Don't you think?" I shoved another dumpling in my mouth, tasting a burst of smoky barbeque sauce. These things were like crack.

"I guess so," he said. "That would just make me hungry. You'd only get one turn on the pole before I'd have to like, run out and eat another bowl of this shit."

"What's your stripper name?" I asked him.

He put a sheet of dark green seaweed in his mouth and swallowed it in one gulp.

I hadn't realized you could eat it. I'd thought it was just for decoration. Now, I picked mine up and nibbled on it tentatively. It tasted salty.

"Well, it's been a long time since I've been up on stage," he joked.

The waitress brought us two tiny shot glasses of sake. Nick threw his back.

"You know how to figure it out, right?"

"Can't say that I do," he said.

"You never did this when you were a kid? You just take the name of your first pet, and combine it with the street you lived on when you were born. And, presto! You've got your stripper name."

He looked out the ceiling-to-floor window onto First, thinking. An Asian woman wearing a bloodred raincoat and matching boots walked past the large window we were sitting next to. A light rain had started, the grayness making the passersby's colors crisper.

"Trouble Pepperidge," he said.

I directed my attention back to him. "What?"

"That's my stripper name. My first pet was a golden retriever named Trouble, and I was born on Pepperidge Street. So, Trouble Pepperidge. It sounds kind of awesome, actually. I think I'd get a lot of work." He winked at me.

We finished our meal and ordered angel cake soft-serve ice cream. It came with two plastic spoons and we shared in a comfortable silence.

"So . . . what would your name be?" he asked.

I thought about it. "Paxil Pear."

He snorted. "Paxil Pear?"

"Yes," I said. "Don't laugh. We had a goldfish named Paxil and we lived on Pear Street in Madison. We still do, actually."

"I'm totally calling you Paxil Pear from now on," he said, grinning mischievously.

"I'll kill you!" I said. "Trouble Pepperidge!"

We both laughed until my stomach hurt.

"Hey, Paxil, you almost done with your food, there?" He had his hands behind his head and he was absorbing everyone in the restaurant watching him. His tattoos filled the room with color.

"Yes, Trouble. Let me just grab my purse."

"You can call me Trouble all you want," he said. "It actually sounds kind of cool. I like it. It's good for my ego. Makes me sound like I'm badass."

"I don't think your ego needs any assistance," I said, sliding off the stool. "It's pretty big already."

Walking toward Avenue C, I tried to be independent by not holding his hand, and he never reached for mine, content to light a cigarette and stroll along. A gaggle of young women ran by us, laughing. One had a veil on, with a sweatshirt that read SOON-TO-BE MRS. REYNOLDS. "Those bachelorette night drinking fests are so silly," I said to Nick. "What's the celebration in just getting drunk and going from bar to bar, armed with penis straws? It makes me want to barf."

"She looked pretty happy to me," he said.

He was always like that, saying the opposite of what you thought he would. It was almost exhausting just keeping up with his thought process.

Suddenly, all sarcasm left me. Seeing a bride so happy made me realize just how fucked up my love life was.

"What would you call me, if you were referring to me?" I asked Nick. I knew bringing up our relationship was a bad road to go down, not to mention early, but curiosity overruled me. I wanted to see what Nick would say.

"Um . . . probably Harper?" he said, his brow furrowed.

"No, like if Marty or John or someone asked what I was to you, what would you say?"

"Oh, now I see what you mean," he said, sighing. "I would tell them you are my dear friend, someone very important to me," he said. His words felt like tiny steel hammers.

The black and gray clouds were swirling even faster as we walked past Mud, which was still open, a cheery bar of golden light coming from underneath its door. A storm was definitely brewing and now my mood decided to match it.

It started to drizzle. Wet pitter-patter splashes on my face like tears.

"Nick, if you fuck someone they're no longer your friend."

He flinched at the word "fuck." I was walking faster than him; he had to jog a little to keep up.

"That's a fact."

"Well, what would you like me to call you? Does everything have to be so complicated?"

"Nick, *life* is complicated."

He was silent for several blocks; I thought we'd dropped the subject.

"How about lover?" he said, putting his hand on my lower back to steer me away from a bunch of loud young people weaving toward us, probably NYU kids in search of a nearby bar where they could drink underage.

"'Lover' sounds like someone who smokes clove cigarettes and doesn't shave underneath their armpits," I hissed at him. Just then, a crack of lightning flashed very near and we both jumped. I sucked in breath. Nick craned his neck to look up at the sky and the pulse in his throat beat in rhythm with the rain. The thunder rumbled, the only thing louder than the traffic horns. It was as if someone pushed aside a curtain, as suddenly it was pouring rain; the sound was a symphony. The aroma of the wet pavement, a cross between a wet dog and overturned soil, reached my nose.

He reached out for my hand then, and his skin was so deliciously warm I instantly stopped being mad. We ran the rest of the four avenues and seven blocks to his apartment, hooting like maniacs. "I love the rain!" I shouted to him as he fiddled for his keys in his pocket. We looked like corpses in his front hallway, our skin pasty and lips purpled as if our bones were X-rays, held to light.

Nick went in the bathroom to take a hot shower. I flung off my wet clothes and read a magazine about motorcycles he had by his bed. The models posing on the bikes all looked alike, with their airbrushing and spread legs and blond highlights and breast implants. I counted seven that could all be twins. Septuplets. I learned a few names of the machine's parts, then started to feel my eyelids droop and closed the magazine's cover. I listened to the flowing water outside and then the rush of Nick's shower. By now, his apartment felt soothingly familiar.

Tuesday

When I woke up Tuesday morning, I had a voice mail from Sarah. "Hey . . . Harper, it's me. You've left a lot of slurry drunk-girl messages lately. Everything okay? Lots of love directed atcha from Chicago, girl." I made a mental note to call her later today and assure her I wasn't one step away from waking up with sidewalk imprinted on the side of my face. I would have to tone things down a little. I was starting to wake up every day with a slight hangover—not good if I was going to try to land a new job anytime soon.

There was another text from Lauren: **back home. mom and dad forcing me to go on ugly house drive. when are you coming. agh!**

Smiling, I texted back: **coming home soon promise. you are on own for drive, though. haha.**

One of my parents' favorite things to do is to drive around New Jersey looking for the ugliest houses. My father would get out of the car, snap a photograph, and jump back in, speeding away like he was leaving the scene of a crime. After getting the pictures developed, he'd pin the latest addition onto the refrigerator. He had quite the collection. His favorite ugly houses were those new McMansions being developed all over New Jersey. You've seen them. Additions on top of additions. Roses etched into glass above doorways. Six driveways. Eight-car garages. Pillars slapped everywhere on the house willy-nilly—on the front of a house, side of a house, back of a house. We used to guess which houses belonged to Mafia, suspecting the giant, twelve-bedroom Italian villas erected in small, unassuming neighborhoods. Dad claimed he'd someday put all the pictures into a book. I think the artist in Lauren secretly enjoyed developing an eye for structure by these odd sight-seeing adventures. My mother would bring along snacks like fruit leather and cashews for us, happy to just look out the window and search for Springsteen on the radio. I too secretly enjoyed this time together as a family, though of course I'd groan and roll my eyes whenever the mood would strike Dad and he would tell us all to jump in the car, today we were driving to Franklin Lakes or Short Hills or Mendham. I hadn't been on one of these outings in a few years, but reading the text from Lauren made me remember all the crazy things my parents did to get the four of us to be together.

I rubbed my eyes and realized Nick and I had slept apart from each other, our backs touching and forming the less- and more-than symbols from eighth-grade algebra. He was already awake, staring up at the peaked ceiling. His eyes were burning, his jaw clenched. Through the skylight, I saw the sky was still a dark gray. Like steel wool.

Whatever was bothering Nick, he wasn't going to talk about it. He rolled over and put his head on my belly. I felt maternal, stroking his broad shoulders. I traced his tattoos with the pad of my finger.

We both jumped at the sound of his phone vibrating on the

trunk near his bed. Nick peered at the screen, which lit up. "Marty just texted me," he said.

"What did he have to say?"

"Oh you know, Mr. Manners as usual," he said. He held out his phone: **hey asshole its marty—rose found your passport for tomorrow it was under her couch—tell harper rivers is down for writing about him at harvard you can give her his #.**

"So I guess now you just have to figure out which editor at *The Times* to pitch it to, right?" Nick said. He was nodding, and I found myself getting excited along with him. "I think they'd totally go for it. The press reported him dropping out, but no one knows Rivers is going back to Harvard to get his degree. He's been kind of a hermit for the last few years, but he says he's working on a new album that's going to put Weezer back on the radio, so he'll be at Harvard when it drops. Marty said it's good shit. Hell, everyone's gonna want to write about him, and you can be the first!"

Immediately, I tried to start plotting out what my next steps should be. Did I have any contacts at *The Times* in the Rolodex I'd stolen from my old job? I suddenly remembered the editor from *Us Weekly* who let me cover red carpet events had once worked as a copy editor at *The Times*. I texted him, asking if he knew anyone working in the Arts section, and if so, if he could provide a name and phone number. I knew it was a long shot, but for the first time in weeks I was excited about something related to my career.

"Thank you so much for making it happen, Nick," I said, leaning over and kissing him. I leaned over and dropped my phone back in my purse by the side of the bed.

"No way, Harper, *you* did it. You must have made a good impression on Rivers the other night at the Bowery Ballroom."

"Er . . . I guess so. I kind of thought I'd scared him away by singing Weezer songs to him in my cracked-out voice."

"Nah, he loved it." Then, "Crackhead."

"Ew! You're a crackhead! You probably really do smoke crack, you druggie musician. Like, out of a pipe and everything. You're a professional."

"A professional crackhead? Would I carry a briefcase?"

"Yeah! With business cards and a fax number." I bit him on the shoulder and he pinned me down on the bed and we made out. I loved our mutual corny sense of humor. Underneath all his macho bravado, he was a dork. Just like me.

His window was open and I could hear clapping and cheering. I reached out a hand and rubbed the top of Nick's shaved head. Bristles underneath my palm. There seemed to be some kind of race going on, though Alphabet City seemed like an odd location for one.

"I was thinking," I told him. He didn't say anything, but I could feel an eyebrow raise. "You should have a bonus track at the end of your new album."

"You mean like a hidden song?" he asked, turning over and putting his arms behind his head. Six lines of dark blue Japanese writing lined the inside of his right bicep. I wondered if I'd ever find out what it said.

"When I was a teenager, I loved searching for hidden tracks at the end of albums," I said. "It was such a thrill when there would be a silence, then the secret song would start up. I remember finding 'Endless, Nameless' on Nirvana's *Nevermind*; I kept playing it over and over."

"Me too!" Nick exclaimed.

"I just think your fans would like it."

"You're full of good ideas, lady." He kissed my belly button.

"Hey, did you hear the city bought out Coney Island?" he said suddenly, lifting his head.

"Really? I feel like I read that somewhere," I said. "I thought they're, like, restructuring or something, not shutting it down all the way, right?"

"Yeah, it's not really clear yet what they're doing with it," he said. "It's a fucking shame. I like my Coney Island the way it's always been. Dirty, cheap, faded, and fun. We filmed the video for 'Your Dad Definitely Hates Me' there," he said, referencing a song off Hitchhiker's last album.

"I've never been," I admitted.

"What?" He leaped up, nearly falling off the bed. "You're lying to me." He cupped his hands around my face. I laughed, putting my hands on his. The morning light spilling across his face from the window made his features light up like an eager little boy's. His blue eyes shone brilliantly. "You can't possibly be telling me the truth. Coney Island is like the best place on earth. Get your shit, we're going right now. Before they make it nice and ruin the place."

I looked out the window. "But it's kind of a gray day."

"Maybe it will clear up."

"Why don't you put on the Weather Channel and check?"

"I hate checking the weather. I'd rather be surprised."

This unexpected optimism from Nick was what began to sway me. Being around him one can't help but feel plugged in to a giant jukebox that could spit out any record at any time. You might get the Ramones, but then again you could just get Céline Dion singing that annoying *Titanic* song.

I wanted him to persuade me to come. "When I picture

Coney Island I see this washed-out picture of rickety carnival rides and hypodermic needles littering the place," I said.

"Well, lemme tell you, lady, you are dead wrong. It's fucking paradise, and we're going right now."

"Can I at least take a shower?"

"No." He was dressing me, pinning down my arms so he could zip up my jeans. I kicked him very close to his balls and he grabbed my foot, licking its bottom like a Popsicle.

"Gross!"

I continued to fight him as hard as I could but he was much stronger than me. Punching and kicking and squirming around on the floor with Nick made me short of breath but also felt so good, like a release of tension.

I finally was able to grab his arm, twisting the skin back and forth. "Indian burn!" I yelled.

"Fuck!" he said. "What are you, eight years old? That's dirty fighting. And politically incorrect."

"Ah, and I've found your weak point," I said.

"Are you talking in a weird Australian accent for any reason?"

"None in particular."

"Okay, just thought I'd ask."

He managed to get me dressed, and even put my bra on right, closing the clasp on the first try. This was Nick at his finest: spontaneous, sweet, and fun.

Outside, we watched the runners, their toned legs and bright white sneakers passing us in a blur. They looked like the epitome of good health, and I momentarily entertained the idea of becoming a runner, perhaps even training hard enough to enter the New York Marathon. I watched a pert woman wearing only a sports bra and shorts with the number 35 drawn on her stomach jog by, and my gaze wandered from her over to Nick, her visual opposite in a black leather motorcycle jacket so worn it was almost gray, black Carhartt jeans, black Dr. Martens, and a scowl. Not a health nut, my Nick. "What's so funny?" he asked me, knocking his shoulder into mine gently like a kid in the schoolyard.

I had another moment like Monday when I feared the motor-cycle subject would come up again and I'd have to wuss out, but luckily you can take the D right to Coney Island from West Fourth Street so we walked across Tompkins and down St. Mark's to the train. Nick took every pamphlet handed to him by the guys who ran the tattoo shops along the street.

I found two seats by the window. The train was only half full. We passed graffiti-covered buildings, factories, Spanish super-markets, and auto body shops as we left Manhattan and headed into Brooklyn. People got off the train until it was just the two of us, a tiny beam of sunlight pushing past storm clouds and slanting through the windows to dance on the floor as the sound of the train sailing over the tracks filled the space surrounding us. As we went over bridges, from the position of our seats we couldn't see the track anymore; as a result, when I looked out the window it was as if we were flying. My guts flip-flopped; I'd never been on a subway ride this bumpy before. I grabbed Nick's hand and held it, small paw inside huge paw. I rubbed my thumb against the thick skull rings he had on his middle and ring fingers. "They're kind of lame, but they work great for opening beer bottles," he said, looking down at them.

I stared out the window, running my thumb over his wrist, feeling tendons like cables underneath. We weren't exactly hold-ing hands, but close. It seems crazy, that you can sleep with someone, but then holding hands seems like a bigger step. Something about that just isn't right.

When we got off the train at the Coney Island stop, it started to drizzle lightly. We walked a block and were on Mermaid Avenue. I pointed to the sign, smiling. "They have a parade here every year to kick off summer," Nick said. "Everyone dresses like some sea creature. People go wild! It's awesome."

"We should come next year for it," I told him, but he was looking at all the buildings and didn't appear to hear me.

A large yellow sign boasting NATHAN'S FAMOUS HOT DOGS SINCE 1916 loomed in front of us as we headed toward the boardwalk. I'd heard about their hot-dog eating contest over July Fourth. A blue pickup truck parked on the street had both a MADE BY, DRIVEN BY, AND PAID FOR BY AN AMERICAN bumper sticker and also one that said: MY KID BEAT UP YOUR HONOR ROLL STUDENT, which Nick liked. Storefront fast-food joints were littered in front of us. The closest one was Gregory and Paul's, which had white signs in the front advertising HOT KNISHES, ITALIAN SAUSAGES, ITALIAN ICES, SHISH KEBOBS, COLD BEER.

Another read: DREAMLAND. "That's the old Astroland," Nick said, sauntering toward the boardwalk that made up Coney Island. DENO'S SNACK BAR was decorated around the edges with tiny red lights, which were off now. "You should have a corn dog," Nick said, walking over to Nathan's. "They are yum."

"*You* are yum," I said, kissing him on the shoulder. "What's a corn dog, anyway? Like, corn on the cob with bread around it?" Nick stopped in his tracks.

"No way, dude. You don't know what a corn dog is? For your entire life, you've been missing out on one of the world's most exquisite culinary delights. Didn't you ever go down the Jersey Shore during your summers?"

I didn't want to let on that my family summered in Cape Cod. It sounded too posh compared to the Jersey Shore. A flash of guilt ran through me. I wasn't being myself with him. I heard Lauren in my head, who always kept it real even in the midst of her depression, who wasn't afraid of saying what she thought at all times, telling me to be myself and what was the big frigging deal. That Nick was just a boy. The moment had passed, however. "Once or twice," I said. "What is it made of?"

"A corn dog is a *hot dog,* lovingly dipped in cornmeal batter, and deep fried, my friend. If I were on death row and it was time to go to the electric chair, my last meal on earth would be a corn dog." He bought one for three bucks, and held it up to my mouth for a taste. The combination of the salty hot dog and the sweet cornmeal was good, but not to die for.

"It's okay, but I think I'll just have a regular hot dog," I told him, giggling at the genuinely sad look on his face.

I pushed my palm on the ketchup pump. "How is it?" Nick asked anxiously after I took a big bite. "I need to know your immediate reaction."

I made a mock serious-face, pretending to deeply think it over. "Not as good as Hebrew National," I said. "These are too thin. Must be the Jew in me."

"Yeah. More like Nathan's not-so-famous hot dogs," Nick said. "Well, I'm going to have another corn dog. We leave for Japan tomorrow and I'm going to be eating rice and noodles for the next few weeks, so I'd better pig out on American food while I still can."

I frowned. "Are you really leaving tomorrow? I can't believe it."

"Yep. Got to make a living somehow." He grinned at me.

Before I could respond a small boy standing near us suddenly dropped his vanilla ice cream ball, which made a *splat* sound on the boardwalk. He didn't cry, only glanced down at it, surprised his treat had turned on him so quickly.

Nick put his arm around my shoulder. I leaned my head on his shoulder and breathed him in. The fact that he was leaving tomorrow, just when I was starting to feel so close to him, felt alien and wrong. I'd known all along that it was happening, but I'd had the unpractical hope that suddenly he'd announce he'd changed his mind. Nick leaving meant I was forced to move on too, and that made me feel panicky. I'd have to find a job, collect my stuff from Andy's apartment . . . the list went on and on. If one could bottle a day, I wanted to do that right *now*. I wanted to stroll along this boardwalk with Nick forever.

A thin old man wearing only a wife-beater strolled past us with his scruffy-looking dog.

"He must be cold," I said.

Nick smiled at me, the lines on the corners of his eyes crinkling. "Do you always worry about everyone, Harper Rostov?"

"I suppose I do," I said, and he gave me a squeeze.

"I like that about you," he said. "You're very caring." It seemed like kind of a bland compliment, like calling someone "nice" or a "team player," but I was pleased nonetheless. I tried to cheer up. My melancholy mood was going to ruin this perfect day.

"I tried to start a movement in college to call those shirts husband-beaters," I told him as we walked toward the sand. The boardwalk was run-down from use over the years, with large nails sticking up everywhere like a pirate ship. It looked as though the planks could yawn wide and swallow you; they bent and creaked too much, showing us glimpses of the sand below.

"I made a sign and got the other two staff members of *Thrash* to march up and down College Avenue with me," I continued.

"Did it catch on?"

"Not really. I don't think anyone really got what we were talking about. It's hard to say whether calling them 'wife-beaters' is a negative phrase or not."

"I agree," he said. "On the one hand you're belittling a very serious crime."

"Beating your wife," I interjected.

"Right. But on the *other* hand, you're also calling attention to the fact that there are scumbags that really *do* beat their wives, which no one wants to talk about but is a horrible thing that actually happens. Hey, you have ketchup on your chin."

"I do?" I reached up to wipe it off but he grabbed my hand and licked the side of my face.

"Mmm, salty," he said.

We walked down near the water and took off our shoes, Nick hopping on one foot to pull off his boots. He got too close to a nearby seagull, who squawked at him, fluttering his white wings tipped with gray.

"Sorry there, young fellow," Nick said.

It was an unusually warm day, despite the drizzle. Though Coney Island's rides were shut for the season, there were still several families scattered around the beach. An older gentleman around seventy sat under an umbrella, topless in a neon green bathing suit. He had a gold necklace with both a Star of David and an Italian flag, a melting pot of nationality. He was reading one of the *Twilight* books, and looked the type to have been coming to Coney Island for so long he was molded into his chair. As if Nick and I would leave today and go home and get into bed and he'd still be sitting there, smoking his Chesterfields. I dipped one foot into the freezing water, then the other, hopping back and forth. The ocean was so cold the bones in my ankles ached from it. Nick waded in without pausing. Overhead, a small red prop plane flew lazily by. The wind picked up, and made swirls in the sand. A woman walking where the sand was a lighter color above us wore a lily pad-green hat that got blown off her head, tumbling and cartwheeling down the beach. Two young children chased it. Their laughter traveled back to us.

Nick looked funny with his black jeans rolled up. Effeminate. Walking through the waves toward me, he grabbed my elbow and pretended to throw me into the water, but pulled me back to his chest just before I fell. I punched him in the stomach, lightly. He drew me in for a long kiss, sucking hard on my bottom lip. Yum. Was he going to give me a fat lip? I didn't care. He turned me around so my back was to the ocean, and leaned me against his shoulder blade.

"Tell me that isn't fucking beautiful," he said, pointing.

Coney Island stretched out in front of us. The Wonder Wheel with its pastel spokes stood over all of the rides like a full moon, its blue, red, and yellow carts suspended in midair, frozen in time for next summer's crop of people to ride in. To the right, the Cyclone roller coaster stretched out, stark white against the gray sky like a shark's belly. In my ear, Nick said: "In the summer, you can hear the rickety boards creaking under the weight of the roller-coaster car. It makes a 'crick, crick, crick' sound that never leaves your ears."

"It sounds terrifying," I said, whispering. I hated roller coasters, theme parks, crowds.

"It's not a bad life, living here," Nick observed. The light was harsh upon his face, showing all the lines and wrinkles around his eyes and mouth, showing his age. We were up to our ankles in the surf, which felt refreshing between my toes. No one else was in the water. "I suppose once winter sets in it's lonely, but the families stick together, the mother and father work while the grandparents watch the children. I think it would be nice. I wish I could have grandkids to watch over me someday."

"You will, silly," I said, kicking up some water at him. "You'll have oodles of them."

He frowned.

"No, I won't," he said. "I'd have to have a wife first, and I'm a long way away from that. And I'm already old, so I don't think it's ever going to happen. Marriage, being a father, the whole shit show."

Looking at the Wonder Wheel, I didn't say anything. He seemed determined to be negative. I felt a flicker of annoyance.

"I don't think I'd be a very easy person to be married to," he said. "I can't even manage to give Mae what she needs, let alone settle down. I can't do the whole mortgage, pleated pants, retirement plan . . ."

"Just because you get married doesn't mean you have to wear pleated pants," I said, giggling. The mood lightened a little. "What about John? Not a pleated pant in sight in his closet, I'm betting. And you know what? I actually think you'd make a better husband than you think. And you'll be a great dad. I saw you with Miles, he loves you."

He gave me a sideways glance. "Playing with Miles is one thing; actually being in charge of another human life is another."

I thought then of an uncle of mine, my mother's favorite brother. He was in his fifties now, and always got a kick out of wrestling with Lauren and me when we were little, spoiling us with trips to FAO Schwartz and Tavern on the Green when we visited him in his Upper East Side apartment. I'd once asked my mom why he didn't have any kids, and she'd responded: "Harper, not everyone should have children. They're so much work that, believe me, you'd have to *really* want them to get enjoyment out of raising them."

"Who knows, Nick? Someday you might get married and have, like, five kids and ten grandkids and they'll all crawl all over you and you'll tell them about touring around the world and playing in a band. It will be marvelous."

"I've never heard anyone say 'marvelous' out loud before," he said, smiling at me. "You're different, Harper. You're refreshing."

"Why, because I don't ask you if my ass looks fat in jeans or something?" I asked him. He splashed me.

"See? That's exactly what I mean. You're always saying wicked smart, funny things."

I liked the compliment, but it also strangely made me feel uncomfortable. I felt like there was a "but" that could be inserted at the end of his sentence.

Nick surprised me then by stripping off his jeans and jacket and diving headfirst into a wave, even though the water was freezing. The shape of the muscles in his back lingered in my mind after he'd already gone under the water. It was a bigger wave than he'd thought and he caught it right in the face. He came up sputtering and laughing, his gray boxers clinging to his body. I handed him the towel I'd taken from his bathroom before we left.

"I can see your frank and beans," I told him.

"Jesus, Harper," he said, toweling off and grinning at me.

A woman wearing a light green parka was walking her dog nearby, and Nick asked her if she knew whether the Coney Island Circus Sideshow was open. "All the freaks left way back in August," she said. I noticed she was missing most of her upper teeth.

"We're still here though," I told Nick cheerfully. "Where is the building where they perform?"

"It's within walking distance," he said. "Want to go have a look?"

We walked across the sand, which felt cold and crunchy under our feet like granola. Nick held his jeans in one hand and had wrapped the towel around his waist. "I haven't been there for years, but I remember loving this one act with this guy, I think his name is something totally normal, like Scott Baker," Nick said. "He hammers these huge nails into his nose, then eats live crickets and swallows lit cigarettes." His face was lit up, and he talked excitedly with his hands. Droplets of ocean water still clung to the five o'clock shadow on his face.

"You're a big Springsteen fan, right?"

"Duh," I said. "I'm from Jersey, whatdoyathink?"

"Well, this one snake charmer, Satina, was featured in his 'Tunnel of Love' video. There's also this chick named Insectivora."

"Does she eat bugs?" I asked. "I think that's mean."

"No, but she does a host of other crazy shit, like sword swallowing, walking on glass . . ." He turned his head to the side, thinking. "Oh my god, and then she can shoot fire out of her pussy! It's insane!"

"Well, that's like a typical Wednesday night for me," I said.

He laughed. Then, "I like you."

My heart soared. "Yeah. You're all right, I guess."

"No. You like me too. I can tell."

"Nicholas Cavallaro! You are so full of yourself." I kicked sand onto his foot and he kicked some back. We chased each other down the boardwalk. When Nick stopped suddenly, I crashed into his back.

Signs with chipped paint decorated the outside of the Circus Sideshow building, which was now boarded up. Each panel took up one whole wall. It was an eclectic sort of beauty; all of Coney Island looked as if it were drawn with a child's crayon. One of the signs read: ELASTIC LADY! which was a contorted woman, her legs like rubber over her head. ESCAPE ARTIST! showed a man in a white straitjacket, his eyes bulging from his head. ELECTRA: POSITIVELY SHOCKING! depicted a woman in a hot pink dress sitting in an electric chair, her hair standing on end. There was a section dedicated to acts from the past, such as a painting of an obese woman wearing a purple sparkly turban. I counted four chins beneath her pretty face. The caption read: HELEN MELON: SHE'S SO BIG AND FAT THAT IT TAKES FOUR MEN TO HUG HER AND A BOXCAR TO LUG HER!

"Hmm, not very subtle around here," I said to Nick.

"They also had all these scary things in jars with formaldehyde," he said. We were both whispering, like one does when stumbling into an abandoned chapel. "Like a real two-headed baby." My arms broke out in goose bumps.

"I don't think I could enjoy watching these people," I said.

"I know what you mean," Nick said. "I've always felt like a freak on the inside, anyway."

"How very Diane Arbus of you."

"Hey, what's worse than a freakhouse without any freaks in it?" Nick asked.

"What?"

"Nothing," he said, looking sad suddenly. I held his leather jacket for him as he put his jeans back on and we walked toward the train and up the steep flight of iron stairs onto the platform.

Just as we were leaving an old woman was pushing her cart

past us. Trinkets and mobiles hanging from it made soft bell sounds.

"Can't let you leave without buying a souvenir," Nick said. "What have you got for the lady?" he asked the woman, who had covered her head with a plastic bag.

Wordlessly, she held up a pair of sparkling green mermaid earrings. I loved them instantly.

"How much are they?" I asked the woman.

"Three dollars," she said. I couldn't place her accent. Poland? Russia? She was slightly hunched over, and wearing bright yellow Croc slip-ons.

"Money is no object!" Nick boomed dramatically, digging in his pocket and coming up with three crumpled bills.

"Thanks," I said, giggling. I didn't want to mention that I was allergic to anything but 14-karat-gold posts in my ears, and therefore couldn't wear the earrings. Saying so would ruin the moment.

It had started to rain big, tear-shaped heavy drops that made *splat* sounds on the roofs of the freakhouse. After thanking the old woman, we rode the subway home, only this time I expected the bumpy ride, and wasn't afraid.

"Who needs the Cyclone when you have the D train," I told Nick.

"That's a great line," he said.

"Why don't you write it down?" I asked him, handing him a Post-it and pen from my purse. "Maybe it will make its way into a song." He scribbled it down, shoving the paper into his back pocket.

"Do you always carry around a paper and pen?" he asked me, amused. He squeezed my leg, just above the knee.

"Well, just in case I have an idea for the novel I'll never write," I said. "Or if something interesting happens I'll jot it down and transfer it into my diary later."

"Are you going to write about today?" His blue eyes were glittering.

I blushed. "Yeah, I probably will."

We entered a tunnel and my body changed. Sitting in my orange plastic seat, I felt pressure on the top of my head and lower back in my seat as the light left and the subway was plunged momentarily into pitch-darkness. Everyone always sits very still when the train rambles through a tunnel, I'm not sure why. A man wearing a red turban across from us wore thin white pants that gave off a slight greenish glow. What was the name of people who wore turbans like that, the word was right there and ready to grasp.

I asked Nick if he kept a journal and to my ears my voice sounded amplified and strange, like I was speaking into a paper towel roll.

"I have a sketchbook," he said. "I've been drawing stuff for the new album cover for months, working on the lettering and shit like that. There's also some lyrics in there, but it's not a day-to-day record of what I do. I'm too busy living to write about it."

"Well, that's not really accurate, right?" I asked. "I mean, a lot of your songs document experiences you've had. Same thing with my writing."

Sikhs, I suddenly remembered. That was who wore the turbans.

"Good point," he said. "See, that's why I need you around, to educate me on all this."

A teenage girl sitting across from us in a flowery dress and pink cowgirl boots was reading a hardcover book. I squinted but couldn't make out the title. On her lap, she had a Duane Reade plastic bag and through it I could see she had purchased a blue-and-white box of Monistat. I had a sudden memory of wandering the aisles with Andy, early in our relationship, when he'd given me a yeast infection. At the time, he'd been growing out a ridiculous Brandon Flowers–type mustache, on which I'd blamed the yeast infection. We'd held hands, laughing, as we passed cough syrups and blood pressure machines. Andy had picked out the three-day box after researching online what product worked the fastest, even ignoring the stares of customers as he plopped it down on the cash register and paid for it. "You can't get an infection from someone with a mustache going down on you," Andy had said, though I'd jokingly blamed the growth on his upper lip for weeks until he broke down and shaved it. Something told me Nick would never act this way with me; if for some reason I got a yeast infection this time I was on my own.

"Where do you want to go tonight, kid?" Nick asked as we exited the train and walked back toward his apartment, ducking under bodega awnings to keep out of the rain. The men who sell moth-eaten books and old records along Sixth Avenue were rolling up all their wares into a large white tarp, chatting to one another in thick Jamaican accents about the storm. It was only five o'clock but the sky was pitch-black. It had rained hard while we were on the subway but now it was only lightly drizzling. The days were starting to get shorter and shorter as fall presented itself. Noticing I was cold, Nick lent me his leather jacket.

"Can I wear your varsity pin too?" I asked him.

Putting my hand up to futilely pull my tangled hair into a ponytail, I noticed the elbow of the jacket had a golf ball–size hole.

"What happened here?" I asked him, pointing to it.

He stuck his finger through the hole, remembering.

"Oh, when Lana left me I was all fucked up on drugs and I drove my bike out to California to try and convince her to stay with me," Nick said, laughing humorlessly. "I wiped out on some gravel in the La Sal Mountain Range in Utah. *Man* that was an awesome ride—the sun, the people I met on the road . . . it was a killer trip."

"What happened when you got to California?"

"Oh, she kicked me out of her house, told me to go fuck myself, she was in love with Tom, the usual. That girl put a fucking dent in my chest that won't ever close."

I felt instantly jealous; this was the first girl, the one who really mattered to him. The tone of his voice was different from when he talked about Redhead; about her he sounded annoyed, like she was a persistent salesman that wouldn't stop calling and trying to sell him better wireless service. No, about Lana his voice became wistful, hurt even. It was a subtle change but I caught it. The fact that there existed a girl strong enough to leave Nick blew my mind—the man was like a human magnet; I couldn't contemplate resisting it. His hands on my body in bed, his talent . . . why would any sane girl prefer another man to Nick? The story of Lana was another clue to the Nick puzzle, and I filed it away to think about later.

As we made our way up the street, I took my phone from my pocket to check if anyone had called, wiping the rain off the plastic display so I could read it. My breath caught as I realized there was a text message from my friend and former editor from my old job whom I'd texted this morning, which held a name and contact number for a woman over at *The Times*: Dana Vila. We sat down on someone's front stoop, which had shelter. He lit a cigarette. I quickly called, wondering if she would still be in. I was eager to give her the Rivers story pitch and get started on my new career of writing about music. A pleasant-sounding woman's voice told me she wasn't at her desk right now, but if I'd kindly leave a message she'd get back to me as soon as possible. If it was urgent news, I should press "0" and ask to be transferred to her colleague. I tried to keep my voice from shaking as I left a message.

"Hi, my name is Harper Rostov and I have a pitch for your section that is timely." I paused, thinking I sounded ridiculous.

Nick made a motion with his cigarette for me to continue.

"I'd like to interview Weezer's Rivers Cuomo. He has a new album coming out in a month, and not a lot of people know this but he's decided to return to Harvard to complete his under-graduate degree. I already have permission from Rivers to be the first journalist to interview him in his dorm." I left my phone number and hung up.

Nick linked his arm through mine, and we walked down Ninth Street. I tried to avoid the puddles but Nick stomped right in them, his boots coming up black and shiny each time.

"Do you think she'll call me back?" I asked him.

"Babe, I just hope you'll remember the little people."

I was in a wonderful mood. I've always loved storms.

"I'm glad I'm not dead," I told Nick.

"Me too."

"Or have an exotic disease that causes researchers to do tests on every part of my body to find a cure for it."

"I'm happy about that too. Also that a flesh-eating virus isn't attacking our brains at the moment." As we walked we both craned our necks to peer into the meticulously kept brownstone apartments with soaring ceilings, chandeliers, and walls lined with bookshelves. Sometimes it's fun to see how the other half lives.

"Yeah. It's just rad to be here with you, Nick."

He smiled at me, tugging me along. It was rush hour.

I was feeling so many emotions at once, pressing at me from all sides. It was like I'd stepped out of a black-and-white existence into color, and the world around me was shifting and changing along with my new life. People pushed past us on both sides and a couple of times I had to step into the street to avoid being mowed over by pedestrians but I felt I was moving almost in slow motion. I wanted Dana Vila to call me back right now and tell me I had the green light to write about Weezer for *The Times*. I wanted Nick to tell me what the hell we were doing with each other. Was this just a fling or were we falling in love? I also wanted to know why whenever I was with Nick it rained. Was Mother Nature sending me a signal?

There was a precarious moment there where I almost told Nick how I felt about him. Whoa! To avoid saying this I literally clapped my hand over my mouth, which earned me a strange look from Nick: I had a pretty good feeling this announcement would freak him out, and things were going so well between us I didn't want to ruin the moment.

"I should do some research on Weezer's history," I told Nick. "Just in case she calls me back, I want to know what I'm talking about." He nodded enthusiastically.

"I'd like to do some work on the cover for the new album," he said. "I'm going to use your idea for the photograph, maybe screen it into InDesign and draw the lettering in later."

"Awesome."

"Hey, want to get a drink before we go to work?" he asked. "To help lubricate the machinery cogs?"

I pulled up the sleeve of his jacket and looked down at my naked wrist, checking the time on an imaginary watch. "Are you sure you don't need to go to an early bird special somewhere? Isn't that what old people do?"

He hip-checked me. "Hey, I might be old but I can still get it up. The day that doesn't work just put a bullet in my head."

"Right. Anyway, without that you're dead to me. So where do you want to go?"

"You pick this time," he said, looking amused.

"How about Lit on Second Ave?"

He cocked his head. "Too hipster. We'll just run into all those assholes from Interpol."

"Okay, how about Hi-Fi? Still a musician hangout, yet not obnoxiously so. Besides, they have pool!"

"I'm in," Nick said.

An hour later, we sat on the same side of a beat-up red booth, our bodies touching. I got red-flagged after playing Coldplay's "X&Y" ("Coldplay is a good band . . . for me to poop on.") followed by 30 Seconds to Mars's "A Beautiful Lie." ("That Leto guy is a real prick.")

He seemed to emerge out of thin air, but suddenly there was a short kid of around twenty-one standing in front of Nick and me, pointing to his T-shirt, which I realized was one of Hitch-hiker's Revenge's. He had crazy, teased hair, like the "Suck and Cut" from *Wayne's World*.

His face was covered in acne, which made me feel bad for him. "Hey, I know all about you!" he exclaimed, seemingly inca-pable of believing his luck. He waved at a few of his friends,

equally dorky-looking guys over in the corner, nursing light beers.
"I have all your records, and I've been to fifty-seven of your con-
certs. I see you guys every time you play New York," he said. He
slid excitedly into the booth across from us. I gave an inward
groan. Nick was leaving for Japan tomorrow; I relished the time I
had with him tonight, and this guy was getting on my nerves fast.

"Hey man, I really appreciate the support," Nick started to
say, but the kid cut him off.

"I'm actually coming to see you guys play in Japan next week."
Spit flew from his mouth as he spoke. "Booked my ticket and
everything. Dude, where are you guys gonna be staying, maybe it's
near me?"

Nick raised his eyebrows, but continued to be polite as pie.

"I don't know yet, man, our booking agent handles all of
that." He leaned back in the booth, and signaled to the bartender
to bring over another round of drinks.

The kid stayed another hour, even inviting his friends over to
do shots of tequila with Nick. I was bored, and made a trip outside, leaving yet another message for Sarah. It had stopped raining, but the canary yellow cabs driving by still had their wipers
turned on. Bumming a cigarette from a girl standing nearby, I
peered in the dirty windows at Nick, who was surrounded by the
nerdy kid and his friends. If I didn't know him I'd think he was
having a blast, the way he smiled at everyone and kept ordering
more rounds of drinks. I called my parents as well, frowning
when no one picked up. It was eight o'clock on a weeknight, and
I knew my mother usually had patients at this time.

When I got back inside the space had cleared out; the kids
had taken off and Nick was talking animatedly with the bartender, a beautiful blond woman in tight black jeans, standing
about five foot eight.

"Ready to get going?" he asked me, smiling and throwing money on the bar.

"Your money's no good here, Nick, you know that," she said. I noticed one of her eyes was blue, the other green.

"You're the best, Nancy. Keep it as a tip, then," he said, grabbing his jacket.

"That kid was a bit much, no?" I asked him.

"We call those people 'punishers,'" Nick said, digging in his shirt pocket for a smoke as we walked.

"Why?"

"There's just this one type of fan that likes to back you into a corner and talk to you all night about music and your band and shit. But that kid wasn't too bad."

We walked through Tompkins Square Park toward Avenue C. There were a bunch of skateboarders practicing tricks, the loud scraping sounds of their wheels reverberating on the pavement. The dog park had two or three dogs milling around. A Great Dane galloped freely, her long legs beautiful like a woman running across a lawn in a silk dress. Night had fallen while we'd been in Hi-Fi, and Nick pointed out the seven stars that make up the Big Dipper in the sky. Instead of looking up, I watched him. It was one of the sexiest things about him; he was interested in *everything*. Once, I read that the stars we see in the sky are imprints of light; the real star burned out ages ago. Maybe tonight was a flash in the universe that had already come and gone. Maybe Nick and I were an affair that was already over and I was merely experiencing the echo of it.

We passed an old woman with a scarf covering her head, and I gasped as the streetlight showed her eyes, which were opaque cataracts, almost as if she were blind. She left me feeling uneasy for blocks.

As we approached the garage underneath his building, Nick stopped short on the sidewalk. "What is it?" I yelled. His face had gone completely white.

"My fucking bike is missing."

His voice was low like thunder. He clutched his stomach, like he was going to throw up. He circled the parking spot diagonal from his hearse, walked around a Ford Explorer and a small red Honda that could hardly block the view of his large Harley. He ran a hand back and forth over his shaved head.

I walked over to him. "What do you mean your bike is missing? Are you sure you didn't park it somewhere else on the street?"

"Harper, I checked it before we left for Coney Island. It's not fucking here." His words shot out like bullets.

I flinched.

"Shit! What the fuck am I supposed to do?" He kicked the Honda's front tire.

I stood there, fear coursing through me. I had been looking forward to spending a nice evening with him, drinking and doing work side by side.

He took his key ring out of his pocket and flung a small silver key at me. I dropped it, stooping down to pick it up. He didn't help me retrieve it. I noticed it had an eight ball attached to it with only one fortune possible on the screen: WHO KNOWS? I wondered if he'd bought it as a joke, and where.

"I'll meet you back here. There's a police station down the street. Go inside. I'm walking there."

"I'll go with you," I said, reaching out to him.

"No! That doesn't fucking help me, Harper. You'll slow me down. Go inside. I'll be back."

Slow him down? Now I was the pissed-off one. Who did he think he was? I recoiled, turned, and walked inside his building's doors. I let myself in and researched Weezer on Nick's laptop while he rode around in a cop car, searching for his bike. In any other circumstance, the image of Nick Cavallaro hanging out with the police would have greatly amused me. However, him snapping at me really pissed me off. This was our last night together, maybe forever. I didn't appreciate being spoken to that way and it left me upset. A bike was just a machine. I was a living, breathing person and I could swear it seemed like he cared more about the bike than me.

Needing some air, I pushed open his windows to let the night in. An ambulance wail sounded from the street, its red and white flashing lights flitting across Nick's apartment walls. The apartment with the green Heineken sign was dark. I felt an ominous sense of dread creep into my heart. I'd gone from slightly buzzed to stone sober the second I realized Nick's bike was actually stolen. I'd lived in Manhattan for almost three years; while I'd heard stories of crime and read about it in the newspaper, I'd never been directly impacted before. The East Village held more freaks than Coney Island, but no one had ever tried to harm me, no one had bothered me. Someone stealing Nick's bike hit me hard. It felt like a bad omen.

When he burst into the apartment several hours later he strode past me, shaking his head when I tried talking to him. I clicked Start and then Shut Down on his laptop and set it down on the rug. He sat on the edge of his bed, head in hands. He looked so pathetically broken that I walked gingerly over to him and took off his boots, enjoying the intimate act of untying his laces and sliding the boots off his feet. I jumped backward when he suddenly punched the bed.

"I can't believe someone stole my fucking bike, I've had her for over ten years," he said.

I sat there quietly, not sure I could say the right things to make the situation better.

"I've been through some real hard times with that bike, ridden her all over this fucking country, the trip to California to try to win Lana back, all the tours I went on with her . . ."

It took me a couple of seconds to realize that by "her," he meant the bike.

"What have I done wrong, for this to happen?" he asked, lighting a cigarette and taking a deep, angry drag on it. "What gods of karma have I tempted?"

I stood up and crossed my arms over my chest. "Nick, some asshole just decided to steal from you, that's all," I said quietly. I felt horrified at the situation, but his shouting was scaring me. He paced back and forth. At one point he held his hands out in the air to me, but let them fall at his sides without saying anything.

"I feel like we're being punished," he said. "Like you left your dude and I left Mae and now we're paying for it." He nodded. "Yeah, that's it."

"Nick, what the . . . ?"

Suddenly, my phone started vibrating in my purse. I was glad for the distraction. I ran over to answer it, pawing through my bag to find it. My finger got stuck on the back of the mermaid earrings Nick bought me. It was my mother, and she was crying so hard I could barely make sense of what she was saying. I put my finger in my mouth. Warm, heavy taste of blood. *Lauren-is-dead! Lauren-is-dead! Lauren-is-dead!* my brain screamed, as it always does when one of my parents calls me out of the blue. I've lived in fear that Lauren would kill herself since she first started getting seriously depressed. My throat felt like someone's hands were wrapped around it, squeezing.

"Mom, I can't hear what you're saying. Did something happen to Lauren?"

She stopped crying then, like a faucet being quickly turned off. "What? Of course not. It's the Tan Lady. Well, Margaret Alloy is her real name, it turns out. She's dead."

I dropped the phone and had to scramble to pick it up. She was still crying, now louder. I could remember only one other time my mother had cried, when I was five years old and brought her a dead baby bird the next-door neighbor's cat had killed. I sighed. It wasn't my sister. But it was still a sad situation.

"How could she be dead when I just saw her in our bushes the other day?" I felt sick.

"She was hit by a car," my mother said. She was now hiccupping between words, and everything she said was punctuated with a guttural gulp. "It was a hit-and-run, the bastards just left her for dead over on Prospect Street."

Nick was staring at me, and I quickly put my hands up to my cheeks, staring at the glistening tears they took away. The Tan Lady had been a constant headache for our neighborhood, for the town of Madison. I'd grown up haunted by her history, the modeling career and family she'd lost. She seemed like a ghost, doomed to wander the streets (often in the nude) applying makeup to her face. The idea of her being dead seemed preposterous; surely she was immortal?

My mother was still talking. "There's a funeral for her, if you can make it."

"When?"

"Tomorrow afternoon. You can take the train home and we'll pick you up at the station. The service is here in town. The Gorskis took up a collection and the neighborhood is paying to have her buried." She choked on a sob then.

"I'll be there, Mom, no problem. Are you going to be okay today, do you need me home now?"

"Oh honey, I'm fine, just very sad for such a wasted life. I wish I could have *helped* her. If she'd only let me *try!*" We hung up with the promise I'd take a train home in the morning. Most of my clothing was in Andy's apartment, but maybe he would let me come by and take some of my dress clothes so I'd have something to wear to the funeral. I'm sure he'd understand if I explained it to him.

Silently, Nick lit me a cigarette. I guess I was officially a smoker now. We lay on his bed on top of the sheets, smoking and staring up at his high ceiling. We didn't speak for a long time. We were both angry for different reasons. When I told him about the Tan Lady, and her death, he let out a long sigh. I reached for his hand, wanting him to hold me, but he got up and started pacing the room again.

"Everything sucks right now. Can you please stop walking around and come here and hold me?" I hated the wheedling tone in my voice. I sounded like the kind of girl I'd normally make fun of.

"Not right now, Harper," he said, walking over to his window.

"When then?" I felt lonely, sad. Needy. Nick let out a long sigh, tapping a cigarette against his palm. *"What?"* I said again. "Stop staring at me like that. You're freaking me out."

"It's just that you cry a *lot,*" he said, his eyes piercing me. I sat up like a rocket.

"What the fuck is that supposed to mean?"

He had one of those neon bouncy balls in one hand that they sell for a quarter in grocery store prize machines, and he was tossing it from one hand to another.

He sighed. Bit his lower lip. "It seems like what you want from me I can't give you." He looked truly pained.

"Nick, that's total bullshit. Besides, I'm not *asking* you to give me anything."

"Harper, but you are." He sat down on the other side of the bed, not touching me. I couldn't believe the night had taken such an ugly turn.

"What is it that I'm asking you to do? Treat me nicely? Let me cry if I'm fucking sad?" The ball went back and forth, back and forth.

"I just think you want me to be your boyfriend," he said. "And you definitely deserve happiness, but . . ."

"And that's not what you want to be someday?" I asked him.

"I don't think I'm capable of it, I've told you that from the beginning," he said slowly, like he was explaining a difficult concept to a small child.

"God, why do you have to be such an *asshole,* Nick? I've never been made to feel so shitty in my life," I said. My nose was running and I wiped it, leaving a trail of snot in a straight line on the back of my hand. I felt sorry for myself. I took a deep breath. Squared my shoulders. Fuck this. I was Harper Rostov. I was from New Jersey. And I was made of tougher stuff than this.

He was starting to look *really* uncomfortable now. Like a little boy trapped in the girls' bathroom, scrambling for the exit.

"Where did this even come from? Because of your bike getting stolen now you're treating me like shit? Have I once said I want you to be my boyfriend? Have I? No. God! You are such a *dick*. Rose and Fiona were right. You are totally full of yourself." I picked up the closest thing to me and threw it, a soft pack of cigarettes that bounced off his thigh.

He offered me a tissue but I turned away from him. "Harper, I care about Mae a lot, you know that, and there's always a chance she and I will get back together. My head is just all fucked up right now and I can't really be much good to you when I'm like this. It's obvious that I'm not the man you need me to be."

"You sound like you're the male lead in a bad romance novel," I spat at him. "Like you have really stupid lines. Like you're the condescending jock and you're just . . . stupid."

"You said stupid two times," he said, trying to get me to laugh.

"I meant it," I said, even though I didn't.

I peeked at him and saw his brows furrowed: I'd hurt him. I reached out then, and he flinched. He looked up quickly, but it was too late. I'd felt the wave of his rejection in that one small movement. "I'd never go after some guy that didn't love me," my mother said once, when I was heartbroken over some jerk in my ninth-grade class. "It's not worth your time," she'd said.

My stomach clenched: We'd had such a great time today; what could have possibly brought this on? I felt angry. Why was Nick the only one who was allowed to be dark and troubled? I'd swung back and forth with his moods like a pendulum for the last six days, talking out his worries about his bandmates, upcoming album, and the underlying deep depression he feels has followed him around like a too-attentive shadow the last ten years. When would I get *my* turn? When would he ask me about what was going on in *my* life? Everything was always about him, his feelings, his mood, his history. What did he know about my most private thoughts and desires? Andy knew I used to pick my nose and wipe my boogers on the back of my bed when I was a kid. He knew sometimes I get so hyper, the thoughts in my head whirling around and around like a top, that I flip around on the bed like a fish until my heart stops racing. He knew I loved three sugars in my coffee, funky socks, the Sunday crossword puzzle. He knew I still thought I might become a professional ballerina someday, even though I was curvy, twenty-three, and had never taken ballet lessons. I felt a small pang for him then, echoing throughout my rib cage.

Nick knew only the most surface things, but not what lay at the core of me. He didn't know anything about my family because he hadn't asked. He hadn't asked and he didn't care. And I'd let him treat me this way, which made me even angrier. Since meeting in Mud, had we not been building toward something? Was I merely a stopover for Nick between relationships, or while he took a cool-off mini-break from Mae?

Nick put an arm around me, seeming to finally realize he was acting like an asshole. "Listen, I . . . it's been a long day." He started listing things on his fingers. "My fucking bike got stolen." He held up another finger. "There's no freaks left in Coney Island."

"My Nathan's Famous hot dog didn't live up to its reputation," I said softly. Then, "Did I tell you I have to get glasses?"

"No way!" Nick said, pulling me away from him so he could look into my eyes, as if he'd be able to tell my eyesight had gone to shit. He looked relieved at this change of conversation. He was more comfortable with lightness; when he was flirting he was in his element. "I make passes at chicks who wear glasses," he said, sporting his infamous grin. When he smiled his entire face changed. It was unguarded, open. I was attracted to him even now despite myself, his strong chin, robin's-egg-blue eyes, bristly cheeks, shaven head, plump kissable lips.

"Well, I think I'll stay away from those passes at this time," I said. "The bed punch was a bit much for little ol' me. I thought I was going to have to pull out my Chuck Norris roundhouse kick on ya head."

"Harper, I'm totally sorry," he said. He stroked my hair, smoothing it down. He looked shameful, like a puppy learning how to become housebroken. "I freaked about my bike getting stolen when in the end it's just a possession. The Dalai Lama says the more possessions we have, the further we get from inner peace. I think we should just listen to some Otis Redding and smoke a joint. This has been one fucked-up end to one of the most beautiful days I've ever spent with anyone."

So that's what we did. The fight had gone out of me and I just wanted to lie down. Tomorrow I could figure out what to do with the rest of my life but right now, tonight, I just wanted to hear Otis sing about sitting down by the bay. His smooth voice washed over us as we passed the joint back and forth. I still felt hurt by our fight but our shoulders touched and the anger was slowly leaking out of my body and into the mattress, through the floor, into the apartment downstairs and the apartment underneath that one, down into the dirt beneath the building where the roots grow. Nick sighed and rested his big, heavy hand softly on my clavicle. The light in the room was a deep purple. The family living across the hallway from Nick opened their door and I heard a woman speaking rapid Spanish to her children, her daughter protesting something in that unique falsetto pitch that little girls have. Their voices became muted as they walked toward the stairs.

Through the window behind Nick, I saw the green Heineken light flicker on, and it gave me a strange comfort. Nick announced he was going to sleep, hunching his shoulders and pulling his T-shirt over his head in one quick motion. The sight of his naked torso gave me a jolt. Nick would always have this effect on me, the stripping of any resistance against him. I saw the shape his body made in the bed, watched his foot twitch. Whatever he was dreaming about wasn't pleasant. I slid out his cigs from his pants pocket and smoked on the balcony, looking at the moon. I watched lights go on and off in other apartments; the night was so dark they looked like little bright boxes, showcasing glimpses of people's lives.

Through one window, a man clutched a coffee mug and laughed at something a tall black woman was telling him. Upstairs from his place, two small dark-haired children knelt at their bedsides, hands clasped in prayer. The smaller kid had Dora the Explorer pajamas on. I smoked for a long time and thought for an even longer time, going inside only when it got too cold. Nick was right about one thing: I did want him to be my boyfriend. If I was to stay sane in this crazy, mixed-up week I had to be honest with myself. I had to admit at least that. I wanted him to love me, really. And he didn't. He didn't, and maybe never would. The possibility of someone not being able to love me had never occurred to me before.

Wednesday

1 had the strangest dream last night, and it played out behind my eyelids as I slowly woke up. Nick and I were back at Coney Island, only it was night. We were running on the sand; the navy blue waves whipping around behind us had whitecaps of froth on their tops. I could see Nick clearly, as the moon was a bright crescent in the sky that cast crooked white lines on the dark water. Coney Island stretched out in front of us, just as it had yesterday, only instead of looking colorful and peaceful, it was black and white and completely deserted. Above the whipping wind, I could hear the faint sounds of the Cyclone slowly making its ascent; the creak of its wooden slats stretching was horrible. Nick grinned at me, only his eyes were sad, haunted, and as he began to enter the water he unzipped his skin and it fell away from him easily like a sheet to expose his gleaming white skeleton. I was paralyzed with fear until he gestured for me to follow him, and I did, unzipping my own skin, running into the violent surf, his bony arm reaching for me. The water felt so real, as did the wind whistling through my skinless rib cage. I followed him farther into the ocean even though I wanted to resist, the waves engulfing me.

When I awoke I got the feeling Nick had been awake for quite some time. He noticed my eyes had opened and he stroked my back, a gesture that felt like an apology. Neither of us said anything, and the silence wrapped around us. Our fight last night was too emotional for two people who had just met less than one week ago. We were like planets crashing into each other in the solar system. We'd gotten too close too fast and it suddenly occurred to me that what had happened between us, everything, was ending. The universe couldn't withstand the electric force that existed between us; surely it would have to send us spiraling back from whence we came.

Nick flipped on the Weather Channel and we watched a woman in a low-cut polka-dot blouse tell us there would be heavy showers in the morning, giving way to sunshine in the afternoon. I wondered when newscasters stopped wearing suits and switched to more colorful and appealing outfits; this lady had on large gold hoop earrings and a funky green stone necklace. I decided change was good, and hoped the male reporters would start leaving their top buttons open on their starched shirts, with just the tiniest bit of chest hair peeking through.

Nick's voice startled me out of my thoughts. "Hey, Harper?"

"Hey what?"

"I've been thinking."

"Don't hurt yourself." It came out harsher than I'd intended.

He turned and kissed me then, hard on the mouth, and I pictured Nick as I'd first seen him at Mud, the way he'd charmed me out of my despondency right after my breakup with Andy. I had this bad feeling deep in my belly that I was back in the eighth grade and my quickie boyfriend was about to announce our quickie breakup. I also felt like I was the losing contestant on a game show, and I was being forced to collect my twenty-five-dollar microwave and smile for the cameras while the winning person grabbed the keys to their brand-new Ferrari. I was the Sad Girl in Nick's song and he didn't even know it. He was on top of me and I enjoyed the weight of him. The realness of him.

I know there were a lot of reasons he and I were wrong for each other but a very small part of me, a tiny seed of hope, felt there were a lot of reasons we could work. I understood his need for creativity, to write words that would resonate with our generation. We grew up in neighboring towns, had both been desperate to break free and move to the city. I shared his love of punk rock, of down and dirty rock and roll, of the history behind all those angsty lyrics. I'd never felt so artistically charged in my whole life as I did in these last few days with Nick; the desire to write about music was reborn within me. I'd spent so long stroking Andy's bruised ego after he lost his job that I hadn't had the fight in me before to jump-start my career, because I didn't want to hurt Andy's feelings if I should get writing gigs he'd have wanted. It was hard to admit even to myself that I'd been that big of a wimp, but there you have it.

"So, what were you thinking about there, cowboy?" I said. I propped myself up on my elbow, covering my breasts with the sheet. I felt suddenly way too naked in just underpants, too exposed and vulnerable. Finality had crept into the room while we were sleeping and lain down between us, put his dirty boots up on Nick's ugly plaid comforter, and settled in. I braced myself for his response. Look, if he hadn't realized my cool self by now, I'd be just fine. I'd walk away without a backward glance. I know it sounds kind of bitchy, but I'd already left one man this week. I could sure as hell do it again.

"I think you should come to Japan with me."

I turned my head around to stare at Nick. Whatever I thought he was going to say, it wasn't *this*.

"Er . . . are you crazy? Last night was . . . kind of a lot to stomach. We've only known each other a brief time and we're already fighting. I don't think that's a good sign."

He looked sad and I started talking fast. "Besides, I have that funeral today, and I think I should really start seriously job-searching. I might go to the library this weekend and do some more research on Rivers, too."

"Well, that's one idea," he started slowly. He started tickling my leg, moving up and up. I slapped his hand away. "Another one is that I put you on the payroll and convince the label to buy your plane ticket, you come on this leg of the tour with us for three weeks, and we'll see all of Japan's cities, countryside, tiny towns . . . we can even break off from the guys and do a few nights just the two of us in Tokyo at the end of the tour, if you want. We go on to Germany from there, but that's when you'll fly home. If you want. Or not. What do you say, gorgeous?"

I was silent, thinking. Trying to look away from his face, which was so open and convincing. I felt like Nick could charm the pants off a ninety-year-old nun with an iron chastity belt, if he wanted to. What did this mean, that he wanted me to come with him on tour? Did he have way stronger feelings for me than I'd realized? Maybe he was in it for more than just a fling?

"Have you ever been to Asia?" he asked.

I thought of Daniela, how she'd seemed less interesting to Nick and me because she hadn't been outside the United States, had never seen Europe. I pictured myself, Harper Rostov, the new Gwen Stefani Harajuku girl with little Hello Kitty barrettes in my hair, totally funky and well traveled and full of colorful stories of the people Nick and I had met together, the cities we'd sped past in taxis, walking together in little gardens, visiting temples. It was a crazy idea, sure, but sometimes those crazy ideas are the best ones.

Nick smiled and I thought of the Cheshire cat in *Alice in Wonderland*. Maybe I'd been down the rabbit hole ever since I entered Mud and met him. So many colorful, bizarre things had happened. He rubbed my foot under the comforter with his own. "What do you have to lose?" he asked. "It's a free trip to Japan. You can't go wrong with that."

I couldn't go wrong with that.

We decided to go get a cup of coffee. Nick's bedside alarm clock read eight thirty. The service for the Tan Lady was at one, so I had plenty of time. I kept thinking about boarding a plane at Newark airport at seven that evening, and laughing a little to myself that I was even considering it. You see, I was someone who had an adventurous girl inside of me just dying to emerge, but up until now I hadn't let her out. When my friends from high school set off for distant colleges or to hike the Appalachian Trail, I enrolled in a university forty minutes away door-to-door from the house I grew up in. Roommates spent semesters abroad or at sea while I spent every weekend driving home to Madison with a basketful of laundry in my backseat because I just plain liked doing laundry at my parents' house *better* than with the coin machines at school.

In Japan, I would be like Scarlett Johansson in *Lost in Translation* minus the loneliness factor. Also there was no way in hell I'd let some middle-aged businessman with a receding hairline pick me up. No, it would be more of the long languid stares out of my skyscraper hotel room, thinking deep thoughts while walking around, and sticking on my broken headphones while lounging about in my underpants on my hotel bed.

The thing is, even if I was horribly lonely . . . well, doesn't that make for great material? No one ever became a famous writer by joining the glee club. I'd have my notebooks and pens with me, and I could start the Weezer article while in Japan. I'd left Andy when I'd become unhappy and bored with our relationship. Didn't that prove how strong and independent I was? So what if Nick would be practicing with his band and I wouldn't see him that much. I'd still have a free trip to Japan. Fuck it. I was going.

We walked up St. Mark's to Mud. There was a light rain shower in an otherwise sunny sky, and a hum in the pavement even though it was so early. I walked along the curb like a balance beam, quickly stepping away to avoid getting splashed by an oncoming taxi. People were on their way to work, wearing sensible suits and black pants with sweater combos. I wondered if I'd ever be dressed like that again, moving quickly as if I had a destination, a grown-up job, a place to be. I looked down at myself: I was still wearing my Springsteen shirt, wrinkled from the rainstorm we'd been caught in the other night. My hair was a mess; I could see its knots and snarls when I held up a lock in front of my face. But for now, this was okay with me.

I lagged behind Nick when I spotted an Uglydoll in one of the shop windows along the street. It was green, had three eyes, and was hideous. I had to have it. Nick walked back to peer in the window with me. "I love those Uglydolls," I told him. We hadn't said much to each other today, as I mulled over his offer, and I was relieved to talk about something so mundane. "They make me laugh."

"Let me buy him for you," he said. "I feel bad for acting like such an asshole last night, stolen bike or no. You can bring him on the plane with you as a traveling mate." Nick's behavior toward me last night seemed like such a small piece of a much larger puzzle, but I decided to let it go.

"Sure, that would be really nice," I said. When he took out his wallet, which was attached to a short chain on his belt loop, he peered inside and shrugged. "I've got ten bucks, can you cover the rest? I'm totally broke right now." It was such a perfect Nick contradictory thing to say that I almost laughed out loud. Hadn't he bragged just the other day how loaded he was? "Let's call him Tres Ojos," he said, sticking him in my purse so his three white eyes peered out. I paid the shop owner the additional few dollars and we took off.

The Talking Heads' "Psycho Killer" was playing at Mud. "I have to take a piss," Nick said as soon as we arrived. He kissed Fiona on the cheek as he passed her and disappeared into the tiny bathroom in the back. Her hair was back to silver now. She saw me looking and winked. "How ya doing, kid?" she asked, making her way over to my table. There was a knowing smile on her face, but it was kind. Was it written all over me, that I'd been bonking Nick this past week? I looked down. Was I wearing a shirt saying I JUST FUCKED NICK CAVALLARO AND ALL I GOT WAS THIS LOUSY T-SHIRT?

I put my head in my hands. "I'm having a bit of a crisis," I said rolling my eyes—an attempt to downplay the emotion in my words. The truth was, I didn't know what the fuck I was doing. When I was living with Andy everything seemed so safe. A straight line from meeting, dating, moving in together . . . I thought in the back of my mind that surely I'd marry him someday. Not right away of course, but sometime in the distant future, like when I'd learn how to balance a checkbook or pay off my college loans or started reading *The New Yorker*.

Fiona sighed and plopped into the vacant seat across the table.

She tossed her order pad onto the table, folding her arms across her ample chest. "Ah, the great Nick Cavallaro has struck again," she said.

I didn't want her to think I'd lost the upper hand. "He actually asked me to leave on tour with the band tonight," I said, fiddling with an empty sugar packet someone had left on the table. "That's exciting, I guess." I shredded it into little pieces. Then again, even smaller.

Fiona puffed out air from her mouth in a quick whoosh that reeked of disdain. Her nose wrinkled as though she'd caught a whiff of something foul. "Why would you want to travel around with a bunch of stinky boys for three weeks? Trust me—I've done it before when I did their sound and it ain't pretty."

"I really like him," I said in a small voice. I immediately regretted it. It didn't even sound like myself. The voice I heard emanating from my throat was like the mouse that lived in Nick's stove, timid. My big, brassy Jersey accent had been put away in a drawer and I just felt . . . girly and vulnerable. This was so clearly not who I am. I leaned forward and banged my forehead on the table. Once, twice.

Fiona put her finger underneath my chin. "Stop banging your head like that, you're going to give your beautiful face a bruise."

I would have been equally shocked if a rhinoceros had charged into the room. Fiona was great, but not exactly complimentary. She wasn't one of those girls you'd meet who would immediately try to be your best friend and say "I love your bag I love your shoes I love your highlights I love your lip gloss I love your fallopian tubes." She was tough and crackly, like a favorite pair of Frye boots you've worn since high school.

"Seriously, it's not just this big dyke that thinks you're

gorgeous—it's everyone in this room!" She made wide motions with her hand in the air.

"Thanks a lot, Fiona," I said, giggling. "And you're not a big dyke," I told her.

"Well I *am,* proud to be, but never you mind that," she said. "Look, Harper, Nick's been a good friend of mine going on fifteen years, but he can be a real shit. Even before Lana left him he was kind of closed off and cold to her, and they were freaking *engaged!*"

I chewed this new information over, sipped my coffee, and stared into Fiona's earnest brown eyes. Someone behind the counter started grinding coffee beans and I had to raise my voice over the noise.

"It just seems like he has so much to give," I said finally. "Like, if he only cared a little more, was a bit more invested, he'd make a wonderful husband or father to the right person," I said.

"Yeah, and if my aunt had balls she'd be my uncle."

A nicely dressed couple sitting nearby turned to stare at Fiona. "What the hell are you looking at?" she said to them. "Go back to the Upper East Side."

"Fiona!" I said, giggling. "They're your customers."

"Oh, fuck them. Anyway, what I'm trying to get across to you is that Nick is not the right guy for *you,* Harper. You're like, I dunno, puppies and sunshine or some shit! I swear you must have a rainbow shooting out of your ass, you're so bright and shiny and wonderful. Rose and I both totally love you. Nick is cranky and immature and a giant pain in the ass sometimes."

Fiona at this point had come around the table and flung her arms around me, her large misshapen breasts smashed against my cheek. "The thing is, he's so punk rock," I said in a muffled voice. Fiona sat back down and rolled her eyes.

"I mean he's, like, revolutionary in an old-school way and I've just never been around someone like that before."

"Harper, I'm only saying this once so listen real good. Being punk isn't about wearing a black armband with a skull on it, or listening to certain bands." She put her left hand, which had at least six rings on it, over her heart. "It's about being revolutionary inside your soul. Being different from everyone else and not giving a shit. Nick's great, but he's just a scrubby guy in a band. *You're* going to be a famous writer someday. The thing that girls don't get about Nick is that he doesn't *want* to be happy. He doesn't *want* a woman who is smart like you and challenges him. He wants a chick like Mae, who comes back to him every time he dumps her, and who quits one waitressing job after another to go on tour with him. That's not you, is it?"

I shook my head.

"Fucking A, you're smart, Harper. You went to college and shit." She started digging at the nose ring in her right nostril, playing with it. "You have, like, a nice family that doesn't hate you and who cooks meals and sits around the motherfucking *dinner* table! Nick left home at sixteen and has been pissed at his parents for twenty years for reasons that no one can even figure out! His whole MO is to be a moody motherfucker. It's what drives him." She reached over to me and clapped me on the back so hard I coughed. "Take the free trip to Japan, but don't go thinking it's your fucking honeymoon."

I gave Fiona another hug.

"Be strong, okay, Harper?" she said. "Don't take any of his shit. Promise?"

"I promise."

"Pinkie swear?"

I laughed. "Pinkie swear." And I held up my pinkie, just like

I had countless times in grade school, and linked it with Fiona's, her cold rings rubbing against my warm skin. She gathered up her notebook and took off, amidst cries of "Check, please," and "Can I get a cup of coffee or what?" It was loud in here what with the music blaring overhead and all, but I heard her shout back something sounding suspiciously like: "Don't get your panties in a twist, motherfuckers."

Whatever happened with Nick, I knew I'd found her and Rose as girlfriends, and I felt lucky because of it. Then, realizing I'd need something to wear to the funeral and I didn't fit in my mother's size-four clothing, I bit the bullet and went outside to call Andy. Nick still wasn't back from the bathroom. I could leave him here and swing by my old apartment to pick up my all-purpose black cotton American Apparel dress, the one that I've shoved in a million suitcases and backpacks and it's still remained wrinkle-free. My heart was sprinting along in my chest.

It rang three times before he picked up. I imagined him seeing the number come up on the screen of his cell phone, his brow furrowing, debating whether to answer. He had a permanent frown crease between his eyebrows.

"Hullo?"

"Hey Andy, it's Harper."

A big pause.

"What do you want, Harper?" He sounded wary.

"Do you remember that Tan Lady who used to stalk my father?"

"Yeah." He had a sports game on in the background; I could hear an announcer's booming voice and cheering. "Of course I do."

Guilt pierced my heart. He was letting me know he knew me, knew my background and past. Reminding me we'd shared so much.

"She died," I said.

Another pause.

"Well, I'm sorry to hear that. Why are you calling? I haven't heard from you in days. I figured you went home to your parents."

I breathed a sigh of relief. He hadn't heard about Nick, or seen us out around the neighborhood. I knew it was irrational to think Andy had hawk eyes that could somehow spot me flitting about with his favorite rock star around Alphabet City, but I hadn't entirely ruled it out either. It was weird to stand here talking outside when I knew Andy was just a few blocks away.

"Listen, I was thinking . . . is there a time today you'll be home? I'd like to come get some of my things." I heard a sound like keys jingling and looked around, wondering where it was coming from, only to discover it was my own leg shaking so hard the change in my pocket was making the sound.

"Do you still have your keys?" Andy asked. I told him I did indeed.

"Why don't you come by in an hour or so and I'll just not be here. You can leave the keys in my bowl on the kitchen counter after you're done packing your stuff." I decided this was not the time to remind him the bowl was mine; it had been a twenty-first birthday present from Sarah and Marc.

"Okay, sounds great. Thanks for being so understanding."

He barked out a sharp laugh.

"What the *fuck* else do you want me to be, Harper, you left me."

I swallowed. "I know you're upset with me, but you don't have the right to talk to me like that," I said, my heart pounding against my ribs. There was a click and the phone went dead. I thought of my mother correcting Lauren and me whenever we cursed.

I knew for sure Andy would never speak to me again; it wasn't in his manner to be forgiving. He was still angry with a girlfriend from eighth grade who had dumped him, even once Googling her in the hopes that she'd turned into a prostitute or was dead. I could only hope that over time he'd meet someone else who was right for him, who would make him realize he and I together had been an ill fit. If I ran into him in the city in the future I would simply try to be as friendly as possible. I knew being friends was not an option; people who state that while dumping someone only do it out of guilt. I just hoped we weren't enemies, that he wouldn't hate me forever, and that in time his anger would cool.

Nick was waiting for me when I got back to our table. He didn't ask me whom I'd been talking to. We talked about the last time he'd toured Japan in the late nineties with NOFX, and how much fun they'd had. This tour I was going on was only with Hitchhiker's, but they were meeting up with other American bands that were also touring Germany at the same time. He'd also decided to do the Fuse interview. "Thanks to you," he said, ducking me on the chin. I nodded, but my head was elsewhere. I wanted to know what the Tan Lady's last thoughts were. How I was going to get into my apartment and see all my old things. Nick kept talking about Japan and how much fun we'd have together, how close we'd get. I watched his animated face, saw the blue in his eyes turn from light to dark as the day marched on. I took the last sip of coffee in my mug, tilting my head back to get all of it.

"Don't you just hate the last sip?" he asked.

"Uh—what?" He'd been talking but I wasn't listening. My thoughts swirled around like sand in a hula hoop.

"Earth to Harper," he said, reaching under the table to

squeeze my thigh and grinning. It was impossible. The man was like a baby. If he smiled, you just *had* to return it.

"It feels like the end of summer," he said.

"Exactly!"

"Let's get you another cup!" He jumped up from the table, nearly knocking it over, and ran to the counter for a refill. Nick's enthusiasm permeated my every pore. I didn't know if the jittery feeling in my belly was from being near him, the caffeine, the idea that I was about to agree to do something crazy. Maybe it was a combination of all of those things. It seemed he'd go on convincing me of things forever. Nick was the tide and I the sand, like in my dream at Coney Island when my skeleton just melted away, and I followed him into the churning ocean, white bones glistening, Nick's face eclipsed by the moon.

This last week had gone by so fast, and yet time felt suspended within me. Fiona and her ever-shifting hair color. My little sister, with life pressing down upon her chest and everything somehow harder for her than it should be. The Tan Lady, her battered and bloodied body finally resting in a plain pine box. Coney Island, the town that waits quietly all winter and the lonely stretch of sand. Miles's perfect swirl of hair. The calluses lining the inside joints of Nick's hands from playing guitar that scraped my skin when he touched me. His tattoos, which I read like a map to his soul.

Nick was in the middle of telling me he only had one pair of pants that didn't have the seat ripped from stage diving when I looked up and said: "Okay. I'll do it. I'll come." The words were out of my mouth before I had a chance to think them over.

He paused. "For real?"

I grinned. It felt right, to be impulsive. After all, wasn't that what this whole week had been about?

"Yeah. I want to come to Japan." Once I'd said it, I felt better. The jittery feeling in my stomach went away. Everything in Mud came into focus: the kid working behind the counter with dreadlocks frying up eggs. The sunlight filtering in the stained-glass window over the back door. The rustling of the bike messenger's newspaper next to me, his many chains and locks looped around his neck like pearls.

Nick scooped me out of my chair and threw me into the air, turning my body so that our necks fit together like Tetris pieces and he kissed me rapidly, all over, not caring that everyone was staring at us. I heard Fiona whistle and yell, "Get a room!" and I had a brief flash of guilt that I wasn't listening to her advice before Nick carried me out into the street, brushing past everyone in Mud and shouting, "Coming through, coming through!" He set me down carefully on my feet, but didn't let me go, hugging me into his barrel chest. His scent was everywhere, that earthy smell of someone who didn't wear deodorant but didn't need to, he was just *that* yummy. Nick's scent was that of a man very much alive, the sweat of living hard, living fast, and not giving in to the man. After all, wasn't everything about the art? I wanted to experience travel, experience buildings I'd never set eyes on, walk down the street and listen to Japanese being spoken by hundreds of people, get lost in a crowded market armed only with my straw basket and a paperback. Despite my reservations about Nick, this opportunity still seemed like the right thing to do.

The flight to Japan was at seven and we agreed to meet at the airport security at five thirty. Nick would call his label and get permission to buy me a ticket. When he kissed me quickly on the forehead, I felt so giddy and happy, it was like a tiny sparrow was inside my heart and flitting about. This feeling quickly turned to dread; I'd have to stop at my old apartment to pick up my things.

I watched him walk away until he disappeared into the crowd. He lifted the hood of his sweatshirt and tugged it over his head, thrusting his hands into the pockets of his tight black jeans. The silver chain attaching wallet to belt set off a spark, like a mini fireball. My body was so used to his that the physical absence of him had me biting my bottom lip not to call out after him for another kiss.

It had been over an hour, so according to Andy, the apartment should be empty. Though I had many things to do between now and getting on the plane this evening, I dragged my feet over to Seventh Street. I spent five minutes looking up at the windows from the street, checking for movement. I would have stayed there forever had the rat who lived among the garbage cans not waddled out from between them and boldly come within five feet of me and let out a long hiss. What the—shit!

After the mouse in Nick's apartment and the groundhog trap under my parents' porch, I'd forgotten about the rat that you have to fight off every time you take the garbage out to the curb in our apartment. It's smaller than a cat but not by much. Andy had figured out some genius way to distract it, something about throwing a stick of gum in the opposite direction, but I'd eaten my last piece already.

I backed away slowly, holding out my hands. "Nice rat," I said. This seemed to only infuriate it further. It was a standoff. It was time to make a stand. I ducked my head and charged, emitting an "Eeeeeee" sound as loudly as I could, and made a beeline for the front door. I swear I could feel the breeze where the rat snapped at my ankle, but I had turned the key in the door and pushed into the entryway before it could bite me. And then—this is the part I still can't quite believe—it lifted the front half of its body in what seemed to me a "Fuck you, lady!" and charged the door, bouncing off the glass and then scampering off back to its garbage-can lair.

I leaned against apartment 1A's door, trying to catch my breath. Each step on the staircase creaked underneath my feet. My heart was still hammering like a hummingbird's. I knocked twice on my door, pressing my ear up against the wood to listen for movement on the other side. When I was pretty sure Andy was gone, I let myself in with my key. The door swung open and my eyes nervously took in everything: the piles of clothing on the floor, empty Jack Daniel's whiskey bottles on the kitchen counter. (At least he was keeping up with the recycling although he seemed to be drinking too much, not that I was one to judge these days.) The cheery wedding invitation for Andy's fraternity brother from Brown was still taped to the fridge—the one that I'd RSVP'd both of us to attend. Running my finger over the raised typeface, it occurred to me how silly Nick would think joining a fraternity was. How utterly *lame* it was for grown men to call each other brothers and paddle each other's asses and do Jell-O shots as a bonding experience.

So much had happened since I was last here. I sat down on the futon and simply took a few deep breaths. In, out. In . . . out. Something was cutting off the breathing from my lungs to my throat. Tears swam in front of my vision. Leaving Andy had been the right decision for both of us; it just sucked being the bad guy. I knew he'd go on to meet someone else who would make him happy, but how to tell him that?

My suitcase was lying in the hallway closet under a large red Rutgers sweatshirt. I tied the sweatshirt around my waist and loaded the suitcase with as much clothing as I could find, including a stretchy black Gap dress. I think it was once meant to be worn as a slip but I'd been using it as a dress forever. Holding it up to the light, I realized it had been washed so many times it was nearly see-through, but it would have to do. I was blindly grabbing things, the alarm clock my dad had bought for me, some Mexican Day of the Dead figurines from my dresser, and yes! my diary, finally, a pack of gum, which I stuffed in my pocket should the rat reappear outside. I came across a pair of oversize Boss headphones we'd shared and went back and forth on taking them. It had been Andy's idea to buy them, but I'd walked all the way to the Best Buy on Broadway and picked them up. We'd split the cost. I remembered the way they'd envelop his small ears, how happy he looked wearing them. No one ever tells you what to do in a situation like this. For a divorce, it's very clear-cut what stuff you end up with. For my mini divorce, I was left figuring out how nice I wanted to be to a man I was no longer in love with.

I left the headphones on the dresser, searched around my bed and found my iPod, walked outside, and hailed a cab to Penn Station.

I got off the train in Jersey holding my Tres Ojos doll, and walked home. The trees were all shades of orange and red now. Fall was upon us here on the East Coast; I was glad for the change in atmosphere. As I walked, pulling my suitcase behind me, I felt a buzzing in my pocket and realized I had a message. I recognized the voice as Dana Vila's at *The Times*, and I felt my pulse quicken. She told me to call her back right away, and I did so, sitting down quickly on a bench in front of Poor Herbie's restaurant.

"Hi, this is Harper Rostov?" I instantly regretted my tone. "Women make all their sentences rise in pitch at the end," my mother had warned me once. "It sounds as though you are asking a question."

"How are you, Harper? Got your pitch." I could hear people shouting in the background, the sound of a television blaring.

"You have quite the noisy newsroom over there," I said, and she laughed, the lilt in her voice warm.

"We sure as hell do, it's a wonder I get anything done. Listen, Harper, I like your idea to interview Rivers Cuomo." I waited for the "but" in her sentence; it didn't come. "I'd like *The New York Times* to be the first print media to cover him going back to Harvard. Can you ensure this? If so, the story is yours. We're sort of screwed here financially, but hold onto your travel receipts just in case I can swing covering some of your costs." I could barely breathe; I was clutching my cell phone so hard it nearly slipped from my sweaty palm.

"Yeah . . . yes, I can call Rivers and make sure no one else is interviewing him," I said.

"Good. When can you have the story in to me by?" When I paused, she rushed ahead. "How about two weeks? I assume he's going back in the middle of fall semester, so we'd like to run it as soon as possible. Also, you should probably e-mail me your clips from past stories you've written."

"The thing is, I'm going to Japan today," I said. "For three weeks."

Silence on the other end.

Rushed, jumbled words: "I can get some of the research done while I'm away, and also arrange the interview with his publicist for when I get back," I said.

"That might work," she said. "So you can have it in to me in less than a month?"

I assured her I would make it happen. Then I asked the million-dollar question.

"By the way, um . . . are you hiring?" I rushed on. "I mean, I know the economy is in the crapper and everything, but I used to edit this music zine called *Thrash* in college and I got a lot of interviewing experience at *Us Weekly* and I really worship *The Times*. . . ."

She laughed, surprising me. "I love your enthusiasm!" There was sudden static; she must be covering the phone with her hand. "Listen, there are some shifts going on here. They had a downsizing a few months ago, but the paper is actually in the clear now and they did give us permission to do some hiring. Why don't you turn in the Weezer story, and then we'll have you in to the office to meet everyone for an informational interview? We could use more of a female presence in the Arts section, anyway. Especially someone with music writing experience."

I thanked her and then hung up the phone, stunned. Nick had given me Rivers's phone number, and when I called and spoke to him he told me he craved privacy and was only doing this one interview while he finished his degree. I asked him if I could come see him in Boston when I got back from my trip, and he agreed. I was so excited I jumped up and punched the air Rocky style, startling a family walking past me. I ran the rest of the way home, kicking up orange and yellow leaves from the ground and watching them slowly twirl back down.

My mother had a patient, a "Code Banana lady" as Lauren put it when she met me at the front door. When we were little we used fruit to decipher how "crazy" my mother's patients were as they streamed in and out of our house. Code Orange meant the person was friendly and normal, just seeing a therapist to work out the daily struggles of their love life. Code Grape was someone who was only slightly off, but basically fine. Code Banana, as the woman inside her office apparently was today, meant stay the hell away; the person was out of their tree. Lauren followed me upstairs to my room, hugging Tres Ojos to her chest.

"You're not really going to Japan, are you?" she asked me. We were both lying on my bed with our heads hanging over the side, seeing who would be able to stand the blood rushing to their head the longest. She was listening to my old Walkman with the torn-off earpiece and wearing adorable knee-high socks with pink hearts on them, short eighties-style blue running shorts with a white stripe down the side, and a gray Princeton sweatshirt.

I sat up, annoyed. It was eleven o'clock. My father was in the driveway, tinkering on a 1980 Porsche that belonged to the town's head librarian. I could hear him throwing tools around, the shifting of driveway pebbles beneath him as he moved around on the little low rubber scooter with wheels my mother had bought him, after his knees started hurting him. "Lauren, I've never been to Japan. I've never been to any parts of Asia. I think it's going to be awesome."

"Yeah, but you're going to be, like, the only girl?"

"So what? It's not like I need guys to help me survive in this world. I can just do my own thing while Nick is practicing or setting up and doing interviews."

"Okay, as long as you're not going to turn into his groupie," Lauren said.

I felt a flash of anger, but suppressed it. Lauren had never liked Andy, never really been crazy about anyone I'd dated. I thought that might be in part because of jealousy, since she'd never had much luck with guys, never really had a boyfriend.

"I can assure you I am not his groupie," I said. "I'm getting just as much out of this trip as he is. But, enough about all that. What's been going on with you?"

"Well . . . I've been kind of sad lately," she said quietly. "Don't tell Mom, but I've been going to the emergency room at school."

I frowned. "Why?"

She started to cry a little then, which ripped off a little piece of my heart.

"I don't know, I just thought maybe I was dying," she said. "I was convinced they'd find I had a tumor pressing on my brain, or that I had liver failure. I'm still not sure something isn't seriously wrong."

My poor baby sister. Her mind had been turning against her again while I was off getting Nick to fall in love with me and traipsing around the Village, boozing it up. I felt sick to my stomach; hadn't she texted me several times? I'd been only too happy to pretend she was fine.

"The only thing wrong with you is that I wasn't home to take care of you," I told her.

"I don't need taking care of," she sniffed.

I heard the sound of an engine start and wondered if it was the Porsche or my mother's patient leaving. From the sound of the *put-put-put,* I decided it wasn't the Porsche.

"I know you don't, but I'd like to be there for you now, if you'll have me."

"So are you moving home after you get back?" she asked. I hadn't thought it through; I guess I *was* moving home to Jersey, at least until I got a music job, whether it was writing or editing or both. All I could really concentrate on right now was getting on that plane and going to Japan. It felt very Nick-like, to live in the here and now. Not to plan too far ahead, because life was short: You didn't know what was around the next corner. It was a fly-by-the-seat-of-your-pants kind of thinking, and while it scared me, it thrilled me at the same time. Dana Vila's words had enthralled me. I knew with my charm and outgoing personality that if I could just get in there for the in-person interview, I'd be able to convince her to give me a job.

"It looks that way for now, until I can afford to rent a studio in the city."

Through the window I heard dad saying good-bye to mom's patient. A car started up. "Thank *God,* because seriously? I'm like, home from school every weekend and have to deal with Mom and Dad by myself. Last night Mom was going on about how she's having some kind of a 'sexual revolution' at fifty and she's feeling hornier than when she was a teenager. She may have used the word 'randy.' I threw up in my mouth a little."

"Sounds bad," I said.

She looked at me and we both burst out laughing.

Suddenly, Mom came running into the room. She was wearing a slim black pair of pants and a soft three-quarter-length black sweater. On her pedicured feet were cute, black pointed ballet flats with a bow across the toes. It's funny: when I was a kid, I'd always tease her about her all-black wardrobe. "Why don't you wear print dresses and bright colors like Sarah's mom?" I'd moan. "You look like Darth Vader." When I moved to New York, and saw black as the official clothing color of the East Village, I realized Mom was ahead of her time. "You girls have to come outside to see the groundhog," she said, out of breath. "Come on, Harper, we're releasing her soon."

There, next to the porch, was a very pissed-off groundhog. Dad was kneeling next to the cage, making soothing noises. Anna Freud sniffed furiously, wiggling her rump and letting out one gleeful bark. The four of us stood there silently, eyeing the groundhog.

"Shit, we'll have to drive into the woods and release her," Lauren said.

"Don't say shit," my mother muttered. Then, "Shit! What if she has rabies?"

"You just said shit!" Lauren and I squealed.

"Are there really any woods left in New Jersey?" I wondered aloud.

"Lulu, my dear, if you don't mind releasing the groundhog, I thought I'd go for a swim at the YMCA," my dad said. He looked down at his wrist. He was wearing a beat-up black-and-red Mickey Mouse watch. "The funeral for my old nemesis isn't for two hours. Is anyone up for swimming laps?"

I went upstairs and dug through my closet, finally finding a purple Speedo dating back from when I swam on the YMCA team as a teenager. It still fit, thank god, and had a very late-nineties vibe with a white zipper up the front that I pulled up and prayed would hold. I was about ten pounds heavier than I was at sixteen, but I think the weight went to all the good places.

I walked down the hallway and opened the doors of the towel closet. I saw a flash of naked old man, as my father walked past me in his underwear. "Have you seen my bathing suit?" he asked. "Your mother is always hiding things on me."

"Dad! You can't just walk around in your underpants!" They were the dorky ones too, tighty-whities. His stomach hung over them. It was bright white, like a shark's.

"Why not?" he asked, genuinely confused.

"Because! It's just not done! What if I had a friend over? It's so embarrassing."

He laughed. "I remember when you girls were young, your mother had this colleague who was horrified that we walked around nude in front of you. And this is when you were infants, babies! She said it would cause lasting psychological damage. And I ended up with two of the smartest girls in the universe! Her son was one of those, what do you call them, juvenile delinquents? Held up a Taco Bell on Route 46, of all places."

"I definitely have lasting psychological damage!" Lauren shouted from her room.

I giggled, grabbed a towel, and kissed my father on the round bald spot on top of his head.

"I'm getting into the car!" I said.

"Be right there!" Lauren and Dad called out simultaneously.

Downstairs, Lauren finagled herself into the driver's seat and we held on to the sides of our seats for dear life. Lauren is a horrible driver. She's had three accidents just in the last six months, and insurance always comes back that it was her fault. She speeds, she curses at other drivers, she swerves across three lanes to exit. Driving with her is always an exercise in appreciating the mere fact you're still *alive* when you get out of the car.

We came to a stop sign and Lauren didn't slow down to my father's liking. "Watch out!" he yelled nervously when a red Honda pulled up alongside us and made a sharp right turn.

We drove farther along, my father humming, I assumed to reassure himself. The three of us had always enjoyed swimming together, and I felt comforted by all the familiar sights flying by outside my backseat window.

"Watch out!" Dad yelled when Lauren put her right blinker on.

I looked around. Other than a small old woman in a Chevy behind us, we were the only ones on the road.

"Dad! What *exactly* am I supposed to watch out for now? I put my freaking blinker on!" Lauren yelled.

He looked a little abashed. "The woman behind us was getting close to your back bumper, that's all."

"Dad, what is Lauren supposed to do about that?"

"Yeah!" she said. "It's not like I can stop, get out of my car, and wave my arms around to make sure she sees us."

Speaking of seeing, it was alarming just how blurry everything was. I could make out buildings only because I'd memorized the banks, restaurants, and office buildings years ago. Those glasses I ordered would be in next week; there'd be no way out of wearing them. I said a silent prayer the street signs in Japan had really big letters. In English. That I could see up close.

We were there. Lauren slowly pulled into a parking spot as far away from the entrance as she could find and we three got out, slamming the doors. It's a Rostov family tradition; find the far-thest spot from the door. It started out as a joke, Dad always pick-ing the worst possible parking spot, making the rest of us walk ten miles to the door, and it stuck. On the few occasions when I drive I find myself doing it too, finding that one spot next to a Dump-ster, or in the scorching hot sun in the summer. Maybe under an apple tree that dumps crab apples all over your windshield. Some-times a family tradition gets into your bones and stays there.

"See? No big deal," Lauren said, depositing the keys back into Dad's trembling hand. He'd gone completely gray in the twelve-minute car ride to the YMCA.

Inside, the locker room smelled like baby powder and chlo-rine. Old Jewish women walked around completely nude, their floppy breasts and gray pubic hair bushes a strange kind of beauty. Death was closer to them than to me, a fact that seemed to hang in the air like the gossamer strings of a spider's net.

"You have beautiful breasts," one elderly woman wearing a daisy swimming cap said to me, which made me break out in nervous laughter. The woman smiled, sadly. "I did too, once."

"Thank you," I said.

"Harper, you know you've got a great set of tits," Lauren shouted, whipping me on the leg with her towel. I smiled. My love life may be slightly screwed up, but at least I had great boobs. Life could serve it up worse, I guess.

"I'll race you," Lauren said, and we took off. I held my breath for the whole twenty-five yards of the pool, bubbles tickling the inside of my nose. I felt reborn in the water, which, despite having a few hair rubber bands floating around the drain on the bottom, was a clear, clear blue. We played the word game, something we hadn't done since we were little. You duck under the water and open your eyes. Your friend blurts out a word, the bubbles shooting from her mouth and going up, up, up. You feel like fish communicating. Once you think you've got a handle on it, you both push down on your feet and shoot up to the surface, shouting out the word.

Under the water Lauren's hair swirled gently around her face. Her skin was a startling white. I watched her pink mouth open and close, open and close.

I felt the rough cement on the bottoms of my feet as I pushed through the water. A small child did a cannonball off the diving board, the sound of its spring echoing throughout the room. I felt the boom of his splash beneath the water.

"Armpit!"

Lauren wiped the water off her face. Droplets clung to her hair and sparkled a veil of diamonds. "I said Andy Warhol. I always win this game. I think you're going deaf as well as blind."

I splashed her.

Later at home we all stood on the porch of my parents' house, waiting for Lauren to appear. Going anywhere in my family is a dramatic, angst-filled event, even when my sister isn't driving. No one is ever ready on time. Dad looked at his watch. My mother swept her hand through a spiderweb that had attached itself to the mailbox. "No spiders there," she said to us. "They must be out hunting."

"They're going to come back to no house," my father said.

She rolled her eyes at him. "Aaron, if it were up to you we'd have spiders living all over our house." She then leaned into him, receiving a kiss on her forehead. I watched them. Their teasing was such a part of the makeup of their marriage. I wondered if I'd ever have that level of familiarity with anyone. Living with Andy, I'd felt we were strangers passing each other in the hallway. Like two people sitting opposite on a train. And now, with Nick, the teasing was there but would this last?

Lauren finally emerged from the house, her hands fluttering inside her purse and pulling out large, heart-shaped red sunglasses that she affixed to her face.

"Don't wear those inside the church," my mother said to her as we walked to her gray Volkswagen in the driveway.

"I'm Orthodox, I can wear whatever I want."

"You're not Orthodox. You're just Jewish," my mother said.

"I can drive," Lauren offered.

"No!" we all shouted.

We all piled into the car just as I realized I'd left my purse on my bed, inside. "I hate my ADD!" I shouted, slamming the car door.

Lauren cranked down her window by hand. "It's better than depression," she said.

My mother rolled her window down and stuck her head out. "Neither disorder is better or worse," she said. "They're both hard."

My father banged his forehead on the steering wheel, emitting a soft *tweet*.

The Tan Lady's service was held at the Grace Episcopal Church in Madison. No one knew if she had a chosen religion, and this was the house of worship for the Gorskis, who, along with my parents, contributed the most to her funeral arrangements. It was a very pretty old stone church with a bright red door, set up on a hill overlooking all the cars driving on Madison Avenue. It looked like the whole town had turned out; the Tan Lady must have peed and pooped in a lot of people's bushes. A woman from the National Coalition for the Homeless gave a very moving speech. She stood at the pulpit in a purple suit, which clashed with her bright red hair. Sitting a few feet away, my dad caused a few heads to turn by honking his nose loudly into a handkerchief.

"Dad's crying," Lauren whispered, tickling my ear with her breath. "Even though the Tan Lady, like, kicked his ass twice."

I clapped a hand to my mouth but a giggle snuck out. Lauren snorted. My mother pinched me on the back of my hand, hard.

It was a closed casket. I knelt in our pew and did the sign of the cross as everyone else had. (I never knew what to do in these situations until my mother pointed out that often non-Jewish people put on yarmulkes at Jewish weddings, so now I always do the sign of the cross when I'm in a church for an event, out of respect.) On top was a picture in a photo frame. I realized it must have been the Tan Lady back when she was a professional model. She had that eighties fluffed-up hair in loose waves around her face, huge Angelina Jolie lips with a light pink sheen, and an intelligent spark in her eye. It was her eyes that convinced me this was the same woman I'd seen in dirty rags. She had brilliant green eyes the color of the Heineken sign across the street from Nick's apartment. There was no mistaking this was the same woman. My arms broke out in goose bumps.

I sat back down in the pew, flabbergasted. To me, the Tan Lady's backstory of having been a famous model was one of those suburban myths, like the tale that you can chuck an infant into a pool right after they come out of the womb and they'll instinctively know how to swim. Or, if you say "Bloody Mary" in front of the mirror three times while spinning around, she'd jump out and kill you.

The fact that she actually *had* been a model made her eventual self-destruction that much more sad to me.

I looked around the room, wondering if every man I saw was perhaps the Tan Lady's husband from the life she'd led before going mad. How long had he held on, hoping she'd change? That she'd take her medications, stay and fight for their life together? How broken his heart must be. Because of Lauren, I had a great amount of compassion for mental illness; I also felt proud my mother had tried for so long to help the Tan Lady. At the time I'd thought it was a bit extreme, inviting her into our house again and again, but now I understood my mother's intentions better.

When the woman from the homeless organization began with a Dalai Lama reading, I was surprised by how moved I felt by his words. I thought of Nick then, how he'd quoted him just after his bike had been stolen.

She had a soft voice, and I leaned forward in the pew to hear her: "I believe that the purpose of life is to be happy. From the moment of birth, every human being wants happiness and does not want suffering. Neither social conditioning nor education nor ideology affect this."

I slumped down, overcome with emotion. Oh, what had my search for happiness entailed? This past week felt so *hard*. Being with Nick felt easy, but now that I was away from him, from his hands wandering my body and his blue eyes and his gravely voice and his . . . just his *world* that's so amazing with Rose and Miles

and Fiona and his hand on my leg underneath the table at Mud . . .
I finally allowed myself to grieve my breakup with Andy, who
had done his best to make me happy, but wasn't the right fit for
me. I didn't understand either man. Nick seemed to be perpetu-
ally unhappy, though the source was so complicated I thought I'd
never really understand it. I flipped through this week in my
mind, each day sketched in black and white and taking up entire
frames in my head, like a comic book. The last page was blank.
Where did I go from here? I could handle only right now, today,
sitting on this hard bench in this beautiful church, saying good-
bye to a troubled woman who had once shit in our flower bed.

I watched the neighborhood I'd grown up in fly by out the window on the car ride home. I put my palm against the cool glass,
my fingers covering the blur of green lawns and cars in driveways
and blue mailboxes and brown tree trunks. My flight was in four
hours. It could be the best decision I'd ever made or I could be
like one of my mother's spiders, and come home to find that I had
no home at all, no future, no structure. Was growing up always
this confusing? I closed my eyes and when I woke up I was in our
driveway. Lauren had covered me with her coat.

The End

(Or the beginning, depending on how you want to look at it!)

It was three in the afternoon by the time I unfolded my cramped body from the car and walked inside to pack. I ran around my room, making sure I had my cell phone charger. Dad asked me if I had my passport thirty-six times. Anna Freud followed me, her hot breath on the back of my legs. I was going to Japan! How rad was that? The coral reefs in Okinawa. The Buddhist temples. The tea ceremonies. Dinners presented in beautiful wood boxes. It was the losing-your-virginity kind of excited: You want it to happen, but you're scared it's going to hurt. A thought lurked just around the corner in my mind, darting out of my grasp like a silver minnow in cool, running water. Had I forgotten something? "Yourself," my subconscious whispered. "Shut up!" I called back inside my own head. At least I thought it had been, until Anna Freud shot me a fearful look and ran out of the room, her ears flat on her head. I followed her to the kitchen.

I called Nick to make sure he was on the road. "*Konnichiwa*, Harper!" he said, picking up and letting out a long cough. His voice sounded impossibly deep, like he'd somehow smoked a pack of cigarettes and drunk a handle of gin in the few hours since I'd seen him. I could hear the strains of the Cure's "Boys Don't Cry" playing over the deep rumble of the hearse's motor.

"Marty is saying bon voyage to New York by sticking his ass out the window at the people on the Big Apple tour buses," Nick said.

"I *so* wish I were there," I said sarcastically, but he didn't pick up on it.

"Soon enough, dear girl, soon enough. Hey, we're meeting at the airport at six, right?"

I held the phone away from my ear and stared at it.

"Are you serious? We talked about this a few hours ago. We're meeting at five thirty." I was feeling guilty about asking my dad to drive me to the airport. He'd had to cancel dinner plans with a friend.

"Okay, okay. Got it. Five thirty." He was quiet a moment. "On the plane, right?"

"Nick! At the fucking security check. Meet me at the security check-in line at five thirty." I tried to laugh a little. "Stop smoking pot and mooning people and maybe you guys will actually make the plane on time."

"Hey, Harper, I'm sorry, babe. There's just so much to remember with the equipment and the passports and the luggage and the stage guys and I didn't sleep last night and I was e-mailing with the tour manager in Nagoya, and she didn't seem to have her shit together so it's just fucking mayhem over here. And I can only find one of my shoes and someone borrowed my leather jacket."

Anna Freud was looking at me inquisitively. "Should I go?" I whispered to her. I realized she was not trying to send me telepathic doggie messages by staring at me soulfully like I first

thought but was instead nodding toward her treat tin. I tossed her
a peanut-butter-flavored bone.

"I can't wait to see your stunning face every morning I wake
up in Japan," he said.

My shoulders relaxed. "I can't wait either," I told him.

"We're meeting at the gate, right?" he asked.

"Nick, what the hell is wrong with you?" I shouted, vibrating
with tenseness all over again.

His deep chuckle came through the phone. I could imagine
his big mouth grinning with a cigarette dangling from it. One
hand casually palming the skull on the wheel. "That time I was
kidding," he said. "Gotcha."

"You're a dork," I said, shaking my head.

"Hey Harper?" Nick said.

"What now?"

"You are going to have a great time with me, I promise. Hey,
maybe we'll get you a kimono, only if you promise not to wear
anything underneath it."

I smiled, and closed my phone. My dad came into the kitchen
then. He opened the back door to let Anna Freud outside for a pee.
The little bits of hair he had around his scalp were sticking out in
different directions and I smoothed them down, kissing him on
his bald spot. "Thank you for taking me," I said.

"I just hope this guy is worth it," he said.

"I'm not going for *him*," I said. "I also get to go to Japan for
free! I can tell my grandkids about this trip someday. I'll take
thousands of pictures, write about it in my journal, go sightsee-
ing. I'm psyched."

"What are you going to do all day when he's playing in whatever the hell that band is called? Half-eaten Sandwich?"

"Hitchhiker's Revenge, Daddy. Wouldn't you have gone at my age if given the chance?"

"Of course I would have," he said. "Hell, life's short."

I hugged him, breathing in the smell of his freshly laundered T-shirt.

"It's a once-in-a-lifetime opportunity," I said. "I get to see a part of the world I've only read about. We're going to have a driver and see so much of the country. It's going to be amazing. I'll write you guys e-mails whenever I can."

"Just be careful," he said. "There's only one Harper Rostov."

I went outside and threw my bag into the Volvo's trunk. Nick had mentioned I should pack light since they needed most of the room in the van once we got to Japan for their instruments and sound equipment. I'd agonized over which clothes to bring. I took my Canon Rebel 2000 camera, a sixteenth birthday present, brown cowgirl boots, one pair of jeans, purple corduroys, my anti–Bon Jovi T-shirt, and a red-and-black Rutgers sweatshirt to represent. I also took my notebook to start collecting ideas for my Weezer story.

I spent the ride to JFK airport looking out the window. We took 78 East to 95 North. The sun was just starting to set, flashing its orange beams onto the side of my face. The sky seemed endless, the clouds pink and purple dreams floating in midair over steel factories and eighteen-wheeler trucks. The skyline of Manhattan came into focus like an apparition, the point of the Empire State Building a needle point reaching toward heaven.

"Don't lose your head," my dad said in my ear when he hugged me in front of terminal four. He'd said the same thing the day he dropped me off at Rutgers, which was forty minutes away. Today I was going around the world. Then, "If anyone tries to sell you a ferret, by all means say no and walk away."

"Um, is there a story behind that advice?"

He seemed to consider explaining, but then changed his mind. "Just something I read in the newspaper about a tourist in Chile. Eat a piece of fruit every day and drink bottled water. Also, they may be a little angry still about us winning the Second World War, so if that subject comes up, I'd just suddenly start jabbering about the weather."

"Dad! You are such a wacko. No one is going to bring up war. I'm going to be hanging out with musicians and tour managers and publicists and families of all those people. Would you let me go already? I'll be back in three weeks. It's a once-in-a-lifetime opportunity." I felt like a windup doll that repeats the same phrase; I'd said that line so many times in the last day.

I finally wrestled out of Dad's embrace after a final warning about the mysterious ferret, and headed toward the terminal doors. Just outside, men in blue coats were loading suitcases onto carts so I showed my driver's license, passport, printed ticket, and was good to go. After denying that I'd turned my back should any terrorists want to throw a few bombs into my bag, I was suitcase-free. I could see my breath in front of my face and I realized it was the first day of the year the weather was cold enough to do so. I tucked my fists into my sweatshirt. I felt nervous about seeing Nick again and I ducked into a dimly lit bathroom to pee and apply some clear lip gloss. I arranged my hair into a messy ponytail (one of these days I was really going to brush it!) and set forth to find the guys.

I breathed a sigh of relief when I came around a corner near security and found my group of angsty, black-wearing punk boys. It was a comforting sight, like coming home and seeing your bed. Nick was eating a Snickers bar and plugging his laptop into a wall socket. He somehow stood out even in an airport, like a woman wearing a beautiful pink sari walking in a crowd of men in suits.

"It's Ms. Harper Rostov!" Marty called out. I laughed, twirling around in a circle.

"In the flesh," I said.

Nick was typing on his laptop and didn't look up. I felt my smile slip a little.

"Hey there," I said, crouching down next to him. Without tearing his eyes away from the screen, he reached one beefy arm out to hug me around the neck.

"This fucking tour manager is killing me," he said.

"What's the matter?" I asked.

He didn't answer. John caught some of the exchange and shrugged his shoulders at me.

"Hey, John and I were about to go buy a shitload of candy," Marty said. He slung his skinny tattooed arm around my shoulders. His palm smelled of nicotine. "If you come along I'll buy you some trashy girl magazines for the flight."

"Marty likes to read *Cosmo*," John said as we set out.

"I like to know twelve different positions to please my man," Marty said.

I shot a glance back at Nick as we walked away toward the nearest Hudson News. He was still bent over his computer, and something about the set of his broad shoulders reminded me of when I'd first met him a week ago in Mud.

"Eh, don't worry about him. He always gets pissy before we leave for tour," Marty said, following my gaze. His arm was still around me and I reached into my purse for my lip gloss as a polite way to shrug him off.

John's eyes were kind. "I think the woman who was supposed to line up a driver for us when we land didn't do so and Nick is desperately trying to rent us a minivan for all our stuff when we get off the plane tomorrow."

"Hey, I'm just excited to see Japan!" I said.

"You are going to have the time of your life, lady," Marty said. He reached for *Maxim,* which showed some D-list actress in a black thong. No surprise there. The inflection in Marty's voice, the way he called me "lady" was all Nick. It was funny, the way the three guys all seemed to speak the same language. It was like they'd been together so long they were in a marriage of sorts, and they'd rubbed off on one another like people who start looking like their pets. I still felt like an outsider to their circle.

"That's what I was thinking," I said, suddenly excited. "I've never been to Asia before, why not go now, you know?"

Marty was giving John shit about his choice of magazine. "*Reader's Digest*? What the fuck? Are you eighty?"

John rolled his eyes and smiled at me. "We're going to have to try and tone down the testosterone for you," he said. "It will be nice to have a girl around to make us not act like complete dickheads."

"Oh please, you don't have to change anything," I said. "I'm just thankful the label is paying for me to come along, it's so nice." I brought a few magazines over to the counter and paid for them.

"I think Nick actually bankrolled it," John said. The guys strode ahead of me as I walked at a slower pace, digesting this new bit of information. Why would Nick lie and say the label was paying for me if they weren't? A rush of warmth ran through me. He probably didn't want me to know he'd gone to the trouble.

As we walked back to Nick a girl of about twenty walked by with a shorter, messy-haired male companion. She had bleached white hair done up in a bun on the top of her head and tied with orange string, which reminded me of Fiona and her crazy hair-styles. She wore a tight black dress covered in white polka-dots and vintage black peep-toe heels. She came to a screeching halt in front of Nick and screamed: "Nick Cavallaro? From Hitch-hiker's Revenge?"

Nick looked up, smiling.

"Look here," she said, hitching up her dress. Marty's eyes widened. Wrapping around her upper thigh was a skull head on a four-leaf clover, the band's symbol I'd seen printed on everything from sound equipment to Nick's guitar to, now, this girl's thigh.

"That's sexy as hell," Marty said. The boys crowded around her.

"Good shading job," Nick said.

"Thank you!" she said, clearly pleased.

I was standing to the side of Marty, trying to keep my some-what fake grin stretched across my face. I felt suddenly plain in my sweatshirt and jeans. It turned out the girl and her friend were on our flight, so I plopped down near Nick and readied my *Us Weekly* and saw that my name was still smack dab right there on the masthead in cool black ink. Copy must have forgotten to remove it. I smiled wryly to myself. Nick caught my eye just then, thinking I'd been smiling at him, did a "hey there" kind of wave.

The loudspeaker crackled and then switched on.

"Flight 987 nonstop to Nagoya is now boarding first-class seating, that's first class only."

For one horrible moment I thought I was going to throw up.

"You okay?" Nick asked. "You look kind of . . . nervous."

"I'm fine. I hate to fly." I was lying. It wasn't the flight. It was suddenly everything else. Leaving my family. Leaving my clothes and books and CDs with Andy. The sadness I'd felt this afternoon at the funeral. The lead I had with *The Times* that could dry up and disappear by the time I got back from Japan.

My seat was between Nick and John. I was glad I didn't have to spend fourteen hours next to Marty, whose crudeness could be a bit taxing. I mean, the guy was almost forty and he behaved like a teenager. Something about the rock-and-roll lifestyle lets you be Peter Pan forever but instead of flying around Never-Never Land you tour all over the world and spend days smoking pot and writing songs in your basement. Part of the adoration Nick's fans felt for him surely had something to do with the fact that he doesn't wake up every morning, put on a tie, and take the subway to work in an office all day. You could see it in the slightly green shade of jealousy in their faces. They're thinking, If he can do it, could I do it too? Just pull a Thoreau and exit what society expects of me?

I could see out the window to the men loading the suitcases onto our plane and I looked for my pink flowery one. The ceiling lights were bright and Nick's face looked haggard. He always looked different, every time I saw him. He was slippery. He was his own ghost. His features seemed to change in different lights—he looked twenty years old to me sometimes, the blue of his eyes arresting, the skin on his body so smooth. And yet . . . suddenly he'd turn to me while we were driving in his hearse or splashing in the waves at Coney Island or right now in the seat next to me and he looked his age, nearly forty, nearly (gasp!) middle-aged. With wrinkles and everything. The stresses of drugs and booze and nonstop travel would rush over his face and I'd remember, Oh yes! I'm young. So much younger than him still. My life is a subway hub that could branch out in so many different routes, crisscrossing orange and pink and green lines, heading out there. Heading anywhere.

There was a whooshing sound as people fiddled with the little knobs that let in compressed air. The steward stood in the aisle dressed in a blue uniform with a matching blue necktie I imagined must irritate him. He was explaining the seat belt system. I couldn't hear his voice so I tried reading his lips, thinking about Lauren and my underwater game. I suddenly missed her so fiercely I pressed my forehead to the seat in front of me. I should focus on the present. John overheard us.

"Wow, you're really paying attention," Nick whispered to me.

"Of course I am. We're sitting in an emergency exit. Its our responsibility to know what to do in case of an emergency," I whispered back.

"You are so cute Harper," he said out of the corner of his mouth. "But if this baby starts to drop out of the sky, we're pretty much fucked."

"Well I don't think like that," I hissed at him, snapping my seat belt closed.

"I'm glad to know someone will actually know what to do in case of an emergency," he said.

"That's me, safety girl."

"Rose is the same way when we travel," John said. "And now with Miles, forget about it. She'd make him wear a helmet if I let her."

"I'm surprised she didn't want to come on this tour," I said.

John laughed. "Aw man, if only. I'd love their company, but I think Rose's touring days are long over. She said we make her feel like shit and ignore her the whole time. She got pissed off at all of us on a trip to South America a few years ago and now only comes to shows close to home."

"Oh," I said. That icky feeling was back in the pit of my stomach.

John leaned closer to me, out of earshot from Nick, who had put his earphones on and settled back in his seat, eyes closed. "To be honest, Harper, I'm surprised you wanted to come to Japan. I mean, I know Nick is paying for it and you'll see some amazing sights, but I just worry you'll be bored out of your mind being on a tiny van with three sweaty guys and five even stinkier stage-hands. Did you bring a good book?"

Before I could answer, he continued: "And if Nick asks you to do our laundry or lug equipment around you have my permission to tell him to fuck off."

"You don't really think he'd ask me to do that, do you?" I asked, shocked. "He wouldn't have the *cojones*."

John shrugged. "Hey, look. That came out wrong. I'm thrilled to have a friend along with us. I just want to be sure you're going to be happy. I know Rose wasn't. We almost broke up on our South American tour. She got so mad at me after one show in Brazil that she tried to maim me with a rubber toilet plunger."

I started giggling, as I could clearly see Rose doing this.

"Being on the road kind of turns us into assholes, though I'm sure Nick had the best intention asking you," he said.

I chewed the flesh on my thumb. I thought of Rose saying "You'd understand how she'd feel, can't you?" about Mae going slightly batty and acting all clingy by going to her house on the chance Nick was there. I wondered if I stayed with Nick long enough, if his fickleness and detachment would turn me mental too. I thought of the Tan Lady, hit by a car, her confused mind finally fading to dark. I thought of smoking a joint on the roof with my dad, while children with dirty bare feet riding bicycles called to one another and the big ball of fire in the sky signaled the end of another day in the suburbs.

I turned to Nick then, and looked into his ocean eyes that

were so blue they were almost turquoise. I hadn't realized he'd been listening to my conversation with John. I was struck for the millionth time how beautiful he was.

"I'm sorry, I just can't do this," I said softly.

"Do what?" he asked, but he knew. It was there, a shared feeling between our chests, like a hug. Like the steam that had wrapped around our bodies in the shower while he washed my hair.

"I don't think . . . I don't think I can fly to Japan with you," I said, bending down to gather my purse and magazines. A few slipped out of my arms and I bent down to retrieve them. Nick tried to help, and we narrowly missed bumping heads.

Once the words were out I felt better, stronger somehow.

"It's just . . . I feel like I deserve someone who really loves me," I said.

I knew John could hear us but he was being polite and turned his head to look out the window.

"Harper, you know I'm really into you," Nick said. He reached out and grabbed my hand. "Everything else will come." I felt the roughness on his palm where decades of playing guitar had made calluses and I gave him a squeeze.

"I know you like me, but this isn't right. This, this trip doesn't feel right to me." How could I say that *he* didn't feel right to me? "Look, I need to get myself together, get a start on my Weezer story, look for a job. I can't be following you around a foreign country. I'm so sorry."

I was standing up and everyone was looking at me: Nick, Marty, John, the fan from the airport and her friend. People in other rows raised their heads. I was the only person standing. Even the flight attendants had been seated in preparation for departure.

"You don't ever have to feel sorry," Nick said, and surprised me by standing and hugging me tightly.

Maybe he had girls boarding planes to Japan and then changing their minds on him all the time, I don't know.

I awkwardly waved at Marty and John, swung my purse over my shoulder, and walked to the front of the plane. I heard a clapping sound behind me and turned briefly. It was Marty, who kept clapping until John reached over and slapped him upside the head. I caught Nick's eye for just a quick flash; he nodded, a surprisingly appreciative look in his eye. It was as if he were saying "Well done."

Here's the thing: Dramatic exits only work in the movies. I had to wait ten minutes standing at the front of the plane while the stewardess phoned the airline peeps still in the terminal. My face was red. The entire front section had a perfect view of my ass, which of course now felt humongous. One teenager with headphones sitting in first class actually let loose with a long "Booooooo." Ten minutes felt like ten hours. To pass the time, I pretended I was at a Springsteen concert and he was saying "Bruuuuuce," which sounds nearly identical. When I was finally approved to depart the plane, my passport was checked twice by the captain himself. "You know the flight is going to be delayed half an hour now," he said. "I'm sorry," I whispered. "I'm so sorry."

When finally released back into the terminal I spent an hour being interviewed by the airport police (hello, post-9/11 airport security!) in a very small, very scary yellow room. A line of handcuffs were hanging on the wall next to America's Most Wanted posters. The cops didn't think my response of "I was making a huge mistake with a guitarist in a punk band who was really not but too obsessed with himself to ever fall in love with me" was a good enough excuse to get up and leave a flight once the doors were already closed and it took a lot of pleading and one uncomfortable call to my parents to convince them I wasn't some nut.

"I'm a good nut!" I told one police officer, who frowned. Joking while being interrogated is probably a bad idea. Good to know.

I don't know how I went from living with Andy to nearly being arrested for running off a plane, but there you have it. The thing is: I had a feeling Nick would be on my mind a long time. The biggest misconception when we are young is that our experiences are superfluous; that they will multiply, happening again and again. That life is an ocean of second chances. But I knew my time with Nick was unique, something I'd tuck away in a corner of my mind, taking out to thumb over later in my life when all was quiet in my house, the kids asleep, the sky dark.

I wasn't angry with Nick. He wasn't such a bad guy, you know. Just a bit naïve. And at thirty-six, he should know better. Maybe wearing a tie and suit every day is considered boring to him, but I think having a steady job, getting married, and supporting a family is a sexy trait in a man. I ain't knockin' it. Nick was *so* exciting I felt like I needed to jump into a sauna and detox for ten years after just one week with him. He was more like a character than like a real person—if I turned him sideways, he'd be paper thin, like a piece of cardboard. A part of me feels like I might have imagined the whole thing. Made Nick up. Maybe I'd never understand what his intentions had been. Surely if he'd only been after sex I'd have recognized the signs and not gotten involved with him. Was I blind to Nick's dark side because I'd just left Andy and was searching for strong arms to engulf me? It may seem like the obvious answer, but I didn't think this was the case. I knew what I was getting into. He was a man covered in tattoos. And what are tattoos, really? They're scars. Scars, for a man scarred on the inside from a past love.

I walked past all of the stores and terminals like my head was on fire and leaving this airport would bring me to water. People streaked past me in a blur and snippets of conversation trailed after them. The nervousness I felt now was so different from the bottomless terror in leaving Andy. It was more akin to anticipation, the way a caterpillar must feel as she wiggles out of her cocoon, stretching out one tentative wing before the other. She's now different, a butterfly. She's changed. I'd left two men in one week and I'd do it a hundred more times if it wasn't the right guy for me. I'd follow my heart wherever it led me, from Mud to Madison and back again.

I caught a cab in front of the terminal right away, which I took as a good sign from the karma gods. The driver had a WELCOME TO CONEY ISLAND postcard taped to his dashboard.

For a second I couldn't breathe. I felt the waves rushing over my ankles, water filling the taxi, the feeling of leaning against Nick and looking back at the Cyclone. The sound of its churning, the wooden boards bending beneath its weight.

"Where to?" the driver asked.

I blinked, swimming back to reality, and flipped open my phone to turn it on and call Dana Vila at *The Times*. I was going to get started on the Weezer story right now, today.

"Where ya going, lady?" the driver said, a little louder.

"New Jersey," I whispered.

"Where? Speak up!"

I shouted it: "New Jersey!"

As soon as I said it, calmness coursed through my body. I felt I was in the right place, at the right time in my life. I felt like (dare I say it) an adult. A woman. I caught my reflection in the driver's rearview mirror: messy hair, freckles, a huge grin slowly spreading across my face.